Once Upon a Whisky:

The Marmaris Diaries:

Louise Bell

LOUISE BELL

More books in the Marmaris Diaries series:

Book 1: The Final Summer of Vodka

Book 1.5: Back in Blighty

Both available on Amazon:

https://www.amazon.co.uk/Louise-Bell/e/B01IPUYNYK/ref=dp_byline_cont_book_1

Parental Advisory - Explicit Content

Not for the easily offended. I swear. Quite a lot.

Copyright © 2017 Louise Bell

All rights reserved.

ISBN:
ISBN-13: 9781521283288

DEDICATION

For the people that unknowingly gave me writing fodder for years to come. Your frappuccino drinking, active wearing ways have made it from simple annoyance and onto paper.
But mostly, this book is for Gucci - my soul mutt, sidekick and best friend in this race we call life. Without him, life wouldn't be as much fun.

CONTENTS

	Acknowledgments	i
1	August	Pg 3
2	September	Pg 32
3	October	Pg 69
4	November	Pg 113
5	December	Pg 160
6	January	Pg 202
7	February	Pg 244
8	Memories	Pg 280
9	About the Author	Pg 282
10	Plea from the Author	Pg 283

ACKNOWLEDGMENTS

Firstly, thank you to Kaz and Dan for proof reading the living be-Jesus out of this book.
Secondly, thank you to Kris from Drop Dead Designs for the countless hours spent perfecting the cover. I know I was a pain and probably your worst client, but luckily I'm on hiatus for a while.
Thirdly, a big thank you to my friends (and frenemies) who have helped me no end by giving me massive character inspo - you know who you are. Although it's probably time for the last few to get around to reading the books. Scrap that, if you see what I have done with you I fear we may be friends no more.
And finally, thank you to the booze. Without your copious amounts of bad influence, there would be no book.

August

Saturday 20th August 2016

Current Location: Villa De Guch Pig, Armutalan, Marmaris

Current Weight: 68 Kilos (Holiday weight)

Time: 21.40pm

Dear Diary,

In case you didn't already know, my name is Lei Lawson.

I'm a: Blogger, Vegetarian, Vodka lover, and in 7 days I will be turning 36 years of age. 36 - Who'd have thought it? I really hoped by now I would I feel more *adult*. Alas, that hasn't happened yet. I still feel like I'm an 18 year old kid dancing all over Marmaris, and tomorrow I will be 80.

Time. It flies by in the blink of an eye but apparently, it's all relative.

At the moment, I'm blond with dark integrated roots, 5ft 6 in height, usually about 10 stone, size 14/16 on top (DD lumps of lard which are the bane of my life) and 12/14 on bottom. I do not have a flat stomach and I have a dinner plate for a face. It's fair to say that I have body complex issues. I mean who doesn't right?

I, like everyone else have vices, but can they really be considered immoral or evil when you enjoy doing them so much? Put it this way, my friend's say I'm a hard-core rager - me on the other hand, well, I suppose you could say that I like to have fun.

I last wrote a diary 5 years ago, back when I was looking for 'The One'. Did I find him? Yes indeed I did, and I will get to that shortly - but for now, I think it would be a good idea to detail exactly why I've decided to start another diary. My last was an eye opener and at times I surprised myself with just how ludicrous my life was. So, this new diary will hopefully show me if I have grown up any. Doubtful springs to mind.

Message for my Mum: PUT IT DOWN NOW. You know what curiosity did to the cat - killed the fucker.

So, for this diary to fulfil its aim I need to lay out a couple of points:

Point 1: I vow to jot down my thoughts, feelings and downright outrageous married girl shenanigans for the next 6 months, and to be totally honest whilst doing so. This will help ascertain if I need to be sectioned when it's all over.

Point 2: My last diary had a goal, and so shall this one. Now that I'm all *adult*, this diary's goal is to be pregnant by the end of February 2017. Shocker I know. Yup, this wannabe socialite wants a sprog of the non-furry variety, and I am giving myself 6 months from now to be up the duff / with child / got a bun in the oven.

I'm not even kidding.

So, how on earth did I get to this stage? What the bleedin' Christ could have happened to make me want a mini me of my very own?

Well, plenty has happened in those 5 long years I have laid diary dormant, and right here, right now I'm going to submerge myself in a catch up, starting with the good shit - who did I marry?

The dreaded ex? Hell no! He was not thought about again after the switch finally flicked. It was like a 'Hallelujah' moment when I finally realised that the tit was just using me. And, he is married to another now. I would wish them all the best because really there are no feelings left, however they are heading for the divorce court. I can only fathom a guess as to why, but I assume it's something to do with the fact that he's a little cunt... #NarrowEscape

So, was it the flaccid tongued Yanki and his ever present-schlong? No definitely not. He got married 2 months after me and I really couldn't be happier for him.

Could it have been The Player then? Not after he tried a three way 5 years ago, absolutely not!

And what about the Dentist that I was so ridiculously infatuated with? Nope, not him either, but it might have been his friend.

Ahh Barış - the buddy of the Dentist that I added on Facebook just to spite him.

Yup - I married the guy that I added to piss another off.

I really did have to kiss all the frogs before I found my very own lobster.

And now?

Well, I still live in the bubble that is Marmaris. As much as I moan about the place, I love it dearly. I can't see myself and Husbando staying here forever; but for now, it's good enough.

Leading me astray along my journey is my American Cocker soul mutt 'Gucci', who at 11 years old you would think would be slowing down a bit. Not a chance in hell. No, my little monster of furry naughtiness is filled with boundless amounts of energy, piss and farts that would make even Satan gag. We are pretty much inseparable. He makes a great travelling companion and we have been on our jolly holidays to Spain together on numerous occasions now.

Team Minger only half exists these days. Jess and I drifted apart some 3 years back. We had a torrent of little fall outs culminating in one god almighty argument while on a boat where she nearly pushed me overboard. As small as she is, she is a strong little fucker. I still think of her fondly, but we are Mingers no more. Since then there have been new friends that have come and gone, one that even tried to wear me as a second skin, but who I have in my life right now I hope are here for good.

Kimmy, Sister and I are still solid, in fact Kimmy was Maid of Honour at my Wedding. I couldn't have made a better choice as whilst I was getting pissed and rocking out to 'Guns n Roses', Kimmy was like a little Hitler on top of it all.

Sister, although no longer repping in Turkey, made it back for my wedding. He was also part of my bridal party and escorted Gucci down the aisle. They made the perfect companions.

My old kissing friend Kaan still knocks about, all be it on a much smaller scale. That's what happens when you get married; your male friends disappear. I put all that snogging down to a blip in the system, and it never happened again.

And my ole aunty like pal Lorraine, she's still here too. We fell out for two whole years, but as good friends generally do, we made up. To be honest I can't even remember why we fell out now, but I know I was livid at the time. Since then we've been on a couple of holidays around Turkey with not one cross word spoken. We have our moments, but I doubt we will fall out again in quite spectacular fashion.

Camilla (the oldest Minger in the world) and I are still very much in contact. She no longer lives in Içmeler but does come for a visit twice a year. In fact I saw her just recently in Blighty when we met up in Chester for a liquid lunch. She will be back again in September for her usual queen of Içmeler holiday.

And finally onto Husbando; Bariş and I have been together for nearly 5 years, meeting at the end of my last diary. Yup, 'The Final Summer of Vodka' really was when I met the man.

He is my polar opposite - He doesn't often drink, prefers being home to being out and is a computer gaming geek. Quite how he puts up with me is beyond comprehension, but I suppose there is some truth to how opposites attract. At 33, Bariş is my toy boy, but let's get one thing straight - I ain't no Marmaris Sugga Mamma.

We dated for 6 months before moving in, and after being together for 3 years we tied the knot.

You may wonder how the proposal went down. I could try to fool my future senile self into thinking that it was all of a fairy tale by candle light with champagne and rose petals, however I would be lying. Bariş did not get down on one knee and there was no ring to propose with. One day back in March 2014 while we were having lunch, we simply decided to get wed. We were already living together and both of us knew that this was it, so why not? We were very 'adult' about it and weighed up the pro's and con's.

Pro: He gets to be married to me.

Con: He gets to be married to me.

Win win right?

Had I have known then what I know now, I guarantee you the wedding would have been a registry office job. If someone had told me just how horrific planning a wedding would be, I would never have taken on such a hideous task. It was awful, just awful. From choosing the venue to choosing the flowers - I hated it all.

But I did get married in the black wedding dress that I always wanted.

It was not to mourn my single life as my Mum would have you believe; I wore it as wearing virginal white is simply not me. Quite how I turned out to be Virgo I will never know.

Looking back now I realise I looked quite dreadful, but certainly not due to the colour of the dress. I should not have been talked into wearing the stupid hoop underneath said dress as it made me look 10 sizes fatter than I actually was, plus it altered its original fantabulous appearance. I also hated my hair as it was NOTHING like what I had shown my hairdresser I wanted. And my makeup? Simply shit.

Yup, it's fair to say that I did not look great on my wedding day.

Thankfully the photographer took such shockingly diabolical photos that we have no evidence of my shit looking self anyway.

And the wannabe pregnant stuff?

Well, since getting wed we have been trying. I say we but I really mean me as Bariş didn't know that was the plan until recently. Now that he knows, he thinks we should wait a bit until we are older. How much older does he want me to be, forty fucking five? As if. I will just crack on with my plan as who knows how long this shit is going to take. With trying since the wedding, one can only assume that I have shrivelled up old vodka pickled eggs, but I remain hopeful as that's just the sort of gal I am.

It's funny 'cos I was never the maternal type. In fact I'm still not, yet I find myself wanting one of my own. I've done a pretty blinding job with Gucci even if I do say so myself, so I look upon it as natural progression.

Fuck me, life has certainly changed.

ONCE UPON A WHISKY

I still party like the ever aging rock star that I am; in fact just recently I stayed out till 7am to the absolute disgust of Husbando. He didn't speak to me for a week after that. That was one of the most productive weeks of my life so far to date.

By all effects, I am probably not an ideal wife, but I am trying.

I do occasionally pine for my old life. Not because I don't want to be married, believe me I do, but because when looking back, my old life seemed epic. Off course I know the good sticks in your mind and the bad is generally forgotten, but even so, my single life was pretty fucking cool.

I don't miss the torrent of tits I managed to get involved with, but I do miss the all weekend drinking benders, not answering to anyone and being spread starfish across my king-size bed. These days it's physically impossible to be spread starfish as I only get the tiniest corner to myself. Yup, Barış and Gucci push me out of bed, sometimes to the force that I have to get up and sleep in the spare room. And if by chance they don't, then Guch aims his arse directly for my face and farts in it all night, not just keeping me awake but also in the constant state of inhaling shit particles.

And if I do what I want now, I have two sets of judgemental eyes on me. I say two sets as Gucci has become a big fat Judas. Oh he bums of Barış something terrible. At first it was cute, but now it's just annoying.

Barış calls him Daddies boy. I call them a couple of cunts.

And that dear diary is where I am going to leave it for today. With just getting back from a 3 week holiday in Blighty, I find myself with a filthy house to clean and a piss infested piglet to walk.

Why can't men clean properly?

What an absolute bastard. House cleaning and me.

LOUISE BELL

Sunday 21st August

Current Weight: 66 Kilos

Time: 12.54pm

Dear Duty-free whisky drinker,

Now safely back on home soil, it seems that my holiday chub is decreasing slightly and my pre-holiday body has started to put in an appearance. I have pretty much starved myself these last few days so I'm glad to see it's not been in vain.

Why is it that I always pile on the pounds when back in the UK? I'll tell you why, because I leave my self control at the airport and I stuff my fat dinner plate face with all the food you can't find in Turkey. At least here I am not able to reach for a bag of Monster Munch every 5 minutes and there is no Cadburys chocolate in sight.

Thank fuck I'm home - I would absolutely be the size of a house if I lived in the UK.

The best thing about getting home was seeing Gucci. I opened the door and he literally peed all over the place. Good thing I was wearing jogging bottoms that were headed straight for the wash!

It was also good to see Husbando. I never miss him when I go away; not because I'm a cold heartless bitch, just because I'm a gal that's too used to her own independence. But it was rather fabulous to see his smiling happy face none the less. Mind you, I think he lied when he said he kept on top of the cleaning as I found one rather large dried Guch wee in the dining room, and by the look of it, it's been there for 2 weeks. Fucker.

Anyway, I've been off the booze for a whole week in preparation for tonight. Yes 'dear diary', tonight I am going to paint the town red with the girls and John. Kimmy being Kimmy probably won't show up. She does this. But that's OK as I'd rather her come along for my birthday drinks next weekend anyway. So tonight I'm sure will consist of the usual suspects: Lacie, Jenny, John and myself.

I have been friends with Lacie for about 5 years. She is a provocative 39 year old divorced vixen of a man eater from London. She is one of those women that you love to hate as she is so friggin' model-esk, but you could never hate this biatch as she is far too down to earth for that - and that's why she was my bridesmaid.

On your wedding day all eyes are supposed to be on the bride right? Not my wedding day. It didn't help that I looked like shit, but Lacie certainly stole the show with her super slender figure, 5 ft 9" height and shoulder length brunette hair. My mate John says he would wear her legs like a scarf if he could, the dirty ole perve.

Am I jealous of her figure? Fuck yes, but I love her so it's OK. Most girls that look like Lacie tend to be pretentious, arseholes even, but not this girl. Nope, this one's a good egg and that's why I'm able to cope with being the fat friend.

Yup, I think it's fair to say that Lacie is my kinda gal. We are rude, nasty and obtuse and that's just to each other. I sometimes wish that I had known Lacie when I was single, however the Universe had a reason for that, and probably a very good one...

Jenny on the other hand, I have known for about a year. Lacie met her through work and slowly started to bring her in on our nights in and out. She looks a bit like a Russian doll with her petite frame and dark hair, but thankfully not a knob with it. Once Jenny said that she was envious of my womanly body as she hated her little boy's bod. I mean, as if - but it was nice of her to say.

I guess we all have our own body issues whether fat or thin.

The 3 of us together is usually hilarious but occasionally explosive, and I'm pretty sure we lead each other astray.

There was this one time (in Marmaris, not band camp), that it all went Pete Tong and I wasn't sure if our threesome would recover. Back in February it was Jenny's birthday, so we started the shenanigans with pre-drinks round at my house at 5.30pm. It was Saturday after all, and pre-drinks are all about getting as drunk as possible so you spend as little as possible when out on the town.

Surprisingly I wasn't the one abusing people that night...

We were girls on a Karaoke mission and having a grand old time of it in 'Il Primo' when Lacie declared she had a 'promise' to get home to. It never fails to amaze me the men that this one picks up. The girl has serious skills on the bloke front.

Jenny saw her arse royally what with Lacie ditching us to get her itch scratched, but Jen really should have known that Lacie, unless void of all men, would never have made it to Bar Street. So in pure Jenny style, the C word was thrown around furiously like a pin ball machine pinging all over Lacie's face. To be clear here, she called Lacie a big old cunt and not in a nice jokey way.

 I cringed.

And with that Lacie fucked off home to her promise, Jenny fucked off home to another bottle of wine and I fucked off to Bar Street with John. #GoodTimes?

The following day was something of a blur. I woke up still pissed and didn't fancy coming down from that high. As any normal Sunday Funday should start, I poured myself a little vodka to keep me right. I called Lacie about a million times but no answer, so I called Jenny and told her to get her glad rags on as we were going out. Our first port of call was Lacie's house. We knocked and knocked and called and called but she was ignoring us.

Calling Lacie a big old cunt is not always a good idea - she takes offence to being called old...

So instead we got some booze and sat on the beach.

Being full on winter, the beach was deserted, but sunny and warm none the less. We spent a lovely 2 hours in the sunshine talking all kinds of shite, and after the booze was finished, we went back to Lacie's - all be it a lot more intoxicated this time around.

We had the great idea to break in should she continue to ignore us, which she did, so we did. Being the fat friend, there was no way I could squeeze my lard arse through the bathroom window, so the Russian doll had to do just that. As she was clambering through, Lacie caught her in full Lara Croft mode and literally shoved her back out whilst in the midst of an epic hissy fit. Well, who could blame her, she had just found Jenny breaking in and all...

Obviously I didn't let Jen take the rap for the whole incident, I'm no shit bag, but it didn't help because after that Lacie and Jenny didn't speak for a month. It was as awkward as arse. Jenny became a recluse, not wanting to speak to anyone, and Lacie was just annoyed with the world.

Eventually, after they let the dust settle and had thrown around enough abusive texts to sink a battle ship, they started speaking. It was touch and go there for a while, but as booze would have it, they sorted their shit out.

So, to put it mildly, Jenny fits right in. We are like the 3 cackling witches of Eastwick, especially when we break out the Ouija Board when pissed.

So, where does John fit in amongst this gaggle of gals? Well, I have known him the longest. Just as Team Minger was disbanding, John and I started our weekly nights out in 'Lighthouse' near the marina. In fact John knew Bariş before I did, and in a weird sort of way it was through John that I eventually hooked up with Bariş. John and I went out one night (after adding Bariş on Facebook), and ended up in 'Davey Jones' rock bar where

Barış was bar man at the time. We hit it off in person and from there on in, the rest as they say, is history.

But back to John; he is from Birmingham, is a good dependable sort, pretty bloody loyal but suffers from random bursts of negativity from time to time. He is not your usual bloke. I think he may have short mans complex - hence the negativity. On the plus side he is very hardworking and comes from the more old fashioned side of life; knows how to treat a lady. Unfortunately the poor bastard can't find a lady, so he gets stuck with the three of us on the occasional weekend instead.

Our little crew knows how to have a good time, and thank God these guys like to party as much as me - well, Jenny and John at least as Lacie usually has some bloke that she sneaks off early to.

So with all of the above in mind, I'm going to make a start on the unpacking (as I couldn't be arsed yesterday), find an outfit for tonight and pour myself a nice big duty-free whisky and diet Coke.

What's happened to my usual vodka?

I still drink it off course, but recently I felt it was time for a change. After all, I'm growing up don't you know.

ONCE UPON A WHISKY

Monday 22nd August

Current Location: Bono Beach, Marmaris Beach Front

Time: 17.11pm

Dear One for the road,

I was just on my way home from visiting Lorraine for a post-holiday gossip and decided instead of going actually going home, to come down to the beach front instead. Was this a wise idea considering the extreme heat? I doubt it, but, here I am shandy in hand, laptop in front and nothing but blue skies ahead.

The only issue is that it's too sodding hot and this vile chair is causing me to have piss sweat. You know the sort of chair, all fake leather making it a nasty heat attracting contraption. I actually look like I have wet myself. Well, it wouldn't be the first time, but I'm currently not intoxicated nor am I crying with laughter.

Piss sweat. What a bastard.

I do not remember much of last night - no surprise there. What was a surprise was to find that Husbando was not speaking to me. Apparently I am the devil in disguise.

No disguise about it dear!!

What have I done that is so terribly wrong this time? Well, nothing. I had a normal night out on the town, came home at 04.30am, and now he is not speaking to me.

Let's take a look shall we;

Whilst getting ready, I poured myself a couple of heavy handed whiskies while living it up listing to Ibiza tunes on Radio 1. How old do I think I am listening to Ibiza tunes for the love of God?? The whisky, on the other hand, shows just how mature I am - only old people drink whisky, so that balances out the Ibiza tunes nicely.

I met up with Lacie and her Mum, John, Sue and Rita in 'Lighthouse' at 9.30pm. Unfortunately Jenny cancelled as she had a 'tummy bug'. I don't believe that for a second and think she chose to ditch us as she dislikes Sue and Rita. They are not my cup of tea either but as they're Lacie's friends, I make the effort. They're older than us and are pretty bitchy towards people younger than them so it makes it awkward to be in their company. I get the feeling they don't particularly like me either, and that's OK because you can't please everyone.

They have not been here particularly long, but think they know it all - you know the sort.

If they were nicer then I would feel bad about Sue's cheating fella, alas they are not, and I don't. What did she expect when getting involved with a bloke half her age that doesn't speak a word of English? I mean why? Seriously..?

I was having a grand old time in 'Lighthouse' doing my best to avoid the bitchy ones; however, Rita was being difficult due to the price of the wine and the size of the glass it arrived in. The wine in Turkey is generally not fantastic, and being that she knows it all you would think she would know to order a different drink wouldn't you?

Other than that, a great night was had - my drinks were flowing mighty well at least.

At about midnight, half the gang dispersed leaving only Lacie, John and me to continue. Had I been a good wife I would have sent myself home at that point, however married or not I am still the last to leave any party, and with that we headed over to the dark and pretty dingy 'Davey Jones'.

I was pretty much pissed at this point so I can't tell you if it was a busy night or not, but what I can tell you is this – I had a bloody good mosh to whichever long haired greasy band was playing at the time. Were they any good? I have no idea. Would I recommend going to see them? Fuck knows.

I was that pissed that when John informed me he was leaving, I told him that me and Lacie were staying with our new Turkish gay best friends that we had just met. I thought what a cute couple the guys made, so I told them so. It was like watching a slow motion horror movie as mortified looks crept across their faces.

My gay-dar must have been pretty pissed too as to my shock and pure horror they told us that they were not in fact gay and wanted to take Lacie and I home.

Well knock me down with a feather. How could I have got that so terribly wrong?

I was making my apologies and telling Lacie that I needed to leave immediately when in walked Kaan. He walked right over and we hugged warmly. I really do love that guy and not in a 'I want to snog the face off him' way anymore, more like brotherly love these days. He suggested going for Soup (a random thing to do after a night on the town, but tots norms here in Turkey), so off we all trotted, minus the non-gay guys that may or may not have sent themselves home for a manly makeover.

By the time we finished in the Soup Kitchen (where you can order any other food type too btw), I still wasn't ready for home. I mean come on, when am I ever? Lacie suggest a drink at her house and I obviously jumped at the chance, so off we 3 headed.

Barış called at 03.32am while we were in fits of laughter at a random drunk conversation, and I was all 'shhhhhhhhhh, Barış is calling' when I should have been like 'say hi to Barış' as he now thinks something untoward was going on what with the deathly silence. I can't fucking win me.

He asked if I was going to drag my sorry arse home - Yes I certainly was, but he annoyed me on the phone, so I decided to stay for 'one more for the road' before finally sending myself homeward bound at 04.30am. This did not bode well with Husbando, especially as he woke to find me asleep on the sitting room floor, fully clothed, shoes on, handbag still on shoulder with Gucci licking my face at 9am.

Fuck all changes in my world, married or not, see?

Like I say, he didn't speak to me yesterday apart from the torrent of texts he sent informing me that I drink far too much and that I am a bit of cunt. I agree with the later part of that statement, but I certainly don't drink too much. I like to party, oh yes there is no denying that, but drink too much? Oh piss off with yourself man...

It's hard to explain to a Turkish husband why I, as a Brit, wish to go out and drink with my buddies. That's where the cultural differences really come into play because a Turkish wife wouldn't dream of committing such an atrocity.

But I'm no Turkish wife now am I...

So, that was Saturday.

Sunday, apart from not speaking to Bariş - Lacie, John and I buggered off for a roast dinner around 5pm. We had to soak up the alcohol somehow and a 'Piccadilly' roast usually does the job. In true Lacie style she was on the white wine while all I could do was look on and sip my Fanta with pure alcohol impending doom bubbling away within.

Ahh yes, the doom does come a knockin' occasionally. Usually when Bariş is not speaking to me.

Today being Monday, and less hung-over than I was yesterday, I decided to get back in the good graces of Husbando, play the good wife for a change and muster up his favourite dinner for tonight. I spent 2 hours cooking the pasta sauce only for him to message me at 4pm to tell me that he was having a late lunch at work and did not require feeding. Fuck sake.

Back to bad wife it is then...

So, here I am. Looking around at the much quieter than normal Marmaris beach front wondering if I should just send myself back off to the UK for another few weeks. At least I won't have piss sweat dripping down my arse crack there...

Tuesday 23rd August

Current Weight: 68.7 Kilos

Time: 17.11pm

Dear Diet girl,

I went to visit my ex personal trainer cum good friend Julia today in Hisaronu. Not the Hisaronu in the Fethiye area, the one that is a 20 minute drive away from Marmaris. It's just gorgeous down there, and she is lucky enough to live right on the beach.

I would still be training with her had she not have moved out to the sticks, and off course there is also the fact that I fucking hate exercise. Not that she knows it, but I looked at it as a blessing when she moved. The most exercise I get these days is working my biceps by raising my whisky to my mouth for a swig and flexing back down again - easy does it with minimal effort, just the way I like it.

Julia is a bit like me; doesn't really care if people like her or not and also finds it difficult to open up emotionally. What a catch gals like us are, right? Urm...

I have known her now for about 4 years. I started training with her a few months after Baris and I got together for the plain and simple reason that the 'love pounds' had started to show. What with that and me quitting smoking in 2012, I had never needed to start training more. Talk about fat cunt walking...

It's fair to say we hit it off immediately. We bonded over the mutual dislike of an ex friend and from there on in a firm friendship was formed. Another reason that I like her so much is that she and her hot hubby Zafer have somewhat of a Noah's Ark going on with their fleet of dogs, cats and pet goat.

Anyway, back to the reason that I went to see Julia in the first place. Did you see today's weight? Yes, my bloody my fat stuff is back. Although I managed to drop a few of Kilos from the UK holiday, clearly my scales are wrong as I'm not 66 Kilos at all - far bloody from it.

Julia has devised a proper diet that allows me 1200 calories a day. Can someone tell me how the fuck am I going to survive on that FFS?

She says I've also to cut out diet coke, beer, foods from tin cans and basically anything processed considering I'm struggling to get pregnant - plus I'm to get in a 20 minute work out 3 times a week. Fuck sake. Life is going to be fun isn't it? I actually feel sorry for Barış. Maybe he should move out for a month?

Somehow, diet pills are looking quite tempting again...

Anyway, this palaver begins on Monday, so as soon as I was back home, I promptly arranged three meals out and a couple of piss ups to crack on with before then - the first one being tonight round at Lacie's. I have forced her to cook a dirty great big pasta and garlic bread combo, I'm bringing the crisps and dip, and to show good faith, I will try (try) to drink water with my whisky. Can't see it going down very well but I'm a trier all said and done. I'll take a bottle of diet coke with me just in case, but force myself I will to do it the right way. After all, I want to be thin again and I want Gucci to have a little brother or sister to torment.

Tomorrow is Husbando's day off however it's going to be neither pleasurable nor fun as we are going to the hospital to find out if I really do have vodka pickled, dried up, shrivelled old eggs, and, to check his man juices.

He's not impressed, but neither the hell am I. When you have a biological clock ticking one can't piss about for too long in the hopes one will get lucky. Nope, it's time to bite the bullet and let the investigative torture commence.

At least he is speaking to me now. Until this weekend at least.

Oh dear, I really don't think he had any idea just quite what he married did he...?

ONCE UPON A WHISKY

Thursday 26th August

Time: 16.58pm

Dear Birthday girl,

Happy F'ing birthday Lei!

Today marks the 15th anniversary of my 21st birthday. Yes I am officially an old cunt. Most people at 36 have pretty much got life figured out. They have careers or kids, and some greedy bastards have both.

Me, I'm still figuring out what I want to be when I grow up...

Jesus, just yesterday I was a fresh faced 18 year old thinking I could rule the world. Now here at thirty f'ing six, I can no longer say that I have a youthful complexion or great hair. I can hide my age no longer with the little lines that have started to appear around my eyes when I smile.

Lacie was kind about it though. She said I could pull off 27 if it was dark and everyone was pissed. That's nice isn't it?

Just listen to me the voice of doom. I need to remind myself that I'm in a much better place than I was on my birthday 5 years ago. My head was up my arse what with the ex texting all sorts of shite, plus I had an uninvited visitor over from Rhodes in the form of 'Big Dickie' (who couldn't get it up), and a Yanki that had recently lost my hip flask (which I still bloody miss). It was a different life entirely back then.

But 'where are the kids?' asks absolutely everyone.

Yes that's right you selfish mo fo's, make me feel worse with my twattish ovaries and hips that are clearly not meant for child bearing. I shouldn't jump the gun just yet as we have not had our test results back from Wednesday's intrusive session at the hospital, however the Doc pointed out that my endometrial wall was not ready for a baby this month. No shit Sherlock as I started my bleed today...

Guess that's another month of not being preggers then.

Barış has not had his 'wanky in a cupy' just yet as we had to go to a different hospital for that. Something about the state hospital not having the equipment for it. Sounds about right. His appointment is on the 1st September, and inwardly he totally hates me for making him do it, but, needs must. After all, it may not be me with the problem...

At least I have tonight's plans to look forward to - Husbando and I and going out for birthday dinner # 1. We always end up in the same little Turkish restaurant 'Kervan' for every birthday or anniversary because the food is just so fit and you can go there in your jogging bottoms or dress up a bit - either way you don't look out of place. We just like it.

But have you ever eaten dinner with a Turk? Maybe it's just my Husbando, but a meal out is not a treat to him. He sees eating as refuelling only, so when he shovels food into his gullet there is no conversation, and when he's done he wants to leave immediately. Tonight he's going to have to grin and bear it as it's my birthday and I will take 2 hours to eat if I want to.

And, after dinner I may force him into a walk on the beach front too. He absolutely hates walking and nearly died of shock when he realised he had to walk Guch while I was in the UK. I'm pretty damn sure Guch didn't get a walk daily so thank God for Kimmy being a good Minger and taking my boy out a few times a week.

Anyway, I have drivelled on about doom and gloom enough for one day. Jesus, when I'm on my period I'm one miserable bitch, but I can be more positive I swear. In fact I tried to kick start the positivity by treating myself to a new doo today. In an attempt to turn back the clock, I decided to go back to being the full blown suicide blonde that I was 5 years ago. Yup, that didn't work.

Let's see if Husbando notices the difference while guzzling his grub tonight. At a guess I'm going to say epic fail.

Monday 30th August

Current Weight: 68 kilos

Time: 15.52pm

Dear Wannabe socialite,

Today marks the start of my proper diet beginning. I have completed 3 birthday meals out and I am glad I don't have to go through another night where makeup has to be worn in the near future.

Husbando and I did indeed have a lovely meal at 'Kervan' and he didn't even kick off when I wanted to go for a walk around the marina afterwards. My new night time sandals did though and cut my feet to buggery. I strongly believe that Barış transferred his soul into that of my sandals that particular evening...

But he noticed my new blonder locks without any prompting! He said it was like being out with a different woman that was not his wife. That's sweet in a weird non-cheating kind of way.

Anyway, Birthday dinner # 2 was on Saturday night down at 'Zola', the new Tapas joint on the marina. What a great evening we had although we very nearly had a change of venue at the last minute. We were convinced that the rival gang (that we hate with a passion) had also booked 'Zola' for Larissa, their gang leader's birthday. Thank God for Facebook check-ins as we noticed just in time they were elsewhere.

My cool A.F birthday club consisted of Lacie, Jenny, Kimmy, Kat, Bernie and John - the token guy. Kat I don't really see each other that often, only on birthdays and special occasions but when I do see her she is always a good laugh. She has been around as long as I have and we remember each other from way back when, although we never really spoke in those days. Only since she started training with Julia a few years ago did we start speaking properly, which in turn lead to us going out occasionally. She also happens to be an old friend of Lacie's, so it all ties in quite nicely. Bernie however I have only just met but liked her immediately.

After 'Zola' (and quite a few toilet selfies) we headed down to 'Lighthouse' and proceeded to drink like hippies. From there we went on to 'B52's' on Bar Street. It is not one of my favourite places to go due to the gangster rap they play repeatedly, so why we ended up there is beyond me. I still don't do gangster friggin' rap. I mean how the hell are you supposed to dance to it without looking racist?

John disappeared at some point; I think it was when he realised that Jenny really was not going home with him - now or ever. He did not say cheerio, but he did buy me a packet of fags for my birthday. You see he gets rather annoyed when I drink and insist on taking a drag of each of his fags. I didn't keep the fags, I gave them to Lacie, as although I take a drag of Johns, I take many more from Lacie.

Talking about Lacie, she ditched us for her latest conquest around 01.00am - but at least she made it till then.

Jenny lasted a bit longer than her own birthday and was out till 03.00am when she decided it was time to go on the ex hunt. She received a tip off that he was down Bar Street and with that, she was gone.

Kimmy and I finally left around 04.00am ish, so for once I got home at a decent hour, and weirdly enough, not crawling on all fours! Husbando was suitably impressed.

So as birthdays go, the night was a good one.

Sunday came and brought with it a hangover that didn't really warrant my non wankered state from the previous evening. Troubling. So I did nothing. Not one thing. I happily lay on my sofa and binge watched 'The Only Way is Essex' and ate leftover birthday cake. 'Twas a good ole day.

Monday brought with it birthday dinner # 3, but this time with Lorraine. It's her birthday the day after mine and we have this long-standing tradition that we always go out for a double dinner together as close to our birthdays as possible. It could not be combined with my birthday club on Saturday night as let's put it this way; Lorraine does not like many people and many people do not like Lorraine.

I actually met Lacie through Lorraine as funnily enough she was her friend first. I didn't really think about Lacie in any other way other than Lorraine's friend at the time - then they fell out. Lacie messaged me a couple of times and we hit it off. From one wine night round at her house we realised that we were the only souls on fire left in Marmaris, and from there on in we became besties.

I know why Lacie decided to stop speaking to Lorraine but I won't tell her that. I don't cope well with upset and I would feel awkward as arse if forced into telling her. So instead, I claim to have no idea what the story is (but it's pretty much because Lacie saw through Lorraine and didn't like what she saw).

Lorraine and I had a nice enough evening with not one drop of booze touching my lips. The reason being that Lorraine gets very judgemental when I drink and it annoys me, so 9 times out of 10 I just don't bother - why waste the calories? Then when the occasional 10th time hits, I go hell for leather and ignore every one of her snarky comments and dance on the table.

She had a drink of course, but just the one as she's pissed from that. I so wish I could be pissed from one drink - what a cheap night that would make.

Anyway, it's fair to say that my diet which started yesterday, went straight out of the window because as well as the pizza in 'Bono Marina', I also indulged in the most delightful coconut milkshake I have ever had over at 'Roberts Coffee Shop'.

So this brings us up to date with today, Tuesday.

I have not overindulged in food today and I am going to make a proper start on this 1200 calorie allowance if it kills me. I am doing well so far, but I kid you not, my will power is not as strong as it used to be...

I have one more night out lined up this week and that's whisky night round at Lacie's on Thursday. After that, I am going to make a conscious effort to stay in over the weekend. This will be a hard task, but needs must because calories seem to find me at every turn. Staying home with bare cupboards really is the only option...

September

Friday 2nd September

Time: 12.54pm

Dear Girl with Husbando misgivings,

I went to Lacie's last night to have a drink and to talk through her issues. Lacie's issues are that of what only a pretty skinny girl can understand, so on me they were lost. She has the choice between her rich ex-husband begging her to come back offering her the life of riley, or, a new wannabe boyfriend offering her the world. So what's a girl to do? If I know Lacie, she'll add a third man in the mix and start a bidding war. #PrettyGirlProblems

If only I could have such problems, alas mine are that of the computer game variety.

Yup, my husband is married to his f'ing computer games.

All was well yesterday before he went to work. I had my PMS head on which must have come around earlier than usual as it took even me by surprise. But still, no arguments were had. He knows me well enough by now to bugger off out of my way when PMS lurks within. And he did, bugger off I mean.

Anyway, I went to Lacie's as mentioned, we had a good old night gossiping, laughing, chatting, etc, and when I got home there were still no arguments, in fact we dived right into some husband and wife private time (and by that I mean sex).

As Barış is on late's at work this week doing his I.T technician thing, he doesn't start until 2.30pm so he stays up late at night playing his damn computer game (which is not code for porn btw), and is currently infatuated with 'World of Warcraft' or some such shite. At the age of 33 too FFS. So basically, what I'm trying to say is that we don't go to bed at the same time when he's on late's. He rolls into bed, square eyes and all, around 4am, waking up a snoring Gucci who in turn wakes me up and then I can't get back to sleep. Selfish eh? Normally after a few bitter insults, a load of tossing and turning and the occasional super early morning Horlicks, I either drift back off or lay there awake 'till I can take it no more. And believe it or not, this is all fine as I'm used to it by now - but when he doesn't come to bed at all, this makes for an angry Lei.

It's fair to say I was fuming when I woke up and realised that he had not slept in bed next to me - his wife. I found the fucker on the sofa. He can't use the excuse that he drifted off playing his game (although the twat tried) as his desktop computer was turned off and the balcony door was locked, so the tit had done all of that, then decided to sleep on the sofa instead of coming to bed. And after we had shagged an all!

He informed me that he fell asleep playing his game on his *mobile phone* whilst lying on the sofa. Apparently he is now that addicted that he doesn't just play one, he has two on the fucking go!

I think I'd rather he'd been watching porn than to lose my man to a children's fucking computer game.

FML...

According to Barış, falling asleep on the sofa is fuck all next to my coming home late and pissed up after a night out with my pals.

Really?!?

He's turning the tables on me the clever cunt... Not clever enough my dear because this argument is not about me! As if he's trying to confuse me with his trickery... Oh no, that's a different argument for a different day - today I win!

So, now he has gone to work leaving me to fester on his shitty behaviour. I'm not impressed and had I been single right now I would have decided to go get drunk for the rest of the day and possibly find a new boy toy.

Alas I'm not so I can't.

Seriously, is it just me that deals with this shit? Sometimes it seems that way when scrolling through Facebook.

Ahh Facebook, quite possibly the root of all evil, but my love for it will never die.

But what about all the pretentious crap people post about their perfect lives, perfect husbands and perfect face lifts? The rival gang are the absolute worst for doing just this. I'm not daft enough to believe their lives really are that perfect, but that doesn't stop it from winding me up. They call themselves 'The Marmaris Elite'. How can one group of knobs love themselves that much?

The elite turds more like it.

At least I haven't got to the stage of requiring a face lift yet. That's one thing to be thankful for today. Larissa (leader of the rival gang), on the other hand apparently got a face lift a couple of years ago. She is only one year older than me! I must admit that she looks alright these days after having gone through one hell of a makeover in the last couple of years, but really, a facelift at my age?

Must be that perfect life taking its toll...

Mind you, I'm sure it wasn't supposed to be public knowledge. One of the gang members was chatting with Lorraine one day and leaked the info accidentally, and now, well everyone knows, much to Larissa's disgust.

I can't help but laugh.

On you go Larissa, fuck off with your fucking face lift and your perfect life, you irritating cunt.

Tuesday 6th September

Time: 15.15pm

Dear Gal about town,

OK, so I have had a mad couple of days what with Sunday Funday and then its hangover to get over, but you will be happy to hear that the Husbando issue is now put to bed. He has promised not to fall asleep on the sofa and I have promised to *try* and come home earlier of a night out. So for now it's all back to normal - until the next time anyway...

So let me tell you about Sunday Funday;

Firstly it's not often that I blow my own trumpet when looking in the mirror, however on that particular day I truly felt that I looked good. I get those days very occasionally when I am 100% sure that the universe has conspired to line everything up just to give me a bloody good day and a bloody good look. This was one of those days.

I had clear spot free skin, I had lost a pound of the fat stuff, I had on my favourite pair of grey bum shaping shorts, a grey vest top that hid the ever-protruding pot belly, a fringed black sleeveless throw over thingy, with my hair looking wicked in pigtails (I kid you not it looked fucking ace, just ask Lacie), and to top it off I donned a grey trilby to complete the look. Honest to god, I rocked it.

We started off our shenanigans around 12.30pm at Lacie's house with me on whisky and Lacie on wine. Over a plate full of Cheddar Cheesy Pasta which was thoroughly delicious (until you live in a country where Cheddar does not exist, it is hard to know exactly how much you will miss it), we got talking about her pretty girl issues and how they may now be solved. Mind you, she changes her mind that often it's hard to know how long she'll stick to said decision.

As it stands today, she is opting for the wannabe and not the ex-husband. He is a nice guy, loves the bones off her and is probably what she needs right now. In my personal opinion he won't stick as he is a push over, but that's not for me to say. So for the time being, the girl has finally got herself a boyfriend! Bravo Lacie, bravo!

Another conversation was the planning of Lacie's fake surprise birthday party that I am currently in full swing of. I say fake surprise as although Lacie she has given me a strict invite list, she is not supposed to know anything about the rest of it. Clearly she does.

Lacie's other friend Natasha has seen her arse as I started the preparations solo. Not my fault as for 2 days in a row I asked to visit her so that we could plan it together but she kept putting me off. Eventually I got bored of waiting. I didn't do it on purpose, but what did she expect?

Back to Funday;

Arriving next was Lacie's wannabe and another of our friends - a great big gay Thomas Cook rep called Dave. Dave is quite a character. He is as friendly as they come but seems to only have one tone to his voice, and that 'dear diary' is monotone. That's fine, really it is, but a bit of enthusiasm wouldn't go a miss when informing us of his 5pm plans for that very day - especially when they involve a gay boy gang bang.

After a ton of selfies, we got our shit together and buggered off to a right little dive of a tourist bar next door to the hotel where Dave work's up on the Siteler side of Marmaris; 'Fantasia'. Pretty misleading name if you ask me...

I wouldn't normally knock about with tourists but Lacie assured me that we were meeting some mighty good ones, so I took her word for it. And sure enough, waiting for us there was Christine and Paul whom I met back in June. They are a good ole pair and like a drink as much as us. Paul greeted me with "has anyone ever told you that you are the spit of Kerry Katona?" Oh here we fucking go, must be the additional weight I'm carrying that has brought these comments back as this was the second time in 2 weeks FFS.

Thankfully we only stayed for 3 drinks and not the entire Funday - that really would have killed my buzz, but at least we got a good discount. The owner fancied Lacie you see. Well, who doesn't?

From there we headed over to 'Faros Beach', one of our firm favourites for a Funday. It's right on the beachfront, quite trendy, a tad more expensive than the tourist dive's, but we like it none the less.

Our banter and antics continued, Dave buggered off to get gang banged and Russian doll Jenny arrived to the party. So far so good, and Lacie only had one funny turn where she got a bit vicious and nasty for a second. Lacie's funny turns happen any time there is more than just the two of us. I'm not sure why, maybe it's me, but by God the girl could turn you to ice when she's on one. Thankfully they are momentary and then she's back to her normal witty self.

What should have been the final call of the day was 'Cheers' bar, also on the beach front. Lacie and wannabe did a disappearing act relatively early, about 8.30pm, with Christine and Paul not far behind, leaving just me and Jenny to continue the party. Which we did.

Bang goes my promise to try and get home at a decent hour of the night because this 'ere mo fo didn't get home until 05.30am FFS.

Where the F do I get all my stamina from?

If we could have found another place to party at that time I may still be out now, two days later...

I blame Kimmy because while in 'Cheers' she text and said that she was in 'Black Mirror' on the pop, so we headed up to join her. Instead of actually joining her group, we took over the karaoke and the whole of the dance floor. The video and photos that Kimmy took are quite horrific and she has been banned from uploading them onto Facebook.

We hit up 'Albatross' too, not that I remember much of being there, but apparently I danced?

At that point we decided it was time to walk to Bar Street as all the bars in the area were closing. To be honest we had absolutely no idea of the time, we just wanted to party. We got down to Bar Street and found it all in darkness, so it must have been about 3.30 – 4am. Instead of going home, we decided to get a couple of beers and sit on the beach instead. Never a good idea at that time of night as we were bothered by every Mehmet, Ahmet and Ali in sight.

No we do not want your phone number, no we are not interested in seeing your puppies and no, we are not lesbians.

Just because 2 gals wish to sit on the beach and contemplate life at 04.30 in the morning does not signify rug munchers.

And when all the beer had been drunk and the sun was a' rising, we decided to go home.

Creeping in through the front door didn't work very well as Gucci being the ever-amazing bark machine came charging up with a wagging tail, a million barks and the need for a pee.

Barış said not one word. Why would he? He was actually in bed earlier than me for a change! And if he ever mentions my being out 'till the butt crack of dawn, that's what I'm going to run with – "Annoying isn't it when someone comes to bed later than you disturbing your sleep".

Mind you, I do tend to do these things slightly more often than when he stays up late playing computer games…

Oh look, bad wife has returned. Let's face the fact here folks, did she ever really leave?

Next weekend looks no better as there may be another Funday on the cards. Yup, the party literally never ends here, but for now I'm not going anywhere until Thursday which has me out for dinner with Lacie, Jenny, Christine and Paul for an early 40th birthday meal for our Lacie. I will try to send myself home after dinner, but who am I kidding, we all know what will happen there...

And with that, I'm off to plan some husband and wife time for tonight as I'm ovulating.

ONCE UPON A WHISKY

Wednesday 7th September

Current Weight: Are you frikkin' kidding me, I'm back to 69 Kilos!

Time: 20.28pm

Dear Stupid spirit calling fool,

Well good evening you fucked up world. What have I done to deserve the horrific mood that has bestowed me today? Is it hangover? Is it ovulation? Is it that I'm a great big fat bag of bollocks?

Pretty much all of the above.

Last night I did indeed get my husband and wife time, so that was all good. Not long after Jenny showed up with beers in hand - also good. I could see she clearly needed to vent so what sort of a friend would I have been if I hadn't of cracked open the whisky and let her vent on? She has some serious ex issues and unfortunately the only way out that she can see is to actually leave Turkey. I understand completely and what with going through similar I totally see where she is coming from, it's just a shame it has come to this. Who knows, she may, just may find the man of her dreams while back home in Blighty.

As booze would have it, we got mighty pissed and I ended up moaning that I missed the good old days where Husbando romanced me instead of his computer games. At this point Barış came out on the balcony to join us for a smoke and Jenny decided to let rip. Barış is quite good in these situations and would never be rude to a friend of mine and took it on the nose. He finished his smoke and buggered off back indoors, not wanting to endure any more 'torture' as he called it, leaving Jen and me in the mood to do a Ouija board.

At 12.30am this was nothing more than a fucking bad idea as we got chatting to the biggest of evil spirits ever, spelling out the name Lucifer -

seriously, I'm not even joking.

Now some may say this was either Jenny or me pushing the coin, but I swear to God it wasn't me, and I'm pretty sure it wasn't Jen. In fact Jen got that freaked out that she grabbed the homemade board (piece of A4 paper), took it out into the street and burnt it right there to a crisp. She then proceeded to throw the coin into the dry canal that runs parallel to my apartment.

After that things started to get a bit odd. I noticed Gucci wasn't his normal happy go lucky little self. When he was trying to eat, he kept backing away from his food giving a little yelp - that boy loves his food as much as I do, so it was troubling to say the least.

Time to call it a day me thinks.

The negativity from our half hour chat with the other side had basically ruined the night's vibe anyway, and my poor ole Guch seemed to be paying the price for it!

Obviously Jenny didn't fancy walking home on her own (who could blame her), so Barış was forced into giving her a lift. She was also concerned about Guch, assuming he had been possessed, so I told her I would let her know how he was in the morning...

While Barış was running Jenny home, I took Guch on the final piss walk of the night. Whilst out a very odd thing happened - as Guch was taking a dump, the street light that we were stood underneath sparked and went dead leaving us in darkness. I hurried Gucci up, bagged up his turd and started the walk back home passing more street lights which also went dead. I'm not afraid to say that I was mighty freaked out and ran the 2 minutes home.

Off course this could have been a power surge, Turkey is after all known for them, but what if it wasn't?

I think it's fair to say we better stop with our spirit calling antics for a while, shits getting weird.

This morning Guch was the same as the night before, so we took him to the vets. I got ridiculously over emotional and bawled my eyes out, but my lovely vet Alev informed me that it was only a gum infection. Unfortunately for Bariş, he caught me teary eyed and went on to call me stupid right there in the vet's surgery - so you can just imagine how I reacted to that... I took an eppy fit off course. I screamed, shouted, called him a right cunt and told him to never speak to me about my boy Gucci ever again. He is, after all, my first born.

This did not go down well. In fact it caused a bit of commotion as the vet had no idea what a cunt was and asked me to explain right at the moment a British woman walked in with her sick cat.

It sounded so funny to hear a Turkish woman say the word cunt that I almost cracked a smile. Almost.

By this point I felt a bit of a knob asking if she could check Gucci over for signs of possession, so I let that one slide and figured that if he continues with his odd behaviour we will look up a pet exorcist online instead.

Thankfully the pills seem to be doing a great job.

Other than the above ridiculousness, we have also been to the hospital to get my blood test results and Husbando's 'wanky in a cup' results. His test was clear - yup, my man has strong swimmers. Apparently I'm still popping out eggs too (good), but what we don't know is if they are getting to their destination (bad). After my next period (if I'm not pregnant before) I have to go to another f'ing hospital for some random dye in my tubes test.

Seriously, what a load of hassle...

Anyway, we have been told to get back on that horse today as I'm ovulating, but what with my foul mood I really can't think of anything worse than sex right now. Plus we are no longer allowed to use lube as apparently it kills off the swimmers! How the hell my shrivelled up old minge is going to let in that creation of a cock without lube I will never know! I've a feeling I'm going to end up with a red raw fanny... Unless he does it Turkish style and spits on my punani of course. I'm not even kidding, Turks are notorious for aiming and spitting instead of cracking on with a bit of foreplay.

Mum, if you are reading this then it's your own fault and I take no blame whatsoever. **PUT.IT.DOWN.NOW.**

Talking about Mum, I've managed to piss her off too as when she called today and asked how the diet was going, I gave her a gob full when she told me that I shouldn't be on 1200 calories a day, that I should ignore the advice of my expert trainer who went to university for this stuff and instead listen to her as she was slimmer of the year at Slimming World 20 years ago.

Righto Mum, righto.

Seriously can my day get any fucking worse?

ONCE UPON A WHISKY

Friday 9th September

Current Location: People Restaurant and Bar, Marmaris

Current Weight: Oh just fuck off

Time: 16.19pm

Dear Girl that just needs hibernation,

Gucci and I decided to escape from the house and come sit in a relaxed environment for a while. I was driving myself stir crazy indoors and couldn't take it any longer. There is no particular reason for this other than the fact that I am one lazy bitch and simply can't face cleaning up last night's aftermath, and if I stay here long enough, Husbando will arrive home from work and do it for me. Well, chance would be a fine thing but it may be cooler when I eventually take my sorry arse home, which in turn may inspire me to start the clean up.

Just what did I get up to to have the house looking like a tramp has gone binning? Well, Jenny turned up at the door (again) at 5.15pm yesterday afternoon with mascara running down her face and a red wine stained vest top. She did not look like the immaculate Russian doll that I have come to know and love. She resembled a guest of 'Jeremy Kyle', but thankfully with teeth.

God love her, she's had more issues with the ex and her mind simply couldn't take any more of it. Obviously on a normal day I would not break out the whisky at 5.15pm, but this was not a normal day and poor ole Jen needed someone to get shitfaced with.

Funny how all my friends think of me when getting shitfaced is required...

So, we drank (a lot), we ate a satisfying meal of beans and cheese on toast (Branston because they were on sale in the import shop), we drank some more, then decided to be wino's on the move and go star gazing on Marmaris beach.

Jenny was hammered; I on the other hand couldn't seem to get even tipsy. This happens to me when friends have traumas. That's a maternal instinct if ever I saw one. Maybe I am cut out to be a Mother after all?

Anyway, I left the house to go star gazing in my non-showered state with not a scrap of makeup and 5 day old unwashed hair. What a minger. And wouldn't you know it, whilst looking like I had been rifling through the skip, we bumped into a guy I had a bit of a crush on years ago down at the beach. Why God - why me?

So you see, it's not really my fault that I needed to run away from the cleaning today.

I have however done a bit more work on Lacie's 40th birthday to which Natasha is still seething. Let it go already..! All I need to do now is pop along to the party shop in town, get some bits then decorate the venue on the day and we are good to go.

Speaking of Lacie, she is another that may have seen their arse from a situation that was beyond my control. Last night we were due to go for dinner with Christine and Paul (the tourists), but I cancelled as I just didn't fancy it. Lacie thinks that Jenny and I ditched her in favour of having a few drinks at my house, and let's face it - that's how it looks, but is not the case at all and I told her so. But Lacie is one stubborn ole cow and was pretty fucking weird about it when chatting to her on Facebook earlier. Let's just hope she has got over it by tomorrow night as we are having girls' night round at mine.

If my face can't tempt her round, I'm sure the ton of booze and food will.

Oh FML, the liver never gets a rest these days does it..?

ONCE UPON A WHISKY

Tuesday 13th September

Current Weight: 68.5 Kilos

Time: 15.31pm

Dear Food and drink lover,

Firstly I need to point out that when I weighed myself earlier I happen to be exactly the same weight as I was 3 weeks ago when I first started this new diet. That's going well then - not!!

It could possibly have something to do with the amount I have drunk over the course of this last week. I've had 4 nights on the booze - 4 fucking nights! That's not like me at all, honest, in fact 4 nights is 2.5 weeks' worth of drinking these days!

So let me explain...

Three quarters of that drinking was down to Jenny. It's safe to say I'm all Jenny'ed out what with seeing her on Tuesday, Thursday and then again for girl's night on Saturday. It ended up being just the two of us BTW as Lacie had me hung, drawn and quartered. Normal Lacie behaviour - always jumping to conclusions, but I know if I give that girl enough space she will pull right in the end. The problem is, I don't understand space boundaries and feel the need to fix an issue immediately.

I was deciding what to message her when a shining beacon of hope arrived on my Facebook in the form of the most excellent post I have ever seen in my life. It was a 'Back to the Future' meme that quoted 'I have travelled to the future and you're still a cunt there'. It was literally just what I was looking for. I sent that over to her immediately and low and behold I received a reply. I knew that would spark a reaction one way or another, and just as I thought, her mood lifted as she replied with a winky emoji.

The next day she was back to her usual vile self and normal life resumed.

Sunday was a lazy day indoors. I did sweet F.A other than watch movies for the whole day. The night was a bit different as I had dinner with Kimmy Minger and her Sisters at 'Faros Beach'.

I may have slightly veered off my diet when I ordered a bottle of Rose wine for myself, garlic bread and a four cheese pizza. Yup, I probably ingested my total calorie count for 4 days in one sitting... And, as booze would have it, it didn't stop there. We headed over to 'Black Mirror' for more drinks. Not one of my favourite places as it's a bit dingy, and well truth be told, it's quite chavy, but hey, I'll go where the drink is.

It always surprises me how extraordinarily well the chav bars do over here. Most wouldn't step foot inside a bar like that in the UK, but here they are packed.

So we had a couple of shots and copious amounts of vodka, and then surprise of all surprises, my old pal Vicky the hardcore party animal calls me up to ask where I am. 5 minutes later she was ordering a drink with us.

When Vicky's on holiday she goes out every single night. I don't know how she does it. I struggle to peel the top lid from the bottom if I have more than 1 night out, but not our Vicky - she parties harder than anyone I have ever met in my whole entire life!

From 'Black Mirror' we headed over to yet another chav fest, 'Albatross'. I don't mind going in there as the drink is cheap, the DJ plays all my favourite tunes and generally you always find people that you know milling about. Yup, that's how it was this particular Sunday evening.

The only point that spoilt the whole night was a nasty drunk vicious ole queen that thinks he is famous all because he is part of a drag act in a bar that shall remain nameless.

Big fucking deal pal.

Why is it that certain queens think they are above everyone else? I've had issues with this two bit hack for a few years now, dating back to 'The Final Summer of Vodka' days, and although I try to bury the hatchet like an adult, this arsehole continues to be a grade A cunt. To put it mildly, I fucking HATE this guy.

And as per usual, we had words. Again.

So with my talons firmly out of joint, I ended up in a new soup kitchen with an old friend. I don't see Robyn that much, we are not bosom buddies or anything like that, but I have always liked her.

So the final hours of being out were spent stuffing myself with the second meal of the night (tomato soup and a ton of bread) while discussing my hate for bitchy ole queens and why Bariş is never seen out with me. Some people think he is a figment of my imagination. Sometimes, so do I.

I finally managed to creep in at the grand old time of 06.15am. I am nothing if not becoming a master at the creep. Even Guch couldn't be bothered to jump off the bed and make a fuss.

And with that, I am going to remove all the food from the house and put myself on a starvation diet. It's either that or diet pills...

Friday 16th September

Time: 23.49pm

Dear Possible PMS,

Well well well how the tables have turned. I usually can't be arsed writing at this time of night however if I don't vent somewhere I am likely to tell two of my friends to go fuck themselves. Talk about sly bitches...

Last week it was Lacie that threw a tantrum due to a misunderstanding, but that was all cleared up - or so I thought. Clearly fucking not as she totally decided to extract revenge in the Laciest way possible...

For quite some time she has not invited Jenny and me to her house at the same time. I have not asked her why and I won't. Jenny and I have not discussed this either, but it is weird don't you think? This week she had Jenny over to her house on Tuesday and then they met up for after work drinks last night (Thursday). I was neither invited nor told about either of those events, however a woman scorned can do better detective work the FBI.

I already had an idea they were together as when I was messaging Lacie last night she was not replying. Only today did I receive a reply and she was all nicey nicey about it. I didn't throw my dummy out of the pram ala Lacie last week 'cos I'm not shit like that, however it hasn't stopped me feeling like a left out twat inwardly.

It's totally revenge right?

I would say that I plan on steering clear of them both for a while, however it is Jenny's leaving Sunday Funday this week (yup, she is actually leaving) and I couldn't possibly not go to that. I don't feel like going, but I know I would be cutting off my nose to spite my face if I didn't, and that's just not the way I roll.

The plan is to get ready at Lacie's with a bottle and go out about 5pm to meet up with Jenny's other friends from work. Hmph, don't fancy that much and so I told Jen that I would get ready at home and meet them out. Funnily enough she didn't put up a fuss, she just agreed. Nice one love.

Whatever they say about 3 being a crowd is totally on the money this week.

I know it's only Friday and I really hope by the time Sunday comes around I'm feeling better about seeing them, because as it stands now, I couldn't care less if I saw either of them ever again. Sly mother fucking bitches.

All the while I'm still arranging Lacie's 40th birthday party...

What a wanker. And just to be clear here - I mean me.

Other than that, I've had a good week so far. Husbando had a couple of days off work for Byram (my least favourite holiday due to the sacrificing of sheep and goats), so he actually put down his computer game and took me out. Well he had to really as he knows I would have started world war 3 with the neighbours as they literally killed a goat right there on the pathway of my apartment block. What makes matters worse is when I took Gucci out for a walk, they had not cleared up the innards of the poor animal and I hadn't noticed the guts and shit left behind because I was averting my eyes from the crime scene; however Guch did and picked up a load of intestines. I nearly fucking died when I saw what he was carting around. The intestines were bigger than him FFS!

As I couldn't cope, I screamed for Barış to come and help. Well, he was as much use as a chocolate fucking tea pot, not wanting to touch the intestines either, but he knew what had to be done. Guch did not want to give up his vile disgusting prize but in the end had no choice as Barış dragged the gross mess out of his gob.

I was ill. Fucking ill.

For a vegetarian like me, this was hell.

I really shouldn't have to be subjected to this on my own fucking pathway, but seeing as I am, why the fuck cant they clean up after themselves?

Selfish mother fucking pricks springs to mind.

On Wednesday we had the best Turkish breakfast ever up at 'Sahin Tepe' on the hill behind the Water Park, overlooking the whole of Marmaris. Some may say that this is a very romantic place to go with your other half. Not us though. We took any last romantic notion out of said breakfast by damn near ignoring each other while our heads were stuck in our phones - Barış playing on his portable computer game and me uploading photos to Facebook.

It wasn't all doom and gloom, when the food arrived we chatted and laughed and then fed the chickens and their babies. We can be mighty nice to each other sometimes, and while scoffing our food, that was one of those times.

After that, I made Barış come clothes shopping with me for a new outfit for Sunday Funday and he didn't moan once.

Thursday was another OK day. We ordered some new oversized cushions for the sofa's (very mature of us), and went and had dinner with his friends in 'Blue Port' shopping centre.

Now it's Friday and I feel like slitting my own chubby wrists. I know why; oh yes, I know exactly why. Half of it is to do with my *'friends'* and the other half is to do with the possible period on its way. I say possible as I am ever hopeful that this will be the month that I get knocked up.

I'm on day 22 of my cycle, so by Wednesday next week I should have started my period. All I can tell you is this; I feel like I'm going to come on, my back has random aches, my nips have the usual twinges and I have some serious over emotional PMS going on totally explaining why I hate my friends right now.

ONCE UPON A WHISKY

So bastard period, do your bloody worst, I dare you.

In other news, my diet has gone well all week. I have not had binge boozing sessions (due to being excluded), and I am finding it easier and easier to stick to 1200 calories per day. Bravo Lei!

So with good work on the diet front, I will bid you adieu and try to lighten up a bit.

Best not put Adele on as that just tips me over the emotional edge and I am likely to jump on Betty 2.0 (my newest scooter), go visit Lacie and hand her the back the knife I've just pulled out of my back.

Tuesday 20th September

Current Weight: 65.2 Kilos! Honest to god!

Time: 12.55pm

Dear Hangover collector,

Hello period pain, good bye chance of being preggers. My period has not actually arrived yet, but is definitely on its evil way. At least that explains the last horrific diary entry.

PMS much Lei?

I absolutely know it was my hormones in overdrive because I'm back to loving my friends again. I should delete it really, but I am a woman and I have periods. Word.

We went out for Jenny's Sunday session and dear God, what a session it was!

I got to Lacie's house for just before 2pm and hit the whisky immediately. Lacie was on the wine and Jenny was nowhere to be found. She didn't actually show up until just before 5pm. By that time I was dancing along in my own little party having a whale of a time.

Eventually we arrived at 'Faros Beach' looking like a crew to be reckoned with. Me in my night time shorts, vest top, military style black gillet, killer wedges (that have totally disappeared and left me with black feet instead) and my blonde locks for once down. Lacie was in skinny jeans, a vest top and killer heels, and Jenny in a black off the shoulder top, tiny night time shorts and killer heels too. Yup, we looked like a girl band that were we not already part of, we would want to be part of.

Five vodkas later and there was a different look about us. A lot less put together, a lot less sophisticated, and a lot more downright disgraceful. At this point Lacie's wannabe came to meet us, and as Lacie always does, she slyed off home soon after that. #ExpectedBehaviour.

The night didn't end there, well, not for Jenny and me. We moved onto 'Cheers' and danced our asses off for the remainder of the evening. There was a brief period where I had a sickly turn and had to lie down on one of the sun beds, but it lasted all of 10 minutes I'm told, and Jenny had the right idea by ordering a bottle of wine for us for when I pulled round.

This must have been where I lost my shoes.

Anyway, pull round I did, plus I drank the wine. Do you know what, I'm quite impressed with my ability to bounce right back from the edge of darkness - that shit takes skills.

It wasn't a horrifically late night - I think I snuck through the door around 4am (14 hours after we had started) much to the delight of one little piss fest of a Gucci monster as I took him out for a late night walk. Bariş was suitably impressed with the time of my arrival and all was well in the world until yesterday when I woke up with possibly the worst hangover I have ever had in my whole entire life. I was green, literally green. Nothing could break the hangover beast.

Normally my entire day and night would have consisted of nothing but laying on the sofa and eating my way through the pain, however I knew that come 6pm I had to start getting ready to go out again - and it was definitely not something that I could cancel as Camilla would have killed me.

Yup, my buddy 'Queen Minger of Içmeler' is back in town and she had organised a Facebook group meet up. She looks after a group called 'Içmeler Lovers' and a few times a year they have these meet ups. Last night was one of those times. So I made myself look as human as I could and hauled ass over to the dark side, and by dark side I mean Içmeler.

I met up with Camilla and Sam Buca (one of the nicer drag queen's that I know) at the 'Vodka Bar'. I wasn't going to drink due to the horrific state of me, but you guessed it, the pig that lurks deep within simply couldn't help itself and I ordered it a beer.

What is it they say about hair of the dog? It's all fucking lies - my shitty hangover remained ever present.

Other than the hangover, the night was a really good one, I didn't disgrace myself and Camilla certainly knows how to organise a piss up.

On the way home, Jenny messaged and asked if I fancied 'one for the road' as she was using the Wifi in a bar near her apartment, passing time. Usually I would never have phoned the ole ball and chain to double check if he minded, however I felt like I might be taking the piss a bit, so gave him a quick call. He was not a happy Husbando and hung up on me after telling me to do what I want.

Righto then, I will.

Reverse physiology never worked well on me, and although I knew I shouldn't do what I want and just go home, I decided to have that quick drink with Jenny instead.

I am a living breathing nightmare to be married to, but hey, aren't all independent strong spirited females?

By the way, it was just one drink and not another bender. I can control myself at times, plus the hangover was at its peak and I wanted to sleep it off desperately.

I put myself to bed around 01.45am, fell into a beer induced kip to be woken this morning to the wonderful sound of hammering rain and no fucking hangover.

Hallelujah!

Anyway the best bit about my week so far is that my diet is finally starting to work! I hopped on the scales earlier to be greeted with a 3 kilo weight loss! Glory days! Now all I need to do is stick to the calories until I get to

60 kilos and I will be one happy Minger!

How ole Husbando is going to feel when I tell him later I have two more nights out planned for this week is another story...

Sucks to be Bariş sometimes.

Wednesday 21st September

Time: 16.00pm

Dear Wannabe single socialite,

Today has not been a great day.

Considering the way Bariş hung up on me, I thought I was going to be in for it when he got home from work last night, but to my surprise he was frosty but not half as bad as he could have been. In fact we sat together quite comfortably and watched a couple of episodes of 'Breaking Bad' before both sloping off to our respective computers. We didn't chat much, but that's not bad considering.

Just before I decided to take my tired arse to bed, I asked if he had any pain killers in his work bag as my back and stomach ache from the impending period had reached the peak of misery. I don't know if he assumed the pain killers were for a hangover or what, but he very sarcastically informed me that if I couldn't take the pain then I shouldn't play the game.

Silly, silly man.

I didn't have a fucking hangover - I had WOMANS FUCKING PAIN. You know, the type of pain that a bastard man will never in his whole life understand nor feel.

I flipped out and have not spoken to the fucker since.

You may think I'm taking this a bit far considering my bad wifeliness of late, however my PMS'ing self can't bear to look at him let alone speak to him. All I can say is the feeling must be mutual.

I swear, the atmosphere in this house is that thick you would need a chainsaw to cut it.

And so it continued;

Bariş knew we had the new cushions to collect today, so when he informed me at 1pm that he was pissing off to his friend's house I nearly, very nearly flipped again. I asked him what on earth he thought he was doing buggering off at that time when we needed to go to town. He said sweet F.A (I mean nothing at all, no reply, nothing) and went out onto the balcony to play his computer game on his phone.

25 minutes later he came back in and asked why I was not ready.

Am I a mind reader? How was I to know that he was waiting for me to get ready?

I thought he was playing his game before going to his friend's house FFS! So to irritate him further I decided to stay seated at my computer scrolling through Facebook for the next 20 minutes before finally getting up to go for a shower. It doesn't take me long to get day time ready but I made sure to drag it out.

When he parked his scooter outside of 'Yilmaz' restaurant in the centre, I asked why we were parking there, to which he grunted "food". So, we sat and ate our sandwiches in total silence, only speaking when I gave him my half of the bill. Then we went to the cushion place, collected and paid for the cushions and came home. I told him I would take the cushions inside so that he didn't need to come in - he got the point immediately and disappeared down the road in less than 10 seconds flat.

I actually hate him right now.

This feeling will subside off course; after all, it's a monthly occurrence - but for the love of God, why is he such an irritating fucker during the least appropriate of times?

Today is possibly the 102nd time I have considered divorce since getting married. Give me 2 days and I will wonder why I took everything so seriously, but right now, whilst in the thick of PMS rage, there is no need for his bag of bollocks.

So, let's sum this shit show up shall we; I came on my period this morning, I have severe PMS, my husband is a cock and I need to get drunk.

Ahh fuck it, I'm going to crack on with planning the 'Girls Gone Wild' Bodrum weekender in November that Lacie and I are have decided we need. That should cheer me up. Just the thought of a 5* Star all-inclusive actually gives me glimmers of hope.

Yup, nothing beats a weekend away on the piss with your bestie to get you back in the spirit of living.

ONCE UPON A WHISKY

Sunday 25th September

Current Weight: 64 Kilos – Woooppppiiiiiiiiiiii!

Time: 19.20pm

Dear Same old, same old,

I have just re-read my last entry and what a sorry state I was in eh? I would love to tell you that all is back to normal, but I would be lying. Not one single thing has changed in 4 days.

It's true; Husbando and I are still not speaking.

It's been nearly a week now. Something may have gone slightly wrong somewhere...

I have not attempted to speak to him because pinning him down has been a bit of a nightmare. I don't blame him as arguments are never pleasant, however we need to break the ice and start somewhere. With my PMS safely in tow, now is the time to get this sorted. I have no idea what I'm going to say, but I'm bored of not speaking.

Yup, it's been a silent week and it's about time that changed.

Friday night was particularly annoying. He came home from work, muttered a quick 'hi' and that was it. I decided to fuck that shit, got my glad rags on and went out with Camilla and Sam Buka to 'Blackpool Bar' to watch the 'Roxy Tart' show.

Seriously, why is drag all that's on offer here?

We had a great time, and it was nice to actually speak to people and my mood lightened considerably. I told them about our 'silent' week and now I wish I hadn't as the looks on their faces said it all - I was being lumped into that 'British wife Turkish husband' unsuccessful marriage bracket.

Arrrgghhhh nooo, that's not it at all!

I got a little lecture from Camilla about making more of an effort to stay home instead of partying and to try to at least keep PMS at bay. Easier said than done, but I will give it a bloody good go. After all, he is my lobster - one that I sometimes wish I could boil alive, but mine none the less.

I had a good night, and when the show finished a friend of mine that now lives in Antalya (who is training to be an airline Pilot) messaged, said he was in Marmaris, and if I was out would I want to go for a drink. Yes please as these 2 were buggering back off to the dark side (Içmeler) and I wasn't quite ready to go home.

Let me tell you about Pilot boy; he is Turkish, ruggedly handsome, a bit taller than me, has dark floppy hair, just the right amount of stubble, smouldering bad boy eyes and the most kissable lips you have ever seen. I think it's safe to say I have an enormous crush on him, but that's alright 'cos he is as gay as they come.

He has a long-term partner and also happens to be going through a bit of a rough patch with his 'wife'. In fact he told me he no longer fancies him and finds himself flaccid. This cheered me up no end. Not because I'm a sadistic bitch that gets off on other people's unhappiness, no, but because it's not only me with husband issues.

So we chatted it out, each one telling our sorrowful tale, we drank, we partied, we went over to Içmeler's one and only night club 'Ambiance', drank some more, went down to the beach with a bottle and then he tried to kiss me.

WTF? I mean - WT ACTUAL F?

What is it with men? You're not even safe with the gays these days!

He puts that attempted snog down to the amount of booze that he put back that night, after all, we consumed a hell of a lot.

But does this mean he considers me manly?

FFS, don't I have enough to deal with as well as adding manly in the mix?

Anyway, I have decided that as long as Barış doesn't go directly to his pal's house tonight from work, this chat is damn well happening. It's simply time. I feel sick at the thought of it. My stomach has been churning all day and has given me a 'nervous belly'. That's a polite way of saying that I've had the shits. I really hate things like this. I hate discussing feelings and emotions. I'm certainly no girly girl when it comes to this sort of stuff. I would rather sweep it under the carpet and forget about it, however I fear the carpet storage is just about full.

Oh life, one minute you're up, the next you're down. I wonder what tomorrow will bring...

Wednesday 28th September

Time: 17.43pm

Dear The good life,

What a difference a few days makes. I have just got back from what I can only describe as quite a romantic day out with Husbando. Yes that's right, we spent the whole day together and not one of us is dead. Progress is being made.

I didn't have the chat with him on Sunday night as I was simply to bitter about it. My head was up my arse and my mind was tired from over thinking. So, I slept on it. I woke up with a clearer image in my weary ole mind, sat Husbando down in the morning and explained PMS to him without the hostility that I felt the night before.

What I was not expecting was his response: "Every time you go out, I think I am going to receive a phone call informing me that you're dead".

Say what now?

He says that I push it to the limit each and every time I go out and why do I need to have that one last drink? Well, I like to party, that's why, but what the bloody hell has this got to do with PMS?

It seems Husbando had been doing some thinking of his own... Clever cunt.

Without going into the full low down of it all, we have both agreed that effort needs to be put in and that we are willing to do the work; me with my booze control and him with being more understanding when I'm PMSing.

I have come to the conclusion that marriage is work. And a lot more work than when simply boyfriend and girlfriend. Whether one chooses to put in the work defines whether the marriage is successful or not, but fuck me it's not half stressful when married to a foreigner.

Yesterday (Tuesday) was an alright day. I managed to fit in a 20 minute workout (even 20 minutes is too damn long when I hate every second of exorcise) and I also went to the 'Ahu Hetman' hospital to see the gynaecologist.

I have decided not to go back to the state hospital as I found their service slightly lacking. The first time was OK, however when I went the second time, the gynae did not check my endometrial wall when he had said he would... I was also due to have dye squirted in my women's tubes, however when they told me the price (650tl), being the doctor that I am, I decided to take matters into my own hands and tell the gynae in the 'Ahu' hospital what I actually believe to be the problem with my not getting pregnant; that being my endometrial wall's thickness or lack thereof it.

Good old gynae humoured me and had a poke around inside and has said that yes, it is indeed on the thin side. He wants to see me again this time next week and if it hasn't grown by then he will prescribe hormones to do the job. He then expertly robbed me of 150tl for a 6 minute appointment.

Anyway, to ease the pain of cash extraction, Jenny came over last night for booze and beans on toast. As Barış was working till 11pm we had time to gossip about everything and talk a bit about Lacie's 40th birthday party looming tomorrow.

F-me that's come around quickly.

And when Barış got home from work, we even convinced him to come to the party. You see, progress...

So this brings us up to today, Wednesday. First things first, we dropped Guch off at the vet as he needed a sheer. I say sheer as it is literally like sheering a sheep when shaving Guch. I could make a coat out of his hair I swear. It would be fucking gross, but I could do it. He also needed to have his gums checked over so we left him there while we went off to enjoy a few hours.

And enjoy we did - I'm not lying either!

We started off the enjoyment with a Turkish breakfast in 'Yunus' on the beach front. Husbando did not get his phone out even once to play his computer game. I however had mine out uploading a selfie of this very rare occasion.

From there we hopped on his scooter and took a leisurely drive out to Yalanci Boğaz right down the other side of Marmaris, very close to where we got married at 'Joya Del Mar' hotel. That area is literally the loveliest of places.

FYI we did not have a big fat Turkish wedding, we are simply not that sort. It was a bit more British style, and instead of the usual Canli music we opted for a DJ.

Weddings here are not as expensive as the UK, but still, when watching the pennies, it's great to have friends that are in the entertainment business that cut us a great deal for their musical services. Our wedding play list consisted of a whole heap of 80's rock and Taylor Swift. Exactly as I had planned.

The Turks that came seemed to enjoy themselves, although were a bit unsure of my moshing on the dance floor. You can imagine the scene - a bride in a great big black dress, pretty pissed up and moshing to Def Leppard. Good times.

Anyway, back to the romantic day out;

We went down to the pebble beach and sat in the sun for a good hour or so. We had a great time finding pebbles to skim in the water.

Bariş - Expert level skimmer.

Me - Sore loser.

Of course Bariş tried to teach me how to skim, but sometimes it's better to give up on a lost cunt of a cause.

And with that dear diary, I'm going for a lie down on the sofa as I'm knackered from all this niceness.

October

Saturday 1st October

Current Weight: 64 Kilos

Time: 17.14pm

Dear Party goer,

I have had the most magnificently disgusting hangover since Lacie's birthday, and even now, two days later, I'm still not 100%. As parties go, it was a good one (I think?); people came, booze was drunk, good times were had with absolutely no shenanigans to report of. Mind you, what sort of party ends with no shenanigans? A fabulous at 40 party, that's what!

Have we all finally grown up? Will there be no more carry-on of a night out?

Fuck no 'cos who could bare that? It's just that this particular night was one of sophistication and maturity. But - it ends here!

We started the night off with dinner in 'Tiffanies' on the beach front. Not one of us had eaten there before, so it could have been a disaster that thankfully turned out satisfyingly well. Thinking back now what an odd thing to do, choose a restaurant we had never eaten in for such a special occasion. Were we drunk?

Anyway, as it happens all was well. Food - good. Company - good. We will eat there again.

As I had done the seating plan, I knew I wouldn't be sitting next to any mo fo's, and let's face it, in every party there is at least one or two. Seating 20 people was actually harder than I originally thought what with this one not liking that one, and that one not wanting to be next to or opposite the other one. And of course I didn't want to be the arsehole that hogged the birthday girl, so I decided not to sit next to Lacie and placed Natasha and Berni beside her instead. Jenny and I were just a couple of seats down, and, at Lacie's request, the wannabe a few seats further as they had not gone public and didn't want to make it obvious. Not a bad seating arrangement even if I do say so myself.

Prezzy wise she got so much stuff! Not that I'm shocked, Lacie is well liked. When it comes to my birthday I generally get fuck all. Now this could be because I have never got into the gift giving scene, or it could be because people don't like me enough to buy me something - either way I'm missing out.

As it was my besties 40th, I couldn't very well not buy a gift, so I went halves with Bernie. We opted for real perfume, a silver bangle and a plaque to signify her 40th. Not bad I reckon.

At 9.40pm a select few of us buggered off to the venue for the fake surprise portion of the evening at 'Cuba' bar. We needed to set up and make sure all was in place. As Jenny felt uncomfortable with Lacie's other friends, she came along with me. I'm not surprised as they can be a daunting bunch, and with Jenny being quite new to the scene she has not had to endure many of these group outings before. She also said she felt some odd vibes radiating from Lacie which she puts down to the week before from Sunday Funday. Apparently Lacie wanted me to go home as I had a skin full but Jenny wanted me to stay out. Obviously I chose the second option 'cos I'm a cunt like that.

Anyway, Jenny came with me to set up for stage 2.

I asked everyone to be there for 9.45pm so I was surprised not to see some of the faces that had promised attendance. Needless to say, their names are now mud after discussing them with Lacie - Sue being prime suspect numero uno.

Sue was invited to the dinner along with Rita, however due to work commitments she could make it for the surprise part only. No problemo - in fact better for me as I didn't have to sit through boring conversation with her across the dinner table. Rita messaged and cancelled in advance so I knew not to expect her, but Sue on the other hand didn't show up and didn't message.

Had she had an accident? Had she got food poisoning? Or was this plain and simple payback as Lacie didn't go to her birthday the week before? A total mystery as still no word from her. I know she's alive as she's liking all the party photos on Facebook.

What peaked my interest was, prior to the party during the day, Sue had posted a load of photos with her much younger boyfriend on the beach. I'm not judging her for having a much younger Kurdish boyfriend - I'm judging her for staying with him when she physically caught him cheating.

Yet another resort boy caught out and escapes being dumped. What am I missing?

Why do these young bucks never get thrown out on their arse for being such sly fuckers? I swear I will never understand it. Do they have diamond dicks or something?

I mean, who am I to judge? But still...

Anyway, Lacie arrived at the fake surprise party and looked happy enough, and the rest of the night went down well. Even Husbando kept his promise and joined us! I forced him to meet Lacie's wannabe in the hope they'll become friends because we had already decided it was time to start double dating. Barış took it all in his stride but later reported that wannabe was not his cuppa tea. Each to their own I suppose.

And when Nuri (Bariş's bestie) arrived, this made it all the more fun as Jenny, Bariş, Nuri and I decided to have an after party at our house. When everyone had left the birthday bash we piled into a taxi and set about having a balcony party. I'm not sure what time it started but Jenny and Nuri left at 07.30am ending the night with a pissed-up snog.

And so, now that I don't have the party planning to keep me occupied I need something new to get my teeth into.

Match making perhaps with Nuri and Jenny?

As Nuri is already infatuated, he twisted my arm into arranging a group bowling date, which I have for Monday night. They make a cute couple after all, and if that perhaps keeps Jen in the country for a bit longer then it's all good by me.

Tuesday 4th October

Current Weight: 65 Kilos – Yep I've jumped up again...

Time: 19.43pm

Dear Ex rep girl,

I'm slightly pissed off with the world right now and quite possibly all that dwell on her. It may simply be an early bout of PMS heading in my direction - but wait, haven't I just got rid of a dose of that? Or, it could quite possibly be the fact that Nuri is a complete cock and totally buggered up my bowling plan.

Fucking Nuri...

But before I tell you about him, I will document my week so far;

After my previous diary entry, as well as being hung-over, I was also in the mood to do something that did not involve drinking at my house. FFS it gets so sodding boring, and a Saturday night is certainly not to be had indoors. As Lacie already had plans, I messaged Jenny to see if she had any ideas on what we could do what with Husbando working lates.

Jen is just like me, always up for doing something at a moment's notice, and if it's cheap or free, all the bloody better. 10 minutes later I had jumped on Betty the electric scooter and was en route to collect Jen. We decided to haul arse up the 'Tepe' hill and sit with a bottle of beer overlooking Marmaris and its bewitching night time lights.

Kastro (my car) and I did the very same some 5 years back. Fuck sake, that was a fiasco of a night spent with a young cheese I met on the internet. I had no plans of a repeat performance, but what I did have in mind was a lovely view, a bit of good chat, then home for the night.

What happened was this;

Every Turk and their tourist girlfriend also had the same idea, so instead of our peaceful hour or two we had loud music, Turkish dancing, nut shells being spat out everywhere and a bloke that pulled his knob out right next to us and took a piss. Talk about rotten.com.

When Husbando phoned at just after 10pm it truly was heaven sent. He failed to previously tell me that his winter hours had kicked in and when working lates he now finishes at 10pm. So, I told him where we were and what we were doing, and with that he said come back to the house and let's have a balcony party.

I suppose it was always going to happen so I may as well embrace it.

When we arrived home, we found Husbando and Nuri sat firmly in situ on the balcony already on the beer. What else could we do but join them..?

Once more we were up 'til the wee small hours of the morning, and once more my neighbours complained the following day. They can do one with their complaints because them mo fo's are the worst for noise. Who the fuck throws a wedding and / or army party directly outside our bedroom balcony window a million times a year, deafens us with Çanli music then goes on to complain about a few people on a balcony?

Urm, off you fuck.

Between the street parties and the sacrificing of animals on my very own pathway - I am the best neighbour they could possibly wish for.

Sunday brought with it plans to see Connor Candlish. Yes that sexually issue ridden dude is back in town for a week. I had no plans to drink as I was still feeling the effects of the night before's boozy balcony party, but I'm guessing you know what happened.

I arrived at the 'Saffron' hotel where he was staying at just after 3pm. I was planning on having a coffee, collecting my duty-free whisky then seeing if he fancied a roast dinner - but what happened instead was this;

Connor's fit mate Marty ordered me a cider (why I have no idea as I don't even drink cider), then Connor ordered me beer(s). After I realised a day of drinking was on the cards the brain kicked in and decided that beer and cider were far too calorific to stay on for the duration. The hotel had happy hour with cocktails 2 for 1, so me in my tipsy state thought that for the same price as beer I could have a cocktail - and with that began the start of my horrific Long Island Ice Tea hangover...

We did nothing but stay in the hotel and possibly offend every person in situ, as the more we drank, the louder we got. Ex reps curse a fair bit and are simply no good at being good.

I pitied the people around us.

Connor being a light weight slopped off to bed around 8pm. He pulled a shits trick and buggered off while I went to the toilet - standard bloody Connor. Just as I thought I should probably go home at that point too, Jenny messaged and asked what I was up to. Before I knew it Marty had ordered another round of cocktails and Jenny had joined the drink-a-thon.

I swear, it never fucking ends!

Although it wasn't particularly late that I dragged myself home (02.00am), Husbadno was not exactly happy about it. I had, after all, been out on the pop for 11 hours.

So, yesterday being Monday, after the hangover subsided, I started to get super excited about our group bowling date. Lacie and the wannabe couldn't make it, however we were still planning to go right up until Nuri messaged, said he was super tired from work and he would get back to me if he feels like coming.

Urm, what now?

This is not the type of message to send to a super organised Virgo, oh hells to the no. No fucker was going to keep us dangling - puppets we are not!

And after he had begged me to do it!

I informed him immediately that it's mighty rude to keep the rest of us sitting around waiting all day for him to make up his mind, and that if we were not going bowling then I would make other plans. Nuri, a bloke that likes to assert his control over women didn't appreciate that - but neither the sodding hell did I!

What the fuck is wrong with people!?!

So, we didn't go bowling and I didn't make other plans.

I mean I could have, but by this point I was in a sulky mood and didn't want to darken anyone's doorstep 'cos I'm mindful like that.

Plans with Connor have however been made for tomorrow night and I couldn't be more excited. Nuri on the other hand has realised the error of his ways and has asked to come round tonight with booze. Although he usually would have been more than welcome, I know his game. He doesn't actually want to see Barış and I – Nope, he wants to see Jenny, but he also knows that she won't see him 1 on 1 and will only entertain a group date. So with that in mind, I told Nuri that he had totally fucked up his chances of doing anything group wise this week as I am fully booked, and without me there is no group date.

Ha! Gotta love karma!

Mind you, I'm not lying - although I had no plans for tonight, I certainly didn't fancy drinking as I'm saving that for tomorrow with Connor. Then on Thursday I'm doing 'Taj Mahal' with Lorraine, on Friday I'm enjoying a night in with Husbando, and Saturday its Dave the Thomas Cook reps birthday.

So Nuri, stick that in your pipe and smoke it.

What an underestimating cunt.

Saturday 8th October

Current Weight: 64 Kilos – Up, down, WTF?!!

Time: 16.21pm

Dear Girl that must learn to say no,

Just a quick entry today as I am suffering from a hangover. I know, again.

Whatever will the neighbours say with all the balcony boozing that's been going on of late?

I have spent a small fortune this last 2 weeks what with boozy days/nights in and out, hospital appointments, dinners, birthday presents and clothes that I have decided to not go to Dave the Thomas Cook reps birthday tomorrow night. It's a bugger as Lacie's going and I've not seen her since her birthday last week and I'm dying for a catch up - but, that will have to wait.

I am, on the other hand itching to book our Bodrum weekender for November. As shallow as it sounds, I can't wait to announce our mini break on Facebook. The rival gang are constantly checking in at VIP restaurants and showing off their Facebook envious lifestyle, so it's time we met this head on with some flashiness of our own.

I'm expecting to hear whispers of 'Just who do they think they are' and 'I'm so glad we're not friends with them', when I'm secretly sure that some wish they were because it must get very boring being so stiff, serious and lady like all the time!

We couldn't be serious if we tried - it's simply not possible. We laugh, we banter and sometimes, just sometimes we can be civilised if we have to. Mind you, we don't post posey photos on Facebook and maybe that's our downfall. Our photos are that of a pair of daft fuckers pulling faces and thinking we're funny. Of course we also do the occasional duck face selfie (we are women after all) but nine times out of ten, our posts are usually to be poked fun at.

The rival gangs are nothing of the sort.

If I see one more video of them 'working out' I will scream. And what is it with them donning 'Active Wear' for everyday life? I mean come the fuck on, sling on a pair of jeans when going out for a coffee on a non-work out day.

Wankers.

Anyway, Wednesday I did indeed meet up with Connor and Marty. Uch - Chav bars, whyyyy?! I'm not ashamed to admit that I very nearly cancelled when they told me to meet them at 'Geordie' bar. In all my years here I had never stepped foot in there and probably never will again. I simply don't do dancing waiters with hair gelled sky scraper high - isn't it time for a new look guys, that one's been doing the rounds since '97...

 No, just not my cup of whisky, vodka, tea or even piss.

And to make matters worse, on my third vodka, Marty jumped up to dance knocking all 3 drinks flying - all landing on me (my crotch to be precise). I was flooded with liquid and looked like I'd pissed myself. I was not nearly drunk enough to find it funny, not like them pair of chumps that had been on it all day. Matry tried to make up for it and bought me a drink, but still, I had to walk round for the rest of the night leaving wet patches everywhere I sat and having to explain that I don't have a slack fanny.

FYI, I still managed to stay out till 04.45, pissy crotch and all!

It wasn't as bad as it could have been, and most of the night was salvaged as we finally left 'Geordie' bar and headed over to 'Cheers', then ended the night in 'Albatross' before going for the usual soup run on the way home. There is nothing like a good bowl of tomato soup and lavaş bread at 04.30am to have you feeling like you really are a shitty wife at times.

Will I ever learn the concept of going home to my husband at a decent hour?

Surprisingly on Thursday my hangover wasn't horrific. Thank God as I had a hospital appointment to get too. It's a good thing that vodka doesn't smell otherwise I may have knocked the Gynae right off his seat with my fumes.

Yup, the quest to get preggers continues.

Turns out I was right; my endometrial wall was not thick enough to have an egg implant. I was prescribed some pills to beef it up and sent on my merry way; right after the hospital masterfully extracted another 150tl. But, at least I know what the problem is.

What has pissed me off is all the wasted sex I've had trying to get up the duff. I mean I know it's not really wasted, but when I have forced Husbando into doing it more than either one of us could be arsed during the fertile window, when we could have been all Netflix and chill instead - well, it makes my blood boil. I mean who wants to have sex 3 nights in a row anyway?

To celebrate finding out what was wrong with my shrivelled up ole wall, Lorraine and I indulged in the biggest mound of food you have ever seen over at 'Taj Mahal' curry house. Oh God, do I love a curry! I refrained from having a beer as I literally wanted to stuff my face with Indian and the beer calories (plus Lorraine's whinging about boozing) are simply not worth it.

Booze always used to be exempt from my diets over the years, however with getting older, Julia my trainer has said that it's more so the booze that's the problem...I'd like to think that she's wrong, very wrong - but deep down I know it makes sense...

We took a few selfies and a couple of food shots because that's what people do, and after dinner we had a long walk down to the marina, stopping off for a drink at 'DeDe' restaurant. Once more, photos were uploaded. I mean how could we not when the marina is simply so gorgeous by night? We giggled as we knew we were clogging up people's newsfeeds with both of us checking in and tagging each other, but sometimes it's the simple things in life that bring the biggest laughs.

And after we had finished our attack on Facebook, we took a walk around town then headed back up the beach front home.

After totting up my calories for the day, I realised I had well and truly exceeded the 1200 daily limit, but for the occasional treat I don't mind. Hopefully the long assed walk may have burnt off a few of those sneaky little fuckers.

What I do mind is overdoing it every day, which is what I seem to be doing lately. Every blinking day there seems to be something, like Jenny popping by for a balcony booze session at 5pm yesterday. We were supposed to be starting early so we could get to bed early, but as per usual that didn't happen.

Good intentions are just that - intentions only.

I can't even say it was a great night because it wasn't! We ended up going down Marmaris beach with Barış and Nuri, parking our arses on a pretty filthy section of sand while we did a typically Turkish thing and sipped our home brought booze while eating our jacket potatoes.

There was a tinge of shitness to the night when Nuri asked for glass #2 of my duty-free whisky. Before thinking I literally bit his head off with "FFS Nuri, why can't you just go to the shop and buy your bloody own". As soon as I said it I felt bad, but the damage had been done. He did indeed piss of to the shop to buy his own, and this is totally what he should have done in the first place, but I still felt guilty for snapping.

When he came back I felt the need to explain that firstly I am totally PMS'ing (again) and secondly, due to my diet I can't drink beer so my diet whisky is sacred. I shouldn't have to explain myself as my booze is my booze and how very dare he have asked for 1 glass let alone 2, especially as Barış and Jenny had been to the shop and bought their own...

Seriously, that Nuri can be a right knob.

Let's just say that the universe was on Nuri's side that night;

We came down to the beach on 2 separate scooters and obviously left on the same - Jenny and I on Betty the beast and Barış and Nuri on Barış's scooter. On leaving, Jenny and I didn't get very far as we skidded across the road and I immediately knew Betty had a flat.

I phoned Husbando who then asked Nuri to come back and collect us in his car. While we waited we decided to push ole Betty up to the bike repair shop that thankfully was only just up the road. Nuri and Barış arrived shortly after and took us up to my house. We all took a pew on the balcony and that's when Nuri asked for another whisky.

Is he serious?

At that point I realised that I had to bite the bullet, and through gritted teeth poured him a glass of the amber nectar as a 'cheers for the lift'. I'm still pissed off about it now and he will never get another out of me - that's a promise, because when I woke up this morning I noticed my whisky was three quarters empty and I only opened it last night! Damn it Nuri!

Jenny is leaving soon so all this double dating will come to a stop. Oh wait, no it won't as Lacie is finishing work for the winter on the 23rd of the month and so *our* winter drinking regime will begin.

At least I know my whisky is safe with her...

ONCE UPON A WHISKY

Tuesday 11th October

Current Weight: 63.5 Kilos Whoopppiiiiiiiiii

Time: 13.22pm

Dear Unhappy camper,

As I sit here completing my diary entry for today, I also find myself contemplating life. I really should pour myself a drink while I contemplate as it helps with the process - it's got to be 5pm somewhere right?

Why am I contemplating?

Well, if the last few days are anything to go by I'm sure you would too...

Saturday I did little else apart from clean the house and watch 'The X Factor'. I did not go out but I didn't feel too hard done by seeing as though we had been to the beach the previous night. Bariş refused to watch 'Shit Factor' and buggered off to his friend's house. All the better for me as it's nice to watch TV alone.

Sunday he was off work due to changing days with his colleague. I usually have plans for a Sunday but this week I made sure that I was totally available to do something with the ole ball and chain. Turns out he wanted to do ball all other than see his friends and he made that abundantly clear while we sat in silence over breakfast at 'Yunus'. Not a problem cunto, two can play that game - so I messaged Lacie to see what she was up to. She suggested meeting at 'Faros' at 3pm which I immediately jumped at.

Yup, I was quite happy to leave Bariş with his friends so that they could have the delight of his miserable face - mind you, I'm sure he perked up no end around them... Funnily enough, I certainly did as soon as I saw Lacie.

We chatted, gossiped and not one drop of the hard stuff passed my lips. There would have been no point really as although Lacie was on the vodka Red Bulls, I knew she wouldn't be staying out for long, and if I had had a drink I would be vile going home at 7pm to sit and get sober for the rest of the evening. So, best not to bother.

And when it got to 7pm, Lacie did indeed call it a day. It pains me how well I know that gal.

We did however sort out the details of our mini break:

Bodrum - out. Kuşadasi - in.

Reason being the hotels had better deals on 5* all-inclusive for that time of the year. Plus Kuş is a winter resort which means tourists! I simply can't wait to start the day with a Bloody Mary, brunch with Mimosa's and then work our way through the cocktail list 'till we need to start again or pass out. Yes, that's what a 'Girl's Gone Wild' mini break is all about.

And once 7pm hit, I dragged my arse home for some boring Sunday night TV viewing consisting of 'The X Factor'.

Pretty much nothing else to report other than the brass balls of Husbando. I never have been a girl that can control facial expressions, and try as I might its damn near impossible. So when Bariş asked for a shag, my face simply couldn't control its sheer and utter disgust.

Learn how to be less cuntish over breakfast and then you may get your shag, fuck face.

Monday was a good day. Lorraine and I knobbed off to town and had a pretty decent shopping spree. We stopped off at our favourite little food place 'Yilmaz' to fill our faces before continuing the spree. We also had a lovely walk around the marina with a pit stop at 'Subway' for coffee and a cookie before finally heading home around 9pm. Bariş is back on lates this week so he wasn't due home till 10pm, so it gave me time to walk Guch who was hopping up and down trying to hold in his wee, failing miserably, spraying me with his excitement.

Damn that wee infested dog!

Bariş called at 10.15pm and said he was at his friend's house and would be home in 15 mins. Turkish time means add on another 30, but I really think he was taking the piss when he arrived home at 01.15am - 3 sodding hours later.

I obviously gave up waiting and went to bed around midnight. That's when the rot set in.

I heard his bike pull up first, then I heard him unlock the door, creep in, get changed and then sly his way into bed. He said nothing all the while as he thought I was asleep.

He was wrong, very wrong.

I was lying there with my eyes closed silently plotting his death.

This morning was a different story - oh yes, Husbando tried to creep up my arse. Not in the anal sense as I'm not that kind of girl - I mean he felt guilty and was like a creeping Jesus all nicey nicey. I'm not a morning person anyway, so all I can say is that his brown-nosing antics went down like a lead balloon.

Of course I couldn't help but have a go about the 15 minutes/3 hours and informed him that there is no need to lie about how long he was going to be. Had he have informed me he was going to take the piss I could have done something myself. I could have stayed out with Lorraine a while longer or I could have popped over to Lacie's or Jenny's for a bit, but no; the selfish mo fo told me fuck all so I had to sit there doing bugger bloody all apart from wait for his bastard arse to drag itself home.

Anyway, he is not around right now, he's pissed off to his mate's house to avoid nasty Lei. Best thing he could possibly do as I'm not just nasty, I'm vicious too.

To prove this point I sent him a message informing him how much of a selfish prick he is, you know, just in case he didn't get that from my earlier outburst. Mo fo not even bothered to open the message. I know his game. He does the same as Lacie; reads it when it comes through without having to open it and then not reply.

Crafty cunts.

At least when I go out I don't make false promises about the time I plan on getting home...

So, I'm not a happy camper today, and its only Tuesday. Jesus, what's the rest of the week going to be like...

At least my weight has come down, not that anyone notices.

ONCE UPON A WHISKY

Saturday 15th October

Current Location: Starbucks, Netsel Marina, Marmaris

Time: 14.41pm

Dear Girl and 4 walls,

After watching mindless crap on TV this morning I decided that if I didn't shift my arse now I never would, so fuelled with cabin fever I hauled ass down town. Yup, I have joined the ranks of the wannabe writers, unemployed and the coffee addicted business folk here at Starbucks this afternoon.

So here I am, looking like a skip rat in my baseball cap (because I couldn't be bothered to brush my hair), dark glasses (as I refused to don a scrap of mascara), a pair of black material shorts that I slept in last night and my military style T-Shirt that funnily enough is the only decent thing that I am wearing today - bar the stain I have just noticed above my left nip area. I would have been happy as a pig in shit with my Pumpkin Spice Latte had I not have seen *her*.

Why oh why when you go out looking like a complete and utter tramp do you always manage to bump into someone that you would really rather not? In any normal circumstance I wouldn't give a crap; however *she* is not a normal circumstance. *She* is a fuck face of the highest order and that particular fuck face happens to be Larissa, leader of the rival gang.

Wouldn't you know it *she* looked immaculate - and for once not in Active Wear! With her newly styled rose gold blond locks, black 90's style choker, Nirvana T-Shirt, ripped jeans and the cutest of Chanel handbags which I'm sure is real as that bitch doesn't do Turkey's designer fakes; it's fair to say that Queen Bitch Larissa nailed that look. Cunt.

Off course we happened to bump right into each other.

I was making my way to a table by the window and she was making her way out, making it impossible to pretend that we hadn't seen each other like we usually would. The universe must have lost some love for me, forcing us to stand politely and make small talk.

The fucker looked me up and down, taking in my laptop, scruffy appearance and possible B.O. and said "Just got done in the Gym have you Lei?"

"Yes indeed I have Larissa" I lied, too ashamed to inform her that I had literally been picking my nose in the house before deciding to come out, "and now time for a much-needed coffee and a quick check over my emails before I go home, shower and then rush out for a very important meeting".

Jesus Lei, really?

She did not look impressed and continued "I'm glad to see that you're working out, I noticed from your Facebook photos that you're retaining weight. If you need any help, I can recommend my personal trainer. As you can see, he has done an amazing job".

Oh fuck off with yourself you nasty northern troll.

As I literally couldn't think of sweet F.A. to retaliate with, I had to fake answer my phone while I waved bye (a 2-fingered salute in my head) and walked to the furthest table away from the world and sat my hobo self down.

It's fair to say I'm seething right now, but with myself I must add.

One day my mind won't be so slow to catch up with my mouth. One day I will think of something suitably witty, sarcastic and degrading to say right back to the stuck up ho - but for today, it was game over.

1- 0 to Larissa.

Other than that vile experience, my week has been pretty boring and mundane.

On Wednesday Husbando took me for a sandwich in town and then we went home. Jenny was supposed to come over that evening but cancelled as she had a heavy night up the mountain with beer and a boy the night before. Instead I watched some really shit TV in the form of 'The Gilmore Girls'. Never again.

Thursday was no better. I didn't leave the house once - I simply couldn't think of anywhere to go. I had done my retail therapy on Monday and didn't fancy doing any more, so a day indoors it was. Other than booking our Kuşadadi jolly for the 11th November, I stayed home and emptied my wardrobe of summery items to make way for the winter favourites to come back out from under the bed where they had been hibernating for the summer.

That was all well and good until it was 30 f'ing degrees on Friday and I couldn't find a thing to wear before heading out to meet Lorraine for coffee... I have these stupid ideas at times but FFS it is mid-October; it's not supposed to be this hot still!

Anyway, after I eventually found something to wear, I finally left the house to meet up with Lorraine. We pretty much did exactly what we did on Monday, bar the retail therapy; 'Yilmaz' for soup and 'Subway' for coffee.

Jesus, my life is so damn exciting these days that all I have to look forward to is a cookie at 'Subway' and the watching of 'The X factor' on the weekend - which is exactly what I am doing tonight by the way.

I used to be at least a wannabe socialite. Now I'm just an old married has been. But, all this is about to change with Sunday Funday looming tomorrow! Oh yes, I will be breaking out of this week's shitty rut and partying with the girls in 24 little hours. Jenny has finally got a leaving date so this really will be her last Funday before she's UK bound on Friday.

We have not all been together since Lacie's birthday and we didn't get much chance for the three of us to chat then, so tomorrow is either going to go one of two ways; lots of tears while Jen gets boozy emotional or lots of nasty jibes as there is still underlying issues lurking.

So, watch this space...

18.10pm

I'm back, but ever so briefly.

I got home about an hour ago and decided to put my feet up and watch a bit of 'Nip/Tuck'. Gucci jumped up onto the sofa and made me pet him with my feet. Nothing unusual about this until I looked up from imputing my calories onto my fitness app to find Gucci thrusting into my feet, wanking himself off.

In 11 and a half year of being together, never once has Gucci tried to have sex with me. Lacie yes, but never me - never his Mother. I wouldn't have been so disgusted had I not actually watched the little fucker shoot his load.

With my jaw hanging open in sheer an utter revolt, I gagged as I cleaned up doggie jizz from all over my sofa. This experience was nothing like when he cocked his leg for the very first time, oh fuck no - this 'dear diary', was no proud moment.

I don't think I can ever look at my boy the same again...

At least I have other news to take away the pain;

Mum just skyped to tell me they have booked to come for a month over Christmas! Yey - that means I won't have to lift a finger for a whole month! Kastro will be filled with petrol which will be a first since the last time they came over for my wedding, my fridge will be filled with food which will be a first in 2 months since starting this diet, and Gucci will be walked to within an inch of his life, which will be a first since being in Spain for a month last year. I won't have to cook, I won't have to wash up, I won't have to hoover and I won't have to mop. All I will have to do is enjoy reverting back to my early teen years and let the olds do everything. Oh bugger me I bloody love it when they come to visit. Even Dad brings his tools to service Kastro!

Never mind that they are getting on in years and are not coming to do anything of the sort.

No, never mind that at all...

Yes, life is good again right at this moment. Fuck knows how it will be tomorrow, but for right now, right this minute, it's bloody beautiful, doggie jizz and all.

Friday 18th October

Current Weight: 65 Kilos. I literally hate myself.

Time: 12.30pm

Dear Flip flop's,

I came on this morning. That explains the weight gain. It was not a surprise - this has got to be the first time since getting wed that I absolutely knew I wasn't pregnant and was expecting the river to run red. Yup, now that I know my shrivelled up ole wall couldn't take it, I saved myself the devastating 2 week wait.

I have however started the pills that the Gynae prescribed to beef up the wall, so this time next month I could very well have a bun in the oven. I am nothing if not a glass half full kinda gal.

In other news I'm on day 2 of hangover.

Sunday Funday really took its toll. Don't get me wrong, I had a good time, but is it worth the agony? In high insight, no, probably not.

I arrived at Lacie's house around 5ish for pre-drinks. We had a good catch up, slagged off Larissa and co. then went out about 6.30pm. We started at 'Zola' on the Marina, and with our drinks we ordered a few Tapas. Lacie's tourist friends Christine and Paul were back in town and joined us, with Jenny arriving about 8.30pm.

Laugh we did, but every so often Christine would tell me off for swearing. Don't get me wrong, every sentence is not littered with fucks and bastards, but one does pop out in conversation from time to time. And FFS, it's not as if they have never met me before - they knew what to expect.

Actually, I know I wasn't offending them - I'm pretty sure Christine was trying to prove a point. I think she was trying to establish herself as cock of the walk. This did not bode well with me, I mean how can a temporary tourist decide to be leader of our group? As if.

But did it stop my mouth from carrying on with itself? No, in fact telling me to stop only makes me more defiant.

FYI Jenny was swearing too but Christine said fuck all to her.

This cemented my belief that Christine didn't like competition. *She* must be seen as the leader, and the only way to do that was to take down the gobby, slightly over confident one - me.

In our little circle we have no leader - we are not the rival gang, so just why she wanted to establish herself as such was a mystery, especially with her ridiculously temporary status! It was laughable really, but battle of the bitches none the less. I let her carry on with herself as I couldn't be arsed arguing with a female that had insecurity issues and was quite possibly going through the change...

Another annoyance was the bill.

I asked for the bonus points acquired from the food and drinks to be put on my 'Zola' card. Jenny suggested splitting the points between mine and her card, but that was a crock of shit as she hadn't eaten. Obviously I said no as I would be done out of points and what with her leaving on Friday, she doesn't even need them! Of course Christine took Jenny's side and informed me that her and Paul's points were to go on Jenny's card.

Seriously, what the fuck is wrong with people?

At least I could count on Lacie, and our combined points went on my card.

Jen must have felt bad as after a little while she suggested that we go to 'Zola's' sister restaurant 'Bono' on Wednesday for a final supper and to use the points. I won't see any of those points as there is only 73tl worth and that's enough to cover 1 person's bill alone if that one person is frugal. I have agreed though, as pissed off as I am... Lacie on the other hand flat out refused. I wish I could be like her at times as she does exactly what she wants 100% of the time.

After 'Zola' we headed over to 'Purple Rain' as they make the most delicious cocktails. What delicious cocktail did I order? Whisky and diet Coke. I don't believe in wasting money on sparkly cup additions unless there is a happy hour on, so a plain old whisky was good enough for me.

From there we hit 'Lighthouse', still my absolute favourite of all of the bars around town. Its small, plays excellent 80's rock music, has a pool table, the drinks are cheap and it attracts all walks of life. It reminds me of a surf bar with its ramshackle decor and the shabby chic appearance of the clientele. Yep, 'Lighthouse' is my kind of place.

Lacie's wannabe joined us at this point and I knew instantly that it wouldn't be long before she was heading home, because when the wannabe arrives, it only ever means one thing. I was right, when Christine and Paul were paying their bill, Lacie then paid hers too. So, this left me and Jenny as it always does. We sat and chatted for a while and I could see that Jen was not in the best of moods, so when I asked her what was up, her reply was a bit of a shock. Apparently I had been chatting with Lacie most of the night and not really speaking to her.

Oh arse, there is always bloody something. Maybe if she hadn't of been such a turd about the points..?

Consciously this was not intentional, but can I really be blamed for my sub conscious actions?

Anyway the guilt didn't last long as I suddenly noticed I was not wearing my own flip flops. I was wearing a pair of black flip flops yes, but they certainly didn't belong to me...

Who the, what the..?

We hit Bar Street about 1am, heading directly for 'Back Street Garden' bar as my neighbour had told me earlier in the day that a big DJ party was on that night and to come along as the atmosphere would be excellent.

No DJ party in sight, apparently they had cancelled. Just our luck eh, but we got a free vodka out of it as apparently whisky is too expensive to be given away.

It was that free vodka that had Jenny and I legless. Honest to God. Jen said we were both compos mentis previous to that vodka, but after it we were complete wrecks.

Nice one free vodka, you absolute tit you.

And that was it. Or at least I think it was as my memory blacked out on the first sip of that last vodka.

Apparently I got home at 3am ish which is a rare turn up for the books.

I have suffered though. The headache I've had for the last 2 days has been unreal. Free vodka is never a good idea really is it..?

Jenny is supposed to be coming round tonight. I would cancel, really I would, but the daft mare doesn't have a working phone for me to get in touch with her, and by the time she goes on Facebook, she will already have arrived. FML, the last thing I want to do tonight is drink, seriously, but with 4 days left till she leaves one has to make allowances. Maybe it will fuck up our plans for tomorrow night's dinner? One can hope.

Ahh well, best she leaves the point's card here with me as God intended.

Lacie messaged this morning to inform me that a pair of her black flip flops are missing, however my bejewelled ones are in their place. Bonus!

17.36pm

Well well well, scrap what I said before about knowing I'm not pregnant. I just took my tampon out and there was not a drop of blood on it. I put it in this morning when I noticed 'period wee' - but now, nothing!

I have full blown period pains, I am bloated and I feel horrifically emotional. Not weepy mind u - it's a weird overwhelming sense that I love the ole ball and chain. Highly unlike me to feel such strong emotions.

I have of course thought that this could be the doings of the new tablets which I started this morning after seeing the period wee. I wish now that I had waited to actually give the period a chance to appear like I was supposed to.

To get some clarification I called the Gynae. He said not to worry about it, but he didn't realise that I hadn't actually let the period manifest before starting the tablets.

Why am I always in such a rush?

Although the Gynae is probably right, I'm sat here half convinced I'm with child.

Friday 21st October

Current Weight: 65 Kilos.

Time: 12.01pm

Dear Oculus hater,

Bad day for me weight wise. On Wednesday morning I weighed in and was over the moon to see that I was 63.5 Kilos, so when I stepped on the scales there 2 minutes ago, I nearly had heart failure to see that I had shot up to 65! I have not over eaten or drank (much), so it must be these sodding hormone pills! And to add insult to injury, I'm definitely not pregnant as I am now in the thick of my period. Bad times.

Although it may have disappeared for 24 hours, on Tuesday night it started with a vengeance, and 4 days later, when it would usually be on its way out - it's furiously clinging on..! Another possible side effect of the hormone pills. Oh lucky me.

On an unrelated note, Jenny and I had a good couple of night's worth of shenanigans, Tuesday night being the first;

She showed up around 8.30pm and left the following morning at 6am. What we did in those hours is beyond me. All I know is my first litre of whisky that Connor brought over is now finished with the second opened and near half empty, there was a crumpled-up Ouija Board on the balcony and a Husbando passed out on the sofa.

Wednesday was not good. I woke up starving at 12pm, had a shower, forced Husbando into sorting his face out and then we headed to 'Yunus' for much needed food. Over lunch Barış told me about a new virtual reality thing that they have at the bowling alley. Decision made - off we went to see what this was all about.

It's called 'Oculus' and basically you wear these huge goggles that transport you into whichever game you choose. I chose roller coaster. I should have known at the time that it would nearly kill me...

Honest to God I did not think it was going to be as real as it was. I was standing there, gogs on head, losing balance, riding around on this virtual coaster feeling sicker and sicker by the minute. I felt like I was 15 again and having a major whitey.

After a few minutes I could take no more and ripped 'Oculus' from my head, fell to the ground with white hot sweats and proceeded to throw up all over. That bastard finished me off.

Obviously a mixture of hangover and I want to say vertigo, but 'Oculus' was not my friend. No, 'Oculus' was a cunt.

That'll teach me for being clever with a hangover - I have learnt my lesson, oh have I ever. I was ill for 3 hours following that experience.

I very nearly cancelled dinner with Jenny before realising I would be a shit friend to do such a thing. So, I forced myself to put my face on, did my hair (well covered it with a trilby) and found something to wear that didn't make me look like the bag of bollocks that I felt.

When arriving at beach front 'Bono', we were both in a bit of a state in all fairness; Jen with her realisation that she was leaving in 2 days and me with my 'Oculus' hangover. We did not make for great company. This didn't stop us racking up a bill of 133tl, and that was after we had taken off the 73tl worth of points! Guess which mo fo got stuck with paying that then...

What did I say about those points..?

We were not aware of just who was in the joint that night until much later when we noticed the rival gang in all their glory getting up to leave. The 5 gang members sashayed out of 'Bono' followed by wafts of various perfume and bitchy attitude's. Of course they all looked immaculate but I always think that an ugly soul can't be masked by makeup and good clothes...

They each looked over, nodded in our general direction and I swear I caught wind of a few shitty comments about my trilby. I had neither the will nor energy to bother with any kind of retort as my hangover and period had knocked seven shades of shite out of me.

Just you wait, my day will come...

Thursday had me living in the depths of hell.

Oh, how I suffered. No more booze for me for a while. Oh wait, I have a date with Kimmy on Saturday for a big fat 'Taj Mahal' and drinks before it closes for the season. All I can say is no Sunday Funday for me this week, absolutely not. I will behave and sort myself out now, no more binge drinking until we arrive in Kuşadasi next month!

Thankfully at least 50% of said binge drinking will come to an end because Jenny has now gone. Well, she is on her way to the airport so that's as good as gone. She's overstayed her visa and didn't renew her residency permit, so she may have a fine to pay with not a sausage to pay it with. I've told her to message me if she can, however I doubt I'll speak to her until she gets home tonight - unless off course I receive a call to collect her from some dingy Turkish jail in Dalaman. You never know, it could happen!

And finally today I have started to feel slightly better, but I still can't quite manage to do a work out. That's 0 so far this week, a new record for me!

At least impending doom has not struck in a while, although I do feel that if I heard an 'Adele' tune it wouldn't take much.

Fucking periods.

WTF is it with them that has me like an over emotional, non-confidant, beached whale that can't think of a witty come back to mean girls that will be sporting trilbies this time next week?

Tuesday 25th October

Current Weight: 64 Kilos.

Time: 18.03pm

Dear Girl with no social life,

I've had a shite few days since my last entry. Not even dinner with Kimmy helped. Actually, that was the straw that broke the camel's back, not that she knows it...

Basically, our plans were made 2 weeks prior, and those plans consisted of a curry date and a drunken night out. Since when have drinks ever meant diet coke and water?

When I picked Kimmy up en route to 'Taj' I could see she was looking a little peaky, so I asked if she was OK. I didn't expect her to inform me she had the biggest hangover known to man. Of course this was mighty unexpected as she very rarely drinks and knew our night was about feeding our faces and drinking our own body weight in booze - so why oh why did she get shit faced the night before?

She went on to inform me that her boss had taken her and a few others out and she couldn't say no to drinks. Did they tie her up and pry her mouth open by holding her nose to cut off oxygen? NO! You could say no to drinks, you just didn't fucking want to. And I get it, I am very much the same - but don't kid a kidder love...

I mentioned it would have been a better idea to have pushed our night back a few days so we could enjoy it more, to which she informed me that no, she fancied a hangover curry. Talk about a selfish Minger. A heads up would have been nice love, you know, so that I could have done the right thing and cancelled.

I absolutely would rather not have spent the 60 odd tl on my curry when I could have been home, watching 'Shit Factor' and moaning to Barış instead. That was an added expenditure that I didn't need for half a night out! And had I have known it was going to be a 'Taj' only affair I wouldn't have dolled myself up - I would have stuck to my dinner only clothes, I would not have washed my hair 2 days earlier than required, I would have used mascara instead of the false lashes and would not I have used the good foundation.

Selfish, selfish, selfish Minger.

Oh colour me not impressed, not at bloody all. But to make matters worse, I was home by 10.15pm. What sort of wannabe socialite is home by 10.15pm on a Saturday night? This fucking sad act, that's who.

FML, why couldn't she have just cancelled?

OK, so we had a nice catch up, this much is true - but that didn't stop me sitting there silently seething while she brought me up to speed with what's been going on.

Being the outspoken kinda gal that I usually am, I could have said something, anything, to make her realise the error of her ways. Other than the 'why not cancel' comment, I said sweet FA. Why? Because firstly I am a knob, and secondly I hadn't seen her for an age and she is leaving for the winter soon.

She has mentioned a night out before she leaves, but before I interpret that all wrong and start getting excited about partying, I need to confirm that she doesn't just mean a cuppa tea and a slice of toast.

I really could do with having some solid plans this weekend, what with Jenny no longer here and Lacie going to Ankara to visit the wannabe's family for the first time - one is starting to feel like a human loose end.

Even John has other plans... Well, it is Halloween weekend and John always goes all out for Halloween. Something else I have not been invited to...

Mo fo. Him, not me.

Talking about Jenny, she did indeed make it to the UK in one piece. She did not have to pay a fine, nor was she jailed. I had images of 'Midnight Express' bouncing around my turbulent mind but thankfully they remained images alone. She is one lucky cow because her transfer turned up late so she found herself rushing to make the flight. This worked in her favour as she got let off by the police and told that she could pay the fine on her return to Turkey - if she ever does...

Anyway, as well as my blaa Saturday night, I also did not have any kind of Sunday Funday. I already knew it wasn't to be, however had I of known the Saturday was going to be such a wash out I would have arranged to go out for at least a couple of drinks. Humph.

So what did I do on Sunday instead? Well I cleaned the house, managed a small work out, went to visit Lorraine for a coffee, came home, took wee infested Guch out that couldn't keep his wee infested legs crossed for 2 bleedin' hours, attempted to sort out more winter clothes from under the spare room bed, failed miserably, left the spare room looking like a bomb had gone off and then watched a new TV show called 'Divorce' with Sarah Jessica Parker. It was an OK kind of day, nothing spectacular but not quite as shit as it could have been.

Monday came and went with me doing not much else other than watching a beauty hack online for painting your nails with glitter polish using a sponge. I thought I would give it a go, got out my spare make up sponge and began. The left hand worked very well indeed; the sponge lived up to the hype and it only took 2 coats to get my nails looking like they had 5 or 6 coats.

The right hand however looked fucking ridiculous.

I had black glitter nail polish literally everywhere - 10 times worse than usual. It looked like someone had projectile vomited glitter all over me. It took me an age to pick off the nail polish from my surrounding skin and I swear it was starting to itch and become enflamed.

Lesson learned, I won't be using the sponge again.

After that fiasco I really fancied a little drink to calm my not so steady hands, but no one was up for it. Barış was home at 10pm and I thought he may fancy getting pissed with me, but no, plain and simple no. So I had a little drink on my own. I really hate doing that as I feel like a bit like a sad ole wino. Who am I kidding; I am a sad ole wino occasionally but needs must. At least it made me feel slightly better about my crappy nails.

I went to bed slightly tipsy, slightly pissed off with life and with a slight amount of impending doom.

Fuck sake doom, what have I done to deserve your visit?

So, this brings us up to today, Tuesday. Another day that I have done pretty much ball all other than pop down to 'Rumours' bar for a coffee (on my todd) just to get out of the house for an hour. Not a bar I would usually frequent, however as I was driving by on Betty the scooter I spied an intelligent looking older chap in there reading a paper and I thought how mature and adult he looked. I fancied giving mature and adult a go so I went to the market, bought myself a magazine and mimicked his look of adultness. Don't think I pulled it off particularly well as I ended up having to use the magazine to swat away the Kurdish waiters that would not leave me alone. Even my wedding ring didn't deter them!

Why is it that a female simply cannot go out on her own without a male thinking it's ok to hit on said female?

Please piss off.

At least the doom is no longer present, but it has been replaced with a weird feeling in the pit of my stomach. I find myself worrying that I really won't have plans for the weekend and I will have another nonexistent one just like last. I find myself worrying that my social circle is becoming ever smaller with Jenny now gone and Kimmy due for the off soon. Who else is left for me to play with other than Lacie these days? Lorraine doesn't do nights out (nor would I fancy drinking with her) and John is becoming more negative by the day, while Lacie would rather be at home with the wannabe than playing out with little ole me.

Can't blame her really, a new relationship needs alone time.

I remember the days when Husbando and I couldn't keep our hands off each other. Seems like a lifetime ago. Mind you, I would rather die than have all that sex again now, eww gross. Chaffed fanny springs to mind.

Shit if I end up with no plans this weekend I'm really going to see my arse. And what with my weight yo-yoing daily, I'm not even going to see a small slender arse...

Seriously, fuck my mother fucking life...

Friday 28th October

Time: 20.35pm

Dear Unicorn puffs,

For the past few days I have been super busy doing fuck all. Yup, winter has arrived and there is not much to do in these here parts. I could murder a drink, really I could. That would remove some of the boredom to be sure. Was that Irish?

Anyway - what boring shit have I been up to since my last entry?

Well, on Wednesday Husbando and I went for a Turkish breakfast (at lunch time) up the 'Şahin Tepe' mountain. We like it up there as you can stuff your face and not be judged for being a great big fatty. Well, they probably do judge us, not for the overeating mind you, but because I am a 'Yabanci' with a Turkish man. They probably think I'm Baris's holiday romance that he is grooming for a load of cash, making me his cash cow. It wouldn't be the first time that I have thought the very same about a couple...

But just to clarify, I'm not.

After that we went into town briefly then came home. Bariş disappeared off to his friend's house for 5 hours while I popped up to see Lorraine as she had had some dental work done and was feeling sorry for herself. While I was there she read my angel cards. She is not a medium or a professional card reader however she gets her own right from time to time and it's a bit off fun.

Between Angle cards and Ouija boards, some may say I'm obsessed...

Good news though, apparently I'm going to get pregnant soon. Well it's about bloody time! I will try not to pin all hopes on this coming month, but wouldn't that be something?

Oh stop it Lei, just because the cards told me it would be soon, doesn't mean it will be this cycle! Or does it?

Thursday was an OK day too 'cos I met up with Lacie. We booked our bus tickets to Kuşadasi and shopped for the same occasion. I ended up with a new pair of grey trousers and a dark green trilby. I like my hats, but WTF, was there nothing else left in the shops to buy for my mini break? The answer to that was no, the shops were filled with shit.

Don't you just hate that, when you have the funds to drop a load of cash on some new outfits and there are no outfits to be had? Nightmare. I suppose you could say that I was lucky to have come out of the spree with anything at all.

I shall trial run my new trousers on Sunday I think. Ahh yes, weekend plans have materialised, finally. Whilst in town with Lacie we bumped into John; he asked what my plans were and when I informed him I had none, he literally jumped for joy. Why? Well, it seems that his friends have decided not to do Halloween as previously discussed as they couldn't find anywhere throwing a party.

Literally everywhere in Marmaris used to get in on the Halloween action but for the last couple of years it has become increasingly difficult to find a bar where you can get Halloween wasted and dress like a slut. Sad but true.

So with that, John and I made a plan to sink a couple of beers. Then, over a Caramel Latte in 'Starbucks', Lacie informed me that her Ankara trip was off and shall we do something on Saturday night instead. FFS, did she not just hear me agree to beers with John? The girl is tall yes, but does she always need to have her head in the clouds?

She then suggested Sunday afternoon down on the marina - so as it stands I have Saturday night out with John and Sunday afternoon out with Lacie. Now there's a good looking weekend if ever I saw one.

We are both getting super excited about our mini break so have dedicated Sunday to deciding which outfits to take and what we plan to accomplish whilst in Kuşadasi.

I have just made myself laugh reading that back, like I was trying to be all mature and well, *decent*. Obviously I am neither of those things, so I shall stop trying to kid myself and call our mini break exactly what it is: One big mother fucking piss up. Truth be told, I doubt we will even leave the hotel - I mean why would we, the free booze isn't located outside of its doors now is it?

Anyway, today is Friday and guess where I have been? Bloody 'Rumours' bar again! I mentioned to my old friend Sandi that I had been down there on Monday and with that she suggested that we meet up there today - so we did. It passed an hour.

When I got home I decided to cook for the first time since getting back from the UK. I used to cook all the time, 5 or 6 days a week. That was until bastardo Bariş informed me that I chew too loud and it makes him feel sick. At that point I stopped cooking for him. Apparently there is a word for people who have that phobia, I looked it up on Google and it's called being a CUNT.

Bravo Google, I couldn't agree more.

As Bariş was on lates, I decided to cook a dirty great big vegetable stew with mashed potatoes. Oh what a splendid idea that was, it went down a treat and I even had seconds. Gucci licked the plate clean and then I felt sorry for him so I gave him his own little bowl of gravy. Absolutely stuffed, the pair of us retired to the sofa to partake in some reality TV watching, choosing the 'Kardashians'.

That's when it started. My tummy let out a god almighty yelp. I looked at my stomach, Gucci looked at me and that's when shit literally happened.

I sharted.

I kid you friggin' not, for the first time in my life, I sharted.

For fear of forever ruining the sofa, I darted to the toilet and that's where I stayed for the next 25 minutes. During this time the noise and aroma coming from my back passage were enough to put me off vegetables for life.

Jesus Christ, that was some '5 a day' cleanse!

What it is it they say, a lady never farts, she just shoots tiny puffs of glitter that sound like a Unicorns laughter and smell like a rainbow? Whoever 'they' are, are fucking liars.

To make matters worse, I went out onto the balcony to top up Gucci's water and the sight that I was greeted with was enough for me to pull my eye balls right out of their sockets. Guch had had his own attack of the bowls. There was sloppy doggie shit everywhere. I couldn't pick it up by paper towel nor by plastic bag as it was the wet finger dripping kind. Nothing else for it, I had to get the hose and bleach out.

FML if this is what veg does for you then you can keep it.

Oh, and Kimmy never did get in touch about plans for this weekend. Good thing I wasn't sitting here waiting for her isn't it...
#SelfishMingerStrikesAgain

November

Tuesday 1st November

Current Weight: 64.5 Kilos

Time: 15.36pm

Dear Baby heffalump,

Well it's Tuesday and day 2 of hangover. At least I am alive, although I barely feel it...

I ended up cancelling Saturday night with John and combining the two outings on the Sunday instead. Somehow, I had the feeling that a hangover may ruin my plans for the Sunday, so I thought better of it. Clever me.

Our Funday started around 3pm with me rocking up to Lacie's with the dregs of my last bottle of duty-free whisky. I was dolled up to the eyeballs sporting my new grey pants, black camisole, black cardi thing, Doc Martin style boots and finishing the look with my wide brimmed black hat, not looking too horrific. That fucker Lacie was still in bed. Mind you, had she not of told me that she overslept you would never have believed that the girl had been catching zzz's. She looked pretty fucking radiant even then.

Damn my beautiful friends.

Why can't I have a normal looking trog as a bestie instead? Surely that would work in my favour if I had an unattractive friend? I may look slightly better in comparison. Yup, it's high time I found myself an average looking friend.

Anyway, it took her all of 12 minutes to make herself look fabulous, and then the drinking began. We chatted, laughed, gossiped and had a great few pre-drinks before heading out to meet John down at our new favourite place on the marina, 'Zola'. What started out as a lovely warm afternoon ended up in all 3 of us wrapped in 'Zola' blankets by 7pm.

Yup, winter has arrived.

From there we strolled along the marina 'till we arrived at 'Lighthouse', where we proceeded to commandeer the music system playing every random tune that we could possibly think of. Who the hell listens to Latin Dance anyway?

I was expecting Lacie to bugger off early, but this was pretty sodding early even by her standards. She stuck it out till 8.00pm. I blinked and the wannabe had materialised just when the night was getting good.

John's friend Steven arrived to take her place, and as far as I can make out, he is a pretty good chap. He is about 45 years old and captain on a yacht. Nice guy, softly spoken and is rather attractive with his salt and pepper hair. You would never in your life believe that instead of taking a girl on a date in a hope to get to know her, that he would rather pay a prostitute instead. He says it's much less hassle and you don't get the clinginess.

But have you seen the state of the Marmaris prozzie's? Most of them are lady boys so it really makes me wonder.

Each to their own I suppose...

As John and Steven wanted to watch the Grand Prix we had to leave 'Lighthouse' for a while in search of somewhere that was showing it. You will never guess where we ended up; bloody 'Rumours' bar again – third time this week! As I had absolutely no interest in watching the Grand Prix, I found the owner of the bar and asked him to let me do Karaoke on my own instead. He agreed to 'silent karaoke', so the mic remained off and the Grand Prix could still be heard. One might say that I was pretty drunk by this point and that I didn't need a mic as the entire bar (indoors and out) heard me shouting my way through 10 Karaoke tunes.

Meatloaf and Roxette have always been firm favourites.

Thankfully the stupid Grand Prix didn't seem to last that long, or, I could have been that drunk that time held no meaning - either way, we piled into a taxi and went back to 'Lighthouse'.

Now I should have gone home at this point. There really was no need for me to go back, absolutely none. But back I went and drink on I did.

That's when it becomes rather hazy. Steven decided he had had enough and sent himself home, with John not far behind. So that left me, on my own, wanting to stay out and party but no one to party with.

So what's a girl to do?

Well, this girl stayed out and partied on her own. For how long I couldn't rightly say what with the whole no concept of time and all, but I checked my call log the following day (day 1 of hangover) and it seems that I called my friend in Istanbul and was on the phone for 45 minutes around 12.30am.

I don't remember leaving the bar, but I do remember going home, silently taking off my makeup, slithering into bed then petting Gucci for a minute before drifting off into a drunken slumber. I did mighty well let me tell you - I am getting this 'coming home quietly' thing down to a fine art.

I woke up with a stinking hangover and decided to stay in bed a while. I caught up with social media and tested the Husbando waters by sending cute pics of me and Guch in random poses over to him. I say 'tested the waters' as what with my drunken memory I had no recollection if he was mad or not. As it happens, he was in a grand old mood and loved the pictures. He then asked if I liked my gift. I assumed he meant Guch had done a turd on the balcony and left it there for me to clean up, fucker. I was wrong. He was actually referring to a present that he had bought and left in the kitchen.

I nearly broke my neck trying to get to my gift, tripping over a load of jackets that were randomly in a pile on the floor.

Was it flowers? Was it chocolates? Oh the suspense was killing me!

It was a box, and although there were pictures on this box I still couldn't make out what the hell was inside. I opened it up but was confused with the contents. The box contained 3 random figurines; a cute little dragon, a witch and a blue Hercules character.

What the actual fuck?

I asked him (Husbando not Hercules) if they were from a film or something, to which he said he had no idea but thought they were cute so bought them. Ahh, how sweet?

I have never received a random gift from Husbando before, but can I just ask - what the hell am I supposed to do with them?

It gets better.

He informed me that there is a stand for them that you plug into the computer and they glow. Sure enough after checking the box again I found the stand, plugged it into the computer, put the random figurines onto the stand and the little fuckers do indeed glow.

OK – so seriously, what am I supposed to do with them? Keep them on display? Or can I pack them away until I spawn a child and give them to him/her when they are approx. 3 years old?

Barış has upped his game.

Alright, so the gift was a bit odd, weird in fact, but it means he is trying and pretty bleedin' hard. So hard that the next little morsel that I am about to divulge shouldn't surprise me, but it did.

When he got home from work he informed me that he had been a clever cunt the night before and took a video of me arriving home pissed. He played it back to me with a smirk on his face that by the end I just wanted to slap right off. The sly mo fo had videoed me staggering out of the taxi, barging into the coat stand sending the lot flying, removing my makeup, then onto a conversation I had with my thumb (yes, my mother fucking thumb), looking in the snack cupboard, filling my face with a bag of Cheetos, updating my Facebook status about being a Honey G supporter, then deleting said status, picking my nose, and finally slithering into bed which went horribly wrong as Gucci was asleep under the duvet on my side and guess which drunken fatty didn't see him? Jesus Christ I nearly squashed my boy! I did go on to pet him like I remembered but it was more of a 'sorry for nearly killing you' than a normal love in.

I was horrified and rather traumatised. Not as traumatised as poor ole Guch, but horrified none the less.

I did not find this footage nearly as entertaining as Barış clearly did. I was *nothing* as I imagined. I mean talking to my thumb! Jesus. I thought I was in an excellent state getting myself bed ready, when all the while I was nothing more than an intoxicated baby elephant that was extremely unsteady on ones feet, knocking shit over and talking to *my best friend* my thumb!

I wondered why all the jackets from the coat stand were littered all over the floor..!

Fucking Husbando and his nasty videography...

I don't think little baby Guch has quite forgiven me yet either. How do I know? Well, that little fucker holds a grudge you see, and when holding a grudge, his favourite thing to do is go on a piss fest. It seems that he decided to piss all over my damn jacket. Yup, out of 1 of mine and 3 of Barış's on the floor, he chose the 1 of mine to cock his judgmental bloody leg on. Judas.

Although thinking about it now, how do I really know that it wasn't Barış cocking his leg...?

Anyway, through my horrific hangover I knew I was ovulating and had to get on the horse so to speak. I couldn't think of anything less appealing than sex, but needs must. Let's see what transpires now that my cards have told me I'm to be preggers soon...

As for this week?

A quiet one ahead with no plans to go out as I want to be in tip top condition for the weekend after in Kuşadadi. All I have in the social diary for now is dinner with Kimmy Minger tonight, where I will be home for 9.30pm, plus an appointment with the Gynae tomorrow for more poking and prodding. Oh joy of joys.

It's going to be a long 11 days without a drop of the hard stuff. Especially as I have PMS due in the next few.

Oh dear oh dear, I see trouble ahead for dear old jacket pissing, sly drunk video filming Husbando...

Saturday 5th November

Current Weight: 63.5 Kilos

Time: 15.48pm

Dear Growing wall,

Facebook Memories: 'On this day' 5th November 2011 my status was: 'Has taken as much as I'm gonna take and would like to add that dentists are vile.'

That was when I wrote my first diary 5 years ago. What a tit - the Dentist. Oh be Jesus, I was obsessed with that fucker. Shocking looking back on it now, but thankfully I have never felt like that again since. Obsessed I mean. I have never been obsessed with Husbando and to be fair I see this as a good thing. Obsession is not healthy but I couldn't have stopped it back then try as I might. I cringe now of course because it's well, disgusting.

Jesus I've done a lot in the last 5 years;

I have moved house twice, given up smoking, holidayed in Spain, UK and America (best trip of my life), made new friends and lost old, met Barış, got married, contemplate murder/divorce on a weekly basis, gained weight, in the process of losing weight and now I'm trying to get pregnant.

Luckily the impending doom doesn't visit as much these days; in fact it's now a very rare occurrence. Must be due to being settled.

So I guess you could say I've had a pretty good 5 years on a whole.

I wonder how much will have changed by the time I'm 40?

And this week?

Well, nothing exceptional happened. Honest to God, it has been a boring week in the life of me.

Tuesday night Kimmy and I had our last dinner together. We ended up going to our favourite Turkish restaurant 'Kervan' and stuffing our faces. As I knew I would be, I was home for 9.30pm. I wasn't annoyed, it was expected, and it was so sodding cold in the restaurant that neither of us wanted to stay there any longer anyway! It was a lovely meal and catch up and a pleasant early night in all.

Wednesday Barış and I went to the Hospital for my endometrial wall check – good news, it's thickened up by 2 millimetres (or whichever unit they measure the thing in). It's still not thick enough to have a sprog implant, it needs to beef up another 2 for that, but the Gynae seems happy with its progress. I'm to go back on Monday for another quick check and he will decide then if I should up the dosage of the hormone pills or carry on with what I already have. I'm getting used to him sticking his probe in my area now, and I even tidied my lady garden for the occasion. I can only imagine what it's like looking up big hairy unkempt muffs all day for a living, so why add to the pain?

Note to self: Remember to prune one's garden - when your fate rests in someone else's hands it's not particularly wise to have an 80's style free spirited scruffy muff to contend with...

From the hospital we moved along to 'Yunus' for a long lazy lunch on the beach front. Its Yacht Race Week so there was plenty to look at on the water. It was mighty nice just sitting in the sun drinking tea and eating toasties with a Husbando that has been absolutely golden of late. It's like he's gone back in time to when we were first dating and has made it his sole mission to be a good husband. I'm finding him to be a pleasure to be around, in fact I'm pretty much bumming off Barış right now. So much so that murder has not crossed my mind for a couple of weeks.

People with suspicious minds may start to question this behaviour and wonder what brought it on. Nope, not me - I trust my lobster. Don't get me wrong, I'm not one of those silly girls that wouldn't believe you if you told me my man were sticking his nib in various ink wells. And I would never go as far to say that my Turk is different from the rest as I don't want my fingers burnt, plus I wouldn't want to look stupid if anything was to happen. However - he is different from the resort boys. He is not a player and takes relationships seriously. As you already know he is the total opposite of me, and if there is a bad one in our relationship, then it's me. I'm the party animal, I'm that girl that can't say no to one more drink, I'm the mo fo that sneaks in at 05.30am while Barış is home babysitting Guch. Thankfully, he trusts me as much as I trust him.

That's the beauty of meeting your man when you're a bit older - one can spot a cunt a mile away because one has dated many before.

So, why is Barış being the doting husband?

Well, we have sorted our shit out because life's too short to be arguing about stupid things. He is learning how to be married to a British party animal and I'm learning how to be a better wife - or, at least to come home more quietly so as not to alert him to the time.

Thursday afternoon I tried out a new hairdresser, a British one at that. I was so pissed off with the state of my hair after the last hair fucker fried it that I wanted to give it a rest. So the new hairdresser rocked up to my house at 1.45pm and didn't leave till gone 6pm. Jesus effing Christ, is that how long it takes to get ones barnet done properly these days?

The end result was that a good 2 inches were cut off leaving me with a Khloe Kardashian long bob, and, to break up the blond she weaved some of my root colour through the hair as it was too fried for bleach.

Damn you Turkish hairdressers!

Verdict - I'm not 100% sure yet as it is a lot darker than I imagined but the good thing is she is coming back on Monday to check on it - so, so far so good.

Unfortunately my track record with hairdressers is pretty fucking abysmal, so for me to be impressed it will take some convincing.

On Friday afternoon Sandi my old pal came round for lunch.

I met Sandi back in 2008 and knew immediately that she was my sort of person. She is 63 years old, has brown bobbed hair, a very laid back attitude and gives excellent advice – not that I needed any that afternoon. When we first met we just clicked and we've been friends ever since. I don't usually see her in the summer as she is super busy at work, but come winter we generally meet up a couple of times a month, and this time was my turn to host the afternoon.

I love women of that age (most of the time). Some can be very judgmental and bitter (usually because they have been robbed of their life savings by a love rat) but most of my older buddies are nothing of the sort.

We chatted for hours without coming up for breath because that's just the way we are.

As soon as she left, Kimmy called round on her way to the airport to say cheerio. We don't do teary farewells, just a hug and a 'hit me up on Facebook when your home' type see off. Mushy Mingers we are not.

So with Kimmy now gone, I am one friend less on the social scene.

Thinking of friends, I must message Jenny, I've not spoken to her recently!

Anyway, this now brings us up to today which is Saturday. I said earlier in the week that I had no plans for the weekend, but I forgot my 'Taj Mahal' feast with Lorraine tonight. It will be a booze free dinner and luckily for her I don't feel like winding her up.

I can imagine every ex pat and their Kurdish boyfriend to be in 'Taj' tonight what with it being their closing weekend. Although I am the social type, I sometimes hate mixing with people, especially when it comes to interrupting my dinner. Forced hello's and small talk really ain't my box of frogs - repping put paid to that.

Lorraine is the same but in more of an extreme way. She would be happy to never bump into another British person again in her life...

And with that in mind, I had better get my arse off this chair, take Guch out for a walk and then look in the wardrobe for something to wear tonight which I'm sure will be a harrowing experience.

Why can't Primark deliver FFS?

ONCE UPON A WHISKY

Monday 7th November

Time: 20.57pm

Dear Pre period bloat,

I don't have much to say. I am annoyed with my body - my near middle aged, tubby, seemingly incapable body.

Why me? Why this body?

I can say in all honesty that I really was not prepared for this all this palaver in the race to get pregnant...

Saturday night was great. Lorraine and I did indeed go to 'Taj' where we have not used a menu for years and the waiters know exactly what we want. Pig out? Yes we bloody did.

We saw a few people that we knew, but thank God not as many as I feared.

As the night would have finished super early if we had gone directly home after dinner, we decided to walk right the way down the eerily deserted beach front until we finally reached 'Starbucks' on the Netsel Marina. It would have been rude not to have indulged in a Pumpkin Spice Latte seeing as though we were already there and it's that time of year after all. So I used my saved beer calories on my Starbucks Latte and indulged my head off. Lush.com

I was home for midnight and ready for some rest what with all the walking. I had 'old woman hip' so I took myself off to Bedfordshire.

Sunday was not spent as Funday - instead I replaced it with another walk, once again with Lorraine. We visited each and every clothes shop in town but ball all caught my eye, and what little did didn't fit my fat self anyway.

Damn me and my pre period bloat!

As well as the bloat agitating me, so was Lorraine. When I spend too much time with her we grate on each other's nerves, rubbing each other up the wrong way. So, that totally happened. I was snapping left right and centre, but she doesn't help the situation much when she claims to know everything. FFS as if I don't know how to pronounce the name of my own Gynae! She reckoned that she was right with the pronunciation and spelling and I was totally wrong...

Righto then.

Note to self: Once per week is more than enough time to be spent with anyone other than Husbando.

And then comes today, Monday. I went back to the Gynae and it's not good news. Stupid endometrial wall has not grown one millimetre, in fact he said it's barely 6 and should be at least 8 by now.

Bloody decrepit old wall.

So, the next course of action is to up my dose of tablets and see him again on day 13 of my cycle. I will do as instructed and pray for the best, after I have completed my tantrum off course.

On the way out of his office I asked for his business card to make an appointment later on. That was not the real reason as I already had his phone number saved. I needed to prove to Lorraine that I was right about the spelling and pronunciation - and prove it I did. I photographed the card and sent it to her.

Did she ask me how I got on at my appointment? No, did she fuck - her reply is exactly what I should have expected: 'Yes that's him, the spelling sounds exactly as I said his name'.

But it didn't. Fucking fact. Fuck off Lorraine.

ONCE UPON A WHISKY

After that my new hairdresser came around to check on my hair.

Verdict: Good.

And she seems like a nice sort, I will use her again.

Other than the above?

Well, I have severe PMS and I hate my shrivelled up old wall.

Thursday 10th November

Current Weight: 64 Kilos

Time: 16.50pm

Dear Girl about to go wild,

Yey, it's nearly holiday time! I simply can't wait to get out of the Marm Farm for a while! As much as I love Marmaris, a few days away from it all will do me the world of good. I'm so sick of seeing ex-pat drama on Facebook and wonder why this has become the norm?

Why - why do ex-pats get so 'involved' over here? Can anyone shed any light on this as it's driving me crazy?

I tell you what, Facebook groups are a danger to be part of what with this one kicking off because that one didn't show up to sell this one some old bit of tat.

It's laughable.

Then this one's friends start a war and that one's friends take it nuclear.

Going out to a simple Karaoke night could end in brawl what with the backstabbing and shit talk of members of the same gang! And don't get me started on doing a simple good turn such as volunteering up at the dog pound... That shit could get you arrested!

I swear it's not the Turks you need to be careful of; it's the ex-pats that would stab you in the back soon as look at you...

Don't get me wrong 'dear diary', nothing has happened to me personally as the older I have got the more I realise that it's wise to keep well out of the drama, however when scrolling through Facebook today I noticed that every second post was about how this one has been gossiping about that one and they don't even know that one to gossip about in the first place.

Funnily enough, Larissa's in the firing line this week. It's about time her shit spreading antics caught up with her ego. Got to love a bit of karma. And can I also add that no one on Facebook, Instagram, Twitter or whatever else cares about your gym session unless you fell off the treadmill and banged your fanny. Just fuck off you active cunt.

And another thing - I am so fucking sick of her crew's endless selfies clogging up my newsfeed. What is it with dusky pink velvet dresses that has them all looking like botox'ed Barbie clones? Cringe, just cringe.

Why don't I delete them? Because as much as I can't stand their stupid selfies, I also want to know what they're up to and see their Facebook rants... I am a woman after all.

Anyway, enough of all that bollocks. I need to be quick today as I have somewhat of a hangover and want to sit my arse down on the sofa and watch 'The Only Way is Essex' with a nice cup of tea and some Digestives.

Have I had a good few days? The answer to that is positively yes.

Tuesday night I went round to Lacie's with what was left of my whisky and a bag of cheese and onion crisps. Firstly we discussed the holiday; outfits, day and night looks, hair and makeup, etc. We now have a plan of what we are doing for each day and night – drinking cocktails and looking fabulous.

Then we went on to discuss husbands, boyfriends and crushes. It seems that Lacie no longer wants to be with wannabe and is now on a one woman mission to land a nice rich business man to keep her in the lap of luxury that she so wants to become accustomed. Well I don't blame her, it's not nice dating someone that is more skint than you.

So once again, Lacie is back on the market. I doubt it will be for long as usually just one blink is enough time for new suitors to materialise in front of her. She's hoping that a decent bloke may pop up over the weekend. In all fairness I'm sure more than one will considering the glorious state of her. I can see my fate already - I will be dubbed the fat friend, only there to make up numbers, or to have the new bloke's average buddy palmed off on.

Bla bla bla – Sometimes I make myself sick.

Wednesday was a random day. Obviously I had a hangover and this left me wanting to eat everything in sight and with it being Husbando's day off, we decided to watch the wind and rain come beating down while we were warm and indoors at 'Yunus', our favourite Wednesday hang out.

I love a good storm here; the lightening show alone is magnificent, however the thunder always put's the fear of God up poor ole Guch.

We had a grand couple of hours down on the front storm watching, and when were got bored we went home. Barış buggered off to his mates house for an hour while I got ready for another outing, this time a couples date night in a near enough stranger's house.

Remember Jenny's last night at to 'Bono'? Well, we got talking to the waiter and he called his wife to come along and we all sat there together dirking and chatting. Eren and Funda called on Monday and asked if Husbando and I would like to go to their house. They seemed nice enough, so why not?

It's awkward hanging out with people that you don't know, especially when you have a Husbando that hates meeting new people, so much so that we nearly cancelled. Instead, we ended up taking the edge off with a couple of whiskies before leaving the house. I can safely say that this may not have been the best of ideas as we arrived late (due to me deciding to have just one more), hungry as I had not made any dinner due to being tipsy, and soaking wet as the heavens had opened and caught us out. Fuck knows what Eren and Funda must have thought when we rocked up.

Couple of cunts?

Anyway, it turned out to be an alright night considering, and Baris really liked them. Me on the other hand, well I was away with the fairies in my own little world, but they seemed OK.

We left at a decent hour of 12.30am and then trawled the streets of Marmaris looking for somewhere to get food on the way home. I stuffed my face with a chip butty.

Nice one drunk me, think about calories much?

So this brings us up to date, today being Thursday, the day before our holidays and I'm far too excited for our 3 day mini break. I have fully packed my huge case, in fact I have totally over packed, but a wannabe socialite needs her options. I will probably curse myself for packing way too much but I would rather that than a complete meltdown for not packing enough.

So for now I shall piss off to enjoy my sofa evening and nail painting.

Hopefully there will be no black eyes or thick lips – Lacie and I can get a bit wild when left to our own devices...

P.S: Lacie hates my new hair. She says there is only room for one brunette in our friendship and as she got there first I need to snap back to being the blonde. #Badtimes

Tuesday 15th November

Time: 16.15pm

Dear Shenanigan starter,

Well, that's me back from holiday - we arrived home yesterday afternoon to a slightly cooler and slightly more sombre Marmaris. Why do holidays always go so fast? The run up to any holiday seems to take forever but the holiday itself always passes in a blink of a bloody eye! After getting everything back to normal at home, it was almost as if it had never happened. How rude!

Would you believe me if I said we were super well behaved and got up to no naughtiness? Nope, neither would I. So here it is in a nutshell;

The journey wasn't particularly pleasant. I hate getting up at the butt crack of dawn anyway so my face wasn't full of the joys of life on Friday morning. Transport wise we had to get 2 busses and a taxi. The first bus was fabulous and had Wi-Fi, free snacks, Tea and Coffee, the lot. The second bus was a hot sweaty dolmuş that got a flat tire half way to Kuşadadi. Of course the dolmuş driver didn't carry a spare, I mean why would he? So, on the dusty roadside that looked like we could have been in the thick of Calcutta, we had to wait for the driver's mate to arrive with a spare (which took about 45 minutes), then for it to be changed (which also took about 45 minutes). Why so long? Well, there were 10 men mulling around consulting Google as they had no idea what to do with the sodding Jack. I kid you not...

When we eventually arrived at the 'Korumar' hotel, Lacie and I were Hank Marvin. Wouldn't you be after that traumatic travelling experience? So after dumping our bags in our rather special room that we paid extra for to have a garden view (that actually over looked a shite ole road and the Devlet hospital), we finally hit the snack bar.

Penis Colada's and Spaghetti - yup, that'll do us.

From Pina Colada's we went on to White Russian's and then onto Brandy's. It was only 5pm and we were already Livin' La Vida Loca. Around 7pm we had had enough of the breath-taking view looking out onto the whole of Kuşadasi and decided to head up to our random road view to continue our drinking and general merriment whilst we got ready for the night's activities.

As previously mentioned, it takes Lacie all of 12 minutes to look her best, yet takes me 2 hours to look just passable - so I had to get started immediately. Lacie continued to live it up on the balcony while replying to her many adoring suitors. I have never seen so many phone calls, texts, FB messages and Whats App's flying around in my life. She was choosing wisely who to reply to, but FYI, she is considering getting back with the wannabe. Mind you, she has stated in no uncertain terms that she is keeping her options open this weekend, and our Lacie is Queen of frikkin' options.

Around 9pm we rolled down to the restaurant. I say rolled as that's just what we did. Both of us rather pissed and once again starving hungry. FFS I had only eaten a couple of hours prior!

If I could eat hotel buffet food for the rest of my life I would be as happy as a pig in shit. It really is my all-time favourite of food to gorge upon. My plate was filled to the max with all the various hot and cold options, plus the soup and French bread I had as a starter, and the variation of sweets I had for afters. OMG yes, I enjoyed my dinner immensely. Lacie had a handful of salad, a bit of rice and grilled Chicken and declared herself full.

Bastard thin friend making me look like a heffer.

From there we headed up to the hotel bar for a few more drinks. We couldn't decide whether to stay in and have a relatively quiet one or head into town for more of a mental one. In the end we took some drinks up to the room to decide from our balcony while we ogled the road and listened to 80's tunes.

Deary God, the crack is literally endless with us. That's what I love about that girl, when we get started with our banter, there is simply no end to how filthy, disgusting and downright degrading we can be. And another solid point in her favour is that although she is thin and pretty, she never ever acts like it and always makes me feel like I am on the same beauty level as her. I know I'm not - she knows I'm not, but she never makes me feel that way.

Drinking turned into singing, singing turned into the daftest balcony dancing I have ever participated in, and then something quite ridiculous happened – our daft dancing antics caused a passing white Mercedes on the shite ole road to slow down and come to a halt. The driver buzzed down the window, informed us that he and his friend liked our dancing and invited us out for Champagne.

Any normal girls would have said 'on you fuck' and kept on dancing, but we are not any normal girls. Lacie told them to pick us up at 12am (30 mins later) and that was that.

Fuck me.

I would like to say that we stood these possible rapists up and fell asleep - alas we didn't; We corrected our makeup, sorted out our hair, went down to meet them, went out for Champagne, then onto a club, then on to an after party - where I left Lacie at 06.30am in the hands of get this: a fucking rich business man - while I jumped a taxi and headed for bed at the hotel.

Were they rapists? No thankfully not, but they were a pair of rich arseholes. Yup, palmed off with the cunty friend - how did I ever know? And what a total dick he was too. Looks wise he reminded me of a slightly older and much uglier Wayne Lineker, attitude wise he reminded me of Donald Trump. Man, what a cock. I dubbed him 'Eski Kaşar' because that's exactly what he was - an old bit of mouldy stinking cheese.

Lacie's guy on the other hand looked like her ex-husband and although a rich arsehole, was as pleasant with it.

'Eski Kaşar' must never have been told no before as the look on his face was priceless when I dished out the knock back. Even if I wasn't married there is no way I would have given the goods to that mo fo. Talk about up one's own arse... When informed that I was not interested, he replied that it was no problem because he had a young bit of stuff flying in the following morning anyway, and as a rule he doesn't fuck girls older than 30.

Well that told me didn't it!?!

I went to bed pissed, randomly irritated, somewhat amused and very bloody tired - waking up with a stinker of a hangover and no Lacie in sight, the dirty ole stop out.

I have now dubbed her 'Slutty Von Slutterson', because let's face it, she is.

SVS rocked up at 11.30am in need of coffee and food, so after a huge gossip about the size of her guy's willy, we pulled ourselves together and headed down to the restaurant for lunch, and would you believe it - Bloody Mary's.

That's it, we were back on it but in a 'classy lady's that drink Bloody Mary's' kinda way. I wonder out of the two of us just who is the bad influence?

And when we could face Tomato juice no more, we moved onto Brandies and Wine instead.

Lacie had given her number to the holiday fling and off course he was smitten. So smitten he called and invited us both out to dinner. I told Lacie about old cunt's bit of young stuff arriving and how I didn't fancy being third wheel, however her guy said that no, old cunt wanted us to all go out together.

Lying fucker, that's all I can say.

When they picked us up at 9pm, O.C was in a vile mood and wasn't afraid to show it. I felt sick from all the Tomato juice and couldn't be arsed with his shit so sat in damn near silence while Lacie and her dude were in deep conversation.

What did I predict about being the fat friend, only there to make up numbers? You couldn't make this shit up...

O.C clearly didn't want to be there and was neither use nor ornament, wanting only to put his 'Eski Kaşar' willy in the 22 year old high society Turkish girl. I didn't want to be there either but I wasn't a cunt about it...

Lacie's guy went on to inform us that O.C was annoyed because I didn't fancy him - not my problem mate, I'm not attracted to shiny objects, plus I'm a married woman now jog on!

But wait - what's his beef? Didn't he say I was too old for him anyway!?! Knob.

Needless to say I requested a lift home, so at 12.30am I left Lacie with her guy, while O.C dropped me back at the hotel. Dirty ole fucker tried his luck again and asked if I wanted to go back to his pad to watch a movie - absolutely not, not if he paid me £1,000,000! There was no way in hell I was going to waste any more time on his rich miserable ignorant arse!

Instead I video chatted with Bariş and Gucci for 40 mins. During this time I may have flashed a boob before passing out mildly drunk in bed.

SVS on the other hand was having a whale of a time at the 'Ramada' hotel for more of the same from the night before, but with just one problem - that dafty had the Marmaris wannabe messaging her all night asking her to send voice clips and photos, etc. Talk about irritating. They are not even back together and he is behaving like a tit.

For obvious reasons she was reluctant to indulge wannabe's requests. What she should have done was ignore his messages and reply in the morning, but she got so irritated that in the end she agreed to send him a voice clip, pressed the record button on Whats App, and just as she did so, her holiday fling started chatting so she stopped the voice clip but it was too late – it sent to wannabe.

Oh SVS, whatever next?

She sent another voice clip directly after thinking that would throw him off the scent, and for that night it did as he was just as intoxicated as her.

When she got back to the hotel the following morning and relayed the story, I pointed out that if that had been me, I would be re-reading and re-listening to the messages when I was sober enough to do so, and sure enough he did.

The phone range and wannabe asked just exactly what the first voice clip was about and all Lacie could do was look on in horror as I mouthed 'TV' at her. He didn't believe it, not one little bit and went on to send her a torrent of abusive texts.

I told her to use my old trick 'it wasn't me', which she did before informing him she was sick of his untrusting shit and if he wasn't going to believe her then he could just fuck off.

Off he fucked for a few hours, before calling with his tail between his legs telling her *he* was sorry and that *he* would never do that again.

JESUS FUCKING CHRIST.

Lacie must have a gold plated pussy because we both understood that wannabe knew the truth.

I knew she could just about manipulate any man to her advantage, but this was like watching the mastermind Hannibal Lecter in 'Silence of the Lambs'.

I was speechless. Fucking speechless.

And so our Sunday continued - booze, gossiping about O.C's stinking attitude, what Lacie was going to do about the wannabe now that she has him wrapped around her little finger, and food - lots of simply amazing food.

We didn't get too pissed as we had to be up and at 'em early the next morning to travel home, which was a lot less of a ball ache than on the way there.

Since arriving home yesterday I have cleaned the house from top to bottom, arranged Barış's clothes by packing away his summer stuff and replacing it with his winter wear, walked the hind legs off Guch, performed my wifely marital duties and looked back on my mental weekend.

That Lacie may be more fucked up than me. Scary.

3 days was quite enough of that carry on. I love my holidays, but any more days like that and I would have had a breakdown.

So, it's time to sit on my arse with a cuppa and catch up on my fave 'Made in Chelsea'. All these shenanigans can cause a wannabe socialite to live a wannabe normal life for a week.

P.S: I was due on my period on Sunday, today is Tuesday. I'm not reading too much into it as I know what my wall can and cannot hold. It's simply not beefy enough yet for a sprog to implant, so I'm thinking that all the binge drinking has delayed my period.

Nice one dick head. And by dick head I mean me.

I also have a cold brewing.

Friday 18th November

Current Weight: 63.2 Kg (I can't believe it either)

Time: 17.15pm

Dear Girl that Googles,

Have you clocked my weight today? Bloody hell, I seem to have lost a pound during my mad weekend of booze and food! Colour me impressed. I also seem to have skipped my period bloat this month, as well as the actual period. Yup, I'm 5 days late and I'm not even joking.

I have the cramps, twinges and stinky farts - just no period.

Do I believe I'm knocked up? Your damn straight I do.

In fact I'm absolutely convinced about it this time. Even the negative pregnancy test yesterday cannot convince me otherwise. Well, it may have done for all of 10 seconds, and then I thought about all the false negatives that people on Google have written about, so off course I'm one of those that don't have enough HGC in my pee yet to get a positive. I know I shouldn't get my hopes up, I really do - but come on, it's looking good right?

I've Googled myself silly over the last couple of days, so let's stack the evidence up here shall we:

Evidence 1: I had a cold brewing. It did not manifest and left me with a stuffy nose. This is an early sign of pregnancy.

Evidence 2: Period like cramps but with no period. This is an early sign of pregnancy.

Evidence 3: The obvious, I'm 5 days late.

So I'm pregnant right?

Have I considered that the hormone pills have buggered up my period? Yes I have. I even called my Gynae and asked him, to which he said no, the pills will not stop the period and should it not have arrived by Wednesday to go back to him for a blood test. I have bought another home pregnancy test and will take it on Sunday morning as I will be a week late by that point and simply won't be able to stop myself.

I have also considered other options:

Stress: Talking to Lacie about this today and she says she has never seen me so relaxed about life, so stress probably isn't the cause of my no show.

Ovarian Cancer: Google, you're a cunt because I, like everyone else, self-diagnose with your help. I told Barış about this yesterday and he just gave me a look that said 'Shut the fuck up Lei' and carried on eating his breakfast. I have not ruled this option out however I would like to point out that when I was in the UK earlier this year I tried to get another smear test done but since it was only 2 years since my last, they refused to do it. I mean what happens if you get the starting of ovarian cancer the day after your smear? Too late to do anything about it 3 years later mate as you'll be dead. Nice one UK NHS system...

At least I have actually considered other options though eh?

Oh fuck it; it will happen if it's supposed to. Either I'm late this month for no apparent reason or I'm pregnant.

Barış said not to bore him anymore with this 'am I or aren't I' chat as he wants a definite either way. Fucker won't indulge me and I don't blame him - I'm like a dog with a bone when I get started.

I've not done much else of anything this week apart from obsess. I mean, wouldn't you?

Wednesday was Husbando's day off so we went to 'Şahin Tepe' on the mountain for brunch. That was nice. Sod all else was done on Wednesday apart from message Lorraine to see what she was up to and then get annoyed with her for being her.

The woman is like my aunty, and with family status comes annoyance - and, not just from my side. We have arranged dinner for Saturday night, but quite why she felt the need to inform me that if it's a big night out that I want then to go out with someone else.

Well Loraine, don't you think I already know that?

How many years have I known her and she thinks she can to talk to me like I'm some sort of chump? All I can say is she wants to hope I'm fucking pregnant so I can't drink as otherwise I'm getting wankered just to piss her off.

Thursday I put the Christmas tree up. I know how early it is, I do have a calendar, but can I help it if I'm filled with Christmas cheer? I credit my jovial mood with being 99% knocked up. Also, I have not done Christmas in Turkey for 3 years as I've been away in either the UK or Spain, and what with my olds arriving early December, I wanted to get it nice and Christmassy for when they walk through the door. God knows it's not going to be Christmassy in Marmaris, so at least let my house have the festive feeling for as long as possible. Plus the trampolining animals of 'John Lewis' have me all of a Christmas tingle.

Today is Friday. Lacie and I went for brunch at the 'Monte Beach' hotel today in Siteler, right on the beach front. It's so serene that end of Marmaris, seriously gorgeous - and then comes this couple of cunts to disrupt the tranquillity.

By Christ, even without booze we were on pretty top form, high fiving each other for every hilarious remark coming out of our troublesome mouths.

Can I add that she bought a pregnancy test today too as she is also late. In a perfect world this would be the best thing ever for us to be pregnant at the same time, I mean how bloody marvellous right? But no, this ain't no perfect world (and it ain't no country club either), and as Lacie has decided a big fat definite no to getting back with wannabe, this is neither a blessing nor a miracle.

After brunch we wanted to shop so went to the newish Mall near 'Kipa' supermarket, which is just dreadful by the way. Talk about a wasted journey. We sat in the coffee shop and bitched about how shite the Mall was, and also how shite the coffee shop was. To the untrained eye it may be considered alright, but no, not to us.

Now I'm home waiting for Bariş to arrive to sort out the Xmas tree lights in case I electrocute myself. One bulb isn't working and it's set off my OCD. I'm sat here contemplating boxing everything back up until the bulb is working, or I have purchased new lights. But can I really be arsed..?

I'll sign off for now as Guch needs a wee and Christ knows that little fucker can't cross his legs.

Watch this space for pregnancy news. Was that a touch of sickness I felt there?

ONCE UPON A WHISKY

Sunday 20th November

Time: 12.23pm

Dear Saturday night Salep drinker,

Firstly, the Christmas tree lights are sorted. Such a small detail can be enough to push this wannabe socialite over the edge, and thankfully Husbando recognised that and got on it ASAP. It was to his own advantage when all said and done, he knows his life would not be worth living if I had to wait much longer.

Secondly, dinner out with Lorraine last night wasn't as awful as I expected, in fact it was quite pleasant really. I decided to be mature and not get wankered. I didn't do my pregnancy test before leaving the house so wankered was not something I could be. I stuck to one glass of Red like the decent human being that I am occasionally.

See how adult I can be when I put my mind to it?

We went to 'Bono Marina' for dinner, onto 'Castle Bar' for coffee with a view, and finally over to Netsel Marina's 'Kahve Dunyasi' for Salep.

Lorraine had been to Fethiye for the weekend and had a great time telling me all about it, but funnily enough didn't once ask once about my weekend in Kuşadasi. I know why all too well – it's because she hates Lacie and won't have her name mentioned, not even to ask if I enjoyed my damn self.

Talk about selfish.

So I did what any irritated individual could and dropped Lacie's name in 10 times while informing her of just how much of an excellent time we had and how we plan to go back before the season starts.

I sometimes feel like I'm in the playground when dealing with Lorraine, and considering the age of the pair of us, it's quite ridiculous. She is the only person on this planet that can wind me up in the way that she does. I get the feeling she's in direct competition with me. I'm thirty fucking six FFS – why would a 65 year old woman even want to be in competition with a gal of my age? Crazy isn't it, but that's just how she makes me feel. Don't get me wrong, I love the woman, I really do, I just wish she could see her behaviour from a different view point from time to time...

Maybe we know each other too well? Or am I giving her too much credit and it's actually a toxic relationship?

Despite all of the above, the evening was pleasant on a whole. At least it got me out of the house.

Of course I filled her in on my 99% sure pregnancy news. It's not the first time I've convinced her I'm pregnant, but this time with being 6 days late yesterday thus far, she seemed pretty damn convinced herself...

I got home at the decent hour of 11.30pm with a severely sore throat, croaky voice and particularly stuffy nose. Yup the lingering cold was still hanging on in there.

Seriously, how many early pregnancy signs does the universe want to throw at me?

Once home I decided to take Gucci directly out for a wee. Although Husbando was home, I know what he's like when it comes to remembering that ole wee infested Guch simply won't wait to go toilet if forgotten.

Needn't have bothered as when I got back in and put my slipper boots on, I walked directly through a puddle of piss.

Barış swears he took Guch out only half an hour before, but I don't quite believe him.

Let's look at the options here shall we:

Option 1: Bariş took Guch out and pissed on the floor himself in a fit of unknown rage.

Option 2: Bariş was too engrossed in his computer game to take Guch out, causing Guch to go on a piss fest to relieve his bladder.

Option 2 it is.

And now I have piss soaked slipper boots making marks all over the house. God damn Bariş and his mo fo'ing lazy arse...!

So this brings us up to today – Sunday.

This morning I woke up at 8am with horrific stomach pains. I didn't need to go to the toilet to realise I had just started my period.

And then came the tears.

The pain today is a lot stronger than my usual period pain which leads me to believe that I am in the process of having a mini miscarriage.

Fuck you life you piss taking joke of humanity.

Why the fuck did I let myself believe that my shrivelled up old wall could house a baby? Google that's why. Do I never learn?

Fuck Google and fuck my wall.

But I won't give up. I know there is a soul waiting for my wall to be fat enough, and who knows, that could be the next cycle. At least I know it's starting to work, right?

So due to this not so happy occasion I've decided to have PJ Sunday on the sofa with Guch watching Christmas films on Channel 5. I may even turn the tree lights on to cheer me up.

So, that's it for today, I'm signing off. Next time I should be back to me again, but for now I'm just going to have a cry and maybe a whisky. After all, I'm usually a hard faced bitch and all hard faced bitches need a cry once in a while...

Oh, by the way, the sore throat and stuffy nose disappeared at 8am when the stomach pains started.

Got to love Mother Nature. Not.

ONCE UPON A WHISKY

Wednesday 23rd November

Time: 16.58pm

Dear Gucci lover,

So, after reading through my last entry and realising how depressed I was that day, I am happy to announce that I'm no longer the sad sack that was writing that then. I'm back to my happy go lucky usual self and realise that a lot of us have these setbacks in life, and one thing's for sure, I will keep on trying.

I have never been a whole week late before, so if nothing else, it means these tiny little tablets are working.

I allowed myself that one and only to wallow, after all, I didn't want bad vibes continuing into the rest of the week as that would have dragged me down day after depressing day. And let's face it, there is enough depressed ex-pats in Marmaris without adding one more to the equation.

Seeing as I could drink again I decided to do what I do best - get pissed with my bestie. So on Monday night I took myself round to Lacie's house with a 1.5 litre bottle of wine as the whisky is now gone till the parents arrive.

I felt like I was joining a party already in progress as what I heard all night was 'bing bing bing' - text messages flying around left right and centre!

Yup, she's hooked him - the Kuşadasi fling is absolutely besotted.

In-between the incessant texting we had a bloody marvellous time chatting shit and high fiving. That girl makes me laugh no end, but the 3 way conversation got the better of me. In fact it got to the point where I stood up and declared I was leaving as the night would be more entertaining platting snot from the comfort of my own home. It's no fun having a conversation on one's own let me tell you...

She finally told him that she had to go, and for 20 minutes after we had a golden time - right through 'till her friend Natasha messaged and seemed to be going through some sort of mental breakdown. Well, that was it for the rest of the night - a total right off. *I* even offered to go up to see Natasha to help her through whichever trauma was happening this week, but no, she wanted Lacie and Lacie alone. Fine by me, really it was, just let me go home!

Given how the night went I obviously wasn't home late. I was in an odd mood and just wanted Gucci snuggles in bed while catching up on 'Cold Feet', but what I got instead was a Husbando that was a chatty Cathy and wanted to discuss every random thing known to man, such as where did the myth about the man on the moon come from.

FML.

I awoke on Tuesday morning to Barış presenting me with breakfast in bed. Well bugger me - that's a first! And, there was no hidden sex agenda either, bonus!

Note to self: Indulge Husbando in random conversations more often.

I met up with Lorraine that afternoon for Christmas shopping. I had no idea what I wanted to buy the olds when I went into town, but by the time I arrived home I think I had pretty much got it sorted. An electric yellow 'Michael Korrs' handbag and purse for Mum, a belt and other bits and bobs for Dad, and, a present for them together which is a Turkish style crushed glass Vase. I'm sure my Mum will like the handbag and if not, I like it enough to use it. Mind you, I never use fake designer merch - not that I use real designer either. No, I'm more of a 'don't walk around with a name on your shit' kinda gal and always opt for the much more subtle and price friendly Primark option because that's just how I roll.

Kaan bought me a real 'Donna Karen' scarf from Italy once. I truly adored it, but I never wore it for fear of losing it. So I created somewhat of a shrine for it right here in the house. It's still as good as new, as let's face it, that's exactly what it is. I could gift it to someone for Christmas and they would love it and wear it and look great with it, but then I would be minus my only designer item.

Ahh well, shrine it is then.

Anyway, all the presents are sitting on my dining room table just waiting for the day that I find wrapping inspiration. I bet'cha they're still there on the day my olds arrive.

Today being Wednesday is Husbando's day off. We did pretty much what we do on any of his days off and went into town, had lunch at 'Yilmaz' and then came home.

While we were having lunch there was a poor young dog chained up next door to the restaurant crying. Bariş being Bariş went over to see him and was there for 15 minutes petting and fussing. Then he did something that shows just how much of a good human he is; he bought 10tl worth of doner meat and took it over to the crying dog.

Another note to self: If ever I have doubts about my dear ole Husbando, remember this event.

Sometimes I look at Bariş and think how lucky Guch and I are to have such a good bloke on our team. Not often mind you as that's not the sort of soppy ole sap that I am, but today Bariş was up there with Mother Teresa. He is now at his friend's house playing computer games and probably won't roll home till late, but do you know what, it's all good.

Yup, sometimes being a foreigner married to a Turk is not so bad. Especially when my Turk is a devout animal lover.

It drives me mad here as most cross the road in fear when they see a little dog like Gucci approaching. Honest to God, they shit themselves.

About 9 or 10 years ago, there was this one guy that I was dating, he calls himself Patrick. Obviously no Turk is named Patrick and I forget his real name, so for arguments sake let's call him 'fucktard'.

Fucktard bought me a ring; I'm not sure if it was for marriage or what as he never did give it to me. He presented me with said ring and went on to inform me that he hates dogs, how he couldn't live with one and gave me the choice between him and Gucci.

I remember looking over at Guch and seeing his sniggering little face. Guch has the best laugh on this planet - I may be the only one that can hear it, but trust me when I say we laughed our asses off when fucktard realised that there was never a choice to be made. We laughed as we watched him stomp out of the house, get in his rich man's Toyota Yaris and drive away.

Rich fucktard was never to be seen again. Unfortunately I can't add 'heard of' as I got many a hilarious text wishing me and my 'shit' dog dead, but hey, we laughed at them too.

As if there could ever be any competition. Ever. With anyone.
#FuckoffFucktard

Plans for the rest of the week:

Right, well tomorrow afternoon Loraine and I are planning a little walk along the beach to a newish coffee shop for cake tasting and probably some drivel about this young bloke she wants to date.

Friday afternoon I'm off to Sandi's house for more cake and a catch up.

And Saturday night I'm round at Lacie's for a 'get pissed and feed our faces' night that I hope won't turn into a 'sexting her Kuşadasi fling' night.

My social calendar is looking quite good for the rest of the week. It's funny how that goes, one week I can sit on my arse day after lonely day, and the following week I have loads of people to see and loads of things to do.

I must learn to spread shit out so that there is always something to look forward to.

Reminder: Schedule a skype date with Jenny for next week.

So, cheerio for now, I best go walk piss fest before he has one.

Monday 28th November

Current Weight: Weighed on Saturday and was down to 63 Kilos!

Time: 15.27pm

Dear Fire starter,

I'm going to start this entry by telling you that I'm pissed off that 'Honey G' got voted off 'The X Factor' last night. Yeah I know, you think I'm a knob. I am of course a knob, but hey, each Honey G loving knob to their own...

So the latter part of last week nearly went to plan - I did indeed meet up with Lorraine for coffee in the newest coffee shop on the beach front, 'Kahve Dunyari'. I liked it there; trendy decor, cool atmosphere, nice wintery beachfront view from the balcony - oh yes, my sort of place.

As it was 4pm and I hadn't had chance to eat yet, I decided to have a late lunch/early dinner instead of cake, so I ordered a savoury crepe. Beauts, just beauts and the coffee wasn't bad either. It's a shame I can't say the same about the company...

As I had only seen Lorraine on Tuesday, we had fuck all new to say to each other so she dished up more of the same expected drivel re this young bloke she likes. This guy is 32, still living at home with his parents and has generally been a cringy cunt.

I do not see the attraction, no not at all.

When I showed my disgust about this dude living at home still, we had the biggest argument ever, right there in the middle of the coffee shop! Everyone turned around and looked it was that bad. Lorraine did not agree with me one iota that it was a turn off; in fact she said that if her parents were still alive she would be living with them too.

I have heard her spout some shite in my time but this has got to be the biggest pile of flaming dog turds I have ever heard come out of her mouth, and I told her so. She was not impressed, but neither the fuck was I. She even told me that if she lived in the same country as her 35 year old son that he would still be living at home with her too. As if!!! The guy may be somewhat of a Mummies boy but come on, give him some credit!

Never mind that the guy she likes is younger than her own son, all she gave a shite about was sticking up for him for living at home! The real wowzer of this situation is that the guy in question has told her that he could get a place of his own quite easily as his employer would cover the rent - So, WHAT THE ACTUAL FUCK is going on in her mind and why won't this dude leave home?

Can you imagine if she went over to his house for a date and had to go upstairs to his room as his parents (who are younger than her btw) are sitting in the lounge watching TV!

FML Lorraine, seriously!??!

So yes, the argument was big, loud and quite uncouth for two grown women to have in public.

Lorraine cleverly calmed herself down and changed the subject. I think she knew there was no changing my opinion. Best thing too as I would have got up, walked out and not spoken to her again until I had forgotten just how stupid she can be, just like the last time. That shit took 2 years 'till I was ready to forget about her ludicrous antics...

It thinks it's best I don't see Lorraine for a while. What is it they say, familiarity breeds contempt?

Friday didn't go as planned but that's not to say it wasn't good. Sandi cancelled cake afternoon as she needed to go to hospital with a friend, so instead I was looking forward to an afternoon with my arse planted firmly on the sofa. That was until Kate (my new hairdresser) messaged and asked if I was home as she was in the area and fancied a coffee.

Thank fuck I had cleaned the house!

She came over at 1.30pm and we sat and chatted, worked out who each other knew, figured out we are both universe freaks and chatted some more. Every time I see that girl I like her more. There are so many weird, fucked up ex-pats living here that I tend to steer clear of most of them, so it's a refreshing change to find that Kate *seems* to be one of us. I am still hesitant of course as I know how it goes here, so until I am absolutely sure that this new friend of mine is not some sort of psycho, then I shall stay on high alert. But so far so good, I like her. So much so that I have invited her to Sunday Funday that Lacie and I have arranged for this week with some other normal (ish) girls.

Saturday was a good one. During the morning I dossed around at home and during the afternoon Nuri (Jenny's ex snogging buddy) came over for some womanly advice. He was talking a load of shite and it all seemed to boil down to the fact that his ex-wife has a new boyfriend and he was jealous. It was a wasted 3 hours because I definitely did not help his situation what with siding with his ex an all. I bet he regrets coming over for advice now!

Thankfully Lacie and I had a friggin' ball that night. She was back on form and there were no daft distractions. She cooked me dinner and kept my glass filled. She knows how to win me over.

We got talking about past mistakes and God knows she has done some fucked up shit in her life, but this new mistake is by far the most shocking. The daft ole mare had made a *video* for the recently dumped wannabe while they were still seeing each other. He was away working and she was horny. The problem she now faces is the possibility of him sharing said video. He isn't trying to bribe her to get back with him or anything like that, however he did show Lacie a video of the girl she replaced doing similar - so now panic is setting in.

I know, how could she be so damn stupid to have done the very same knowing that she had watched his ex strumming away? FFS Lacie, use your head and not your minge for a change!

As I couldn't quite believe what I was hearing, I asked her to show me said video. Jesus fucking Christ, as well as everything else the skinny biatch has going for her, she can now add Porn Queen to her list of achievements! This video was literally that of star quality - it was gob smackingly good. Total cheese, but fan-fucking-tastic. It involved a finger, a dildo, a neat looking lady garden and the backing music of 'Boys II Men'.

If at any point in the future she decided to earn a quick buck, she could sell that video and make a fortune. I knew she was kinky, but this video? I was rendered speechless.

The girl never fails to amaze me, and when I told her to find a way to delete the video she was on it like a car bonnet. Yesterday she simply messaged 'mission accomplished'. I dreaded to ask but it had to be done. Lacie reported that she lured wannabe over, shagged him and while he was in the bathroom cleaning himself up she went through his phone and deleted the video plus other compromising photos of herself too. Good gal. I don't approve of the shagging to delete the video, however it seems that she and the wannabe are possibly now back on because of this shag session.

I can't keep up, seriously, yet I applaud her temptress ways. She takes this shit to another level!

Anyway, other than finding out how Lacie managed to delete the video yesterday, I did nothing much else other than revel in hangover Sunday. I had a PJ and movie day which Gucci was more than happy to indulge in, and we even dragged the duvet off the bed and onto the sofa. Good times.

And now it's Monday. I am bright eyed and bushy tailed but still don't want to leave the house. Barış is on early's this week so I have decided to stay indoors today as it's grey and windy and I may cook dinner for him for a change. Although 3 minute pasta is really great for the diet (seriously it is, each packet only has 387 calories), I'm craving sensible food. Who'd have thunk it? So for dinner tonight I'm making 'Kisir' stuffed peppers and boiled potatoes. Not one of Bariş's favourites as he prefers junk food, but we need our 5 a day occasionally.

I don't have much on this week other than Sunday Funday, wrapping presents, shopping for Bariş's Christmas present and that's about it. Lacie wants to have a sleep over round hers on Saturday night so that we can get ready together on Sunday, but fuck me that could go wrong on so many levels.

Level 1: Not making it to Sunday Funday because we went on some random road trip, or, got wankered. Either way we never reach Level 2 or Sunday Funday...

Best stay home I recon.

December

2nd December

Current Weight: Just fuck off.

Time: 16.17pm

Dear Member of the Cunts Club,

What a boring old week so far! Seriously, it really does go one of two ways and this week has been the shitty side of the second way.

After Monday's entry I decided that I could not be arsed cooking and gave 'Loose Lacie' a call to find out what she was doing for dinner. We decided on the Pide place here in Armutalan and proceed to stuff our faces.

For some reason we got talking about what each of the Marmaris gangs call themselves. There is 'The Marmaris Elite' that the rival gang kid themselves on with, 'The Golden Group' that a couple of our friends belong to, and then there's us, me and Lacie - 'The Cunts Club'. We don't actually belong to a gang, but we are a couple of cunts.

Tuesday was no better, in fact it was worse as I didn't leave the house at all. It rained all day and all night. I decided to cook what I had planned for

Monday and it was also the start of my fertile week so we hopped on the sex train. And that was that.

Wednesday being Husbando's day off, we started the day by heading for grub. That is literally all that happened on Wednesday.

Thursday was much of the same other than I met a lady that I had sold a cardigan to recently for coffee in 'Violets', our local bakery in Armutalan. It was OK and it killed a bit of time. I then headed to 'Kipa' as I was meeting someone there to buy some tree decorations.

Yup, a sad ole week.

Today is Friday and I have managed to leave the house, but for fuck all exciting. Today's task was to go back to the Gynae to have the wall checked again. Bear in mind that I have doubled up my dose of pills prescribed so I'm now on 4 mg of Estrofem a day. My wall should have been at least 8 millimetres by now, but at its largest point it was only just 5.

So, as you can see, no baby for Lei this month.

What the hell is going on with my decrepit old body?

I originally started this diary with the goal of being pregnant by February. We are now 2 months away from my goal date with only 2 more cycles to go; I somehow think I have not given this old body enough time.

I'm on a bit of a downer due to this, but I won't lose hope entirely. Gynae has said I'm to take 3 tablets a day from now on and go back to see him on Monday to check it all out again, and then decide the next course of action. He muttered something about a patch if the wall hasn't grown...

Stupid wall. Stupid non-working pills. Stupid ever hopeful me.

ONCE UPON A WHISKY

Tonight I'm drowning my sorrows with cheap wine and hopefully good company. I have invited Eren and Funda over much to Husbando's delight. Funny how he really likes them.

In preparation for a good night I have spring cleaned the house, bought some crisps and other snacks, plus added more Christmas decorations in the living room to make it look super Christmassy. As they are atheists they don't celebrate Christmas but I bloody do and it looks so cosy that I'm sure they will love it.

I only hope that no one assumes they will be drinking my cheap red wine. What would literally tip me over the edge is if they show up empty handed like most Turks do.

Once, when I was still with my ex back in 2008, his friends came over to my house and raided the fridge without even asking. I was flabbergasted. They helped themselves to booze and food without so much of a 'Cheers'! If that happens tonight, what with my bigger balls these days, I can see the Hulk breaking out.

Oh be Jesus, wish me fucking luck...

22.16pm

So I'm back. The Turks did not arrive. They were due at 9pm and at 8.47pm I got the following message: 'Still in Istanbul, will message when we get back to rearrange'.

Urm, wouldn't you have known like 6-8 hours ago that you were not getting on your flight and would not be making it back to Marmaris today?

What the fuck is fucking wrong with people?!

Even Barış said it was shit. We literally starved ourselves in preparation for all the snack eating that was to take place, but no, why should that bother them? Plus I opened my bottle of red at 8pm which I needn't have done and could have saved that till Sunday's pre-drinks at Lacie's while she curls my hair.

God some people are inconsiderate.

Well, that's them never to be invited again.

And there was me planning our next outing too! I was going to take them to 'Lighthouse' as I'm sure that bar will be right up their street, but I won't now, oh hells no. That bar is mine and I won't share it with them pair of cancellers.

Don't get me wrong, I'm not pissed off that they cancelled; I'm annoyed that they didn't do it in a timely manner, say when they knew they were not getting their flight. It's just plain rude. Especially when I could have left the spring clean till Monday or Tuesday...

Although I have been here forever, I always forget that the Turks do things in their own way. I need to come to terms with the fact that some people are just not as considerate as I am.

Lacie said that they won't believe they have done anything wrong and this is quite normal behaviour. Well it's not and everyone is wrong.

So as the bottle of cheap red was open, I felt like I needed at least two glasses to calm myself down, but I'm on my third now and it's time to find the crisps. Barış and I have managed to eat all the other snacks so they didn't go to waste, but still – it's not the fucking point really is it...?

ONCE UPON A WHISKY

Tuesday 6th December

Current Weight: 63.5 Kilos.

Time: 18.46pm

Dear Miscellaneous drunk bruise collector,

Guess who arrives tonight – Mum and Dad that's who!! Oh the excitement is killing me! Even Gucci knows something's afoot with all the cleaning and general shifting around of things. I don't know who's more excited, me or Bariş? I swear I'm not being sarcastic, but Bariş absolutely adores my olds. I don't know if it's because they are well and truly different to his, or that they are like a comedy duo, but he really does bum off them.

So yes, today has been spent vigorously cleaning and getting their room ready for their arrival, which should be around 9pm ish. They had to fly to Antalya as there are no direct flights into Dalaman in the winter, so have a 4 and a half hour journey ahead of them once they land; which they did about an hour ago.

I expect Gucci to become a little Judas for the next month as when my olds are in the vicinity it's like Bariş and I cease to exist. I swear to God, he literally ignores us - that little fucker knows who will give him food directly off the plate... Mind you, he made himself sick twice yesterday. I'm not surprised as when I came home I found the bin on the floor with the contents pretty much savaged and a pile of puke under my coffee table (that sits on a lovely cream shag pile rug). Yup, the greedy little piglet had gorged himself on bin shit.

The second time he threw up was while we were all in bed asleep. I woke up to find the duvet, Gucci, some of Bariş and my hand covered in sick. It was gross, but Guch seemed to be in good spirits wagging his tail and sniffing his sickly mess.

Bariş spoiled him rotten for the rest of the day treating him like the blessed baby Jesus. I do believe I saw a sneaky glint in Gucci's eye, the genius little sod.

Anyway, what have I been up to for the last few days? Well, recovering from one god almighty hangover but I will get to that shortly.

Saturday I had a home day, but I didn't mind at all as I was on one hell of a girlie mission! I painted my nails and de-fuzzed in preparation for the first Xmas drinks of the month. The de-fuzzing was a task on its own as I hadn't bothered to shave my legs since Kuşadasi being winter and all. That's what's great about being married; you don't need to shave or generally try to impress your other half. No fucker cares if your lady garden is unkempt or you haven't shaved your armpits... Mind you, the lady garden does tend to itch slightly when left too long, but as long as one makes sure to not walk down the street scratching at it then I can go a good month before having to shave that bad boy again. It's not particularly fair on the Gynae of course, having to endure my laziness, especially after vowing to keep it in tip top condition for his work environment - but sometimes it's simply too much hassle to bother with...

Sunday arrived with bags of excitement. I was getting slightly concerned about this as when one expects a good night out it never ends up that way does it? In fact it usually ends in disaster, like most New Year's Eve's.

Thankfully disaster didn't strike, much.

I started off at Lacie's house around 3pm where she did my hair and I tried on probably half of my wardrobe that I took along with me. I hate it when I can't find anything to wear. I didn't even have the option of borrowing something of hers considering my size 12-14 self would never squeeze into her size 8 stash. In the end I found some hideous creation that made me look like the fat friend again. Fucking brilliant.

We were meeting everyone at 5pm in 'Beer Land' so I had time for 3 glasses of cheap red wine first to get me in the mood. If the crack that Lacie and I were having in the house was anything to go by then we were surely in for a good old night.

Wrong.

Our group curse struck again. Fuck knows what I said (or didn't say) but Lacie turned all funny and left. I can't quite figure out if the reason for her leaving was real or not as she is yet to reply to my messages. Before she left she said the Kuşadasi fling had messaged and had arrived in Marmaris a day early. Hmm, truth or excuse?

I knew he was due to arrive on the Monday for 3 days' worth of rich man sex, but had he really arrived early? I won't find out until she is good and ready to talk and clearly she is not at that point quite yet. Standard Lacie.

FYI, the wannabe has not been invited back on the scene as yet. She decided that she wants showering with gifts from the rich fling before she considers taking wannabe back. Only last week she stated loud and proud that she was done with being materialistic - change your mind much SVS?

Our night went on regardless with Kate my new hairdresser, the 2 Deborah's and Petra. One of the Deborah's got that wasted that she went into pissed zone where she simply couldn't talk to anyone, she could only sit and stare. I know the feeling well but it was still entertaining for the rest of us. Kate on the other hand, was knocking 'em back and holding her own, right up until she went to the toilet, threw up and came back with a smidgen of sick around her chops.

I didn't get home too late, they say it was about 1am when we left 'Beer Land', but considering I got to Lacie's at just before 3pm, I reckon that's a good effort on the drinking front.

I haven't checked my internet banking for just how much I spent, but I'm sure it will be over 150tl going by the amount that I threw up at 4am. I couldn't believe it when the first time in years I woke up and just knew I needed to spew. I never spew when I'm drunk, it's just not something that happens. If I didn't know any better, I would wonder if I was up the duff -

but I know the truth on that old chestnut...

So, I am left to assume that the booze was dodgy or the 'blooming onions' I guzzled were not quite right... Either way, I was sick as a dog, but I do thank God for small mercies as I live to see another day!

So, what do I have to show for my Sunday Funday?

A bestie that's not speaking to me, a huge miscellaneous bruise on my back and a sore throat from all the spewing and smoking of everyone's fags.

Nice one Lei, you complete and utter knob.

Monday served up the most vicious hangover I have encountered. Firstly I was still pissed until 2pm. I had to go back to the Gynae at 1.30pm for a quick check up and I can tell you it was literally the last thing I felt like doing. But, I powered through and hauled ass into the shower, tidied up the lady garden, made Barış take me to where I dumped Kastro my beloved car, visited the Gynae and quite possibly knocked him out with my fumes (I seem to recall writing something similar before), got prescribed the patch thing as wall was still no bigger and then came home to get changed before heading into town to meet Lorraine for masses of hangover food.

Note to self: Never lift one finger off the sofa again when suffering that badly.

I was far too hung-over to be taking on so much that day. Mind you, I needed to stuff my face but what I didn't need was to listen to Lorraine as she filled me in on what she had been up to since I saw her last.

I originally thought she was in the process of talking herself out of liking this young boy, but no, instead of talking herself out of him, she has been over to his family home and attended a family fucking barbeque.

What did I predict the other week about her sneaking up to his room like a 65 year old teenager? Yup, that actually happened and that's where they shared their first kiss, I kid you fucking not. I'm not quite sure what my

Mum and Dad would make of this ridiculous situation, but let's hope she doesn't decide to spill the beans over Xmas sodding dinner...

Anyway, after that revelation I wasn't in the mood to do much else. It would have been nice to buy a few new outfits, however the thought of Lorraine with that young boy, plus the added pain of my hangover was indisputably churning my stomach, so home I went instead.

This brings us up to date. It's Tuesday evening and I'm excited. It's Bariş's day off tomorrow so we plan on taking my olds out and about and also filling the fridge. As Bariş is on lates this week we are going to our favourite Turkish restaurant 'Kervan' tomorrow night and then possibly on the weekend Lorraine will join us for food somewhere. I may choose a restaurant that I know she would usually say no to just because she has no choice in the matter. Ha!

So, I'm signing off for now. No doubt next time I write I will be a stone heavier.

FML, good luck to me on this diet while my Mum is in town...

Saturday 10th December

Current Weight: I don't even dare get on the scales.

Time: 15.45pm

Dear Ranting loony,

Just a quick entry today as I feel highly stressed. Yep, my stress levels have peaked beyond recognition and this surly can't be good for my wannabe pregnant body. Don't they say that stress causes belly fat? If that's true then I'm fucked. I already resemble a pot-bellied pig.

Between my parents wearing their shoes in the house walking all over my cream shag pile rugs, to Gucci's small dog antics while out on the beach front, this makes for a tension filled few days.

I had better explain...

We have just got back from what should have been a nice relaxing afternoon sitting on the beach at 'Bono', drinking coffee and chilling, but contrary to what my Facebook photo and status suggested, it was nothing of the sort. Well, I couldn't very well capture the real image now could I? That would be Facebook lunacy!

When walking Guch along the beach in Spain, or sitting in a cafe/restaurant over there, all is calm, all is peaceful - but not here, never bloody here. The reason you may wonder is because dog owners in this country let their dogs run wild off the lead to annoy the living shit out of responsible dog owners (which are few and far between in Marmaris)... I tell no lies when I say that I spent the entire afternoon warding off other dogs in spitting distance of my boy, as being the human kind of dog that he is, Gucci doesn't cope well with other k9's.

So my question today is this: Why are some dog owners so fucking selfish?

Well, I believe it's because they are selfish people in general. I'm mean come on, why let your dog run riot and terrorise others? It's just shit I tell you! Selfish and shit!

So yes, my afternoon was ruined due to 9 loose dogs and 1 stupid dog owner who brought his little dog to sit down right next to us on the beach, even though I informed him there would be trouble.

Did he listen? No.

Did he move over to the free table at the other end, away from the issue? No.

This resulted in Guch having a near heart attack when wanker's dog came within bum sniffing distance. Some may say this is my own fault for not introducing Gucci to other dogs when he was a puppy. I say fuck that. I am a protective Mother when all said and done, and what if another dog bit Guch and he died? You hear about it all the time, so it's not as if it couldn't happen. I would never forgive myself.

So really, fuck that.

Anyway, the coffee, beer and snacks went flying leaving us dripping in snot, slaver and a mixture of liquid.

Thank you selfish fuck face of a dog owner, you utter turd you.

And what's with dog owners not picking up after their doggie dumps? How gross can people get! There is this old guy who lives around the corner from me and every day I witness him taking his dog across the street for a dump, not bother to poop and scoop, leaves said turd sitting in the sun all day so that flies and what not land on it and then start spreading disease. I have told him before to bag it up but the response I get is to mind my own business! That's nice isn't it? But that old fucker doesn't have to step out of his house and into his dog shit like the poor ole lady opposite!

Really - what the fuck is wrong with people??

Anyway, rant over, normal service is to resume shortly.

But first, can I just ask why my parents seem to have an obsession with keeping their shoes on indoors? I'm trying not to get snappy but sometimes I simply can't hold my tongue. I know fine well that they remove their shoes in their own house as they make me remove mine, so what's the deal with this new fresh torture?

I simply don't get it.

I have asked them repeatedly to put their slippers on at the door, but then I turn around to see them trailing dirt all over the house in the very same sodding shoes! I'm losing the will to live, I really am.

Don't get me wrong, Mum has been fabulous what with all the cooking, cleaning, and ironing, and that's why I'm struggling to comprehend what's going on with the shoes?!

My cleaning of the house is usually every 4 or 5 days, however when it got to 2 days I couldn't stand the trail of filth any longer and broke out the hoover!

My somewhat idle OCD has been reactivated, and I fear it is only going to get worse.

I have just re-read the above and I realise that I may need to calm the fuck down.

It's not the end of the world, and other than that all has been great, truly it has. Since their arrival we have been here, there and everywhere on a daily basis. I have enjoyed taking them around and about in the car, and they have thoroughly enjoyed being chauffeured. I have also over eaten just for the sheer fun of it which started off on Wednesday at 'Yilmaz' restaurant for lunch where we indulged in soup and a mound of bread. Usually that's enough to keep me full 'till dinner, but not on Wednesday. When I got home I made a crisp sandwich and then went on to eat my own body weight in food at 'Kervan' at dinner time!

I dare not get on the scales till January - I know I will cry.

My usual light lunches have been replaced with full on meals, and as well as having snacks while out in town, we are also eating great big evening dinners at home too.

It's also safe to say I'm OD'ing on vegetarian products since they brought a ton over for me. My Mum has been cooking up a feast such as Quorn spag bol and Quorn chicken curry, and they have only been here since Tuesday night!

Tonight we are heading out to try a restaurant on the beach front that I haven't eaten in yet - 'Pukka'. It always looks so nice when the rival gang post a million bog selfies in there (cunts), that I thought it was about time I checked it out too.

I have already decided that there is no point in counting calories today (or any other day 'till January) as tonight I'm having Pizza (and probably a dessert), then tomorrow we are heading to 'Asparan' for a dirty big Turkish breakfast on the way to the Christmas market in Datça, then home for tea and all butter scones!

Inwardly I'm crying, but outwardly I'm a slobbering fucking wreck gorging on all this grub and then demanding seconds! Barış is on earlys next week so that means he will be home to eat with us every night and there is nothing more that me ole dear loves is to cook fattening food to beef Barış up a bit.

I'm in trouble and I damn well know it, but by Christ, I simply can't help it.

21.55pm

I'm home from dinner and I'm stuffed. Not just with the massive pizza, but also with impending doom. I can't even blame the booze as I only had one beer what with being out with the 'rents.

To be truthful, when it came to it, I didn't really fancy going out tonight however my olds wanted to go and I didn't want to be a 36 year old wet blanket. Can you imagine me turning down a free meal? Well, I could easily have forgone it tonight...

Anyway, out we went just the 3 of us as Barış was at work and Lorraine turned her nose up at my choice of restaurant. They wanted to be home early to watch the semi-final of 'Strictly Come Dancing' so we went out at 7.15pm to be home in time. We headed for 'Pukka' as planned but as we hadn't made a reservation, we couldn't sit where we wanted to so we got shoved up the side. It wasn't terrible however the lay out reminded me of a school canteen. It wasn't too busy when we arrived which was great, but by the time we left it was a different story - heaving to say the least.

The food was great but the atmosphere was odd and I think this is where the impending doom set in. Or it may have been because my old friend Kaan walked in without acknowledging me.

I didn't notice him arrive as just like an ignorant only child could, I had my head in my phone - but he would most certainly have seen me. He paraded up and down like a fucking peacock 3 times before his party decided on a table, but still nothing. OK, so I didn't exactly jump up and shout 'Hey Kaan, how you doing' and that is possibly where I went wrong, but so fucking what?

Clearly neither of us could be arsed to say hi to each other, so what does that say about our friendship, or lack thereof it?

Bastard friend...

ONCE UPON A WHISKY

Tuesday 15th December

Time: 16.34pm

Dear Wine drinking wannabe,

My head feels like steam is about to start gushing out. Why is it so much more stressful having my olds stay here with me than it is when I go to visit them? I feel constantly up a height and need to get pissed to come back down again. Of course I can't sit in my own house and have a drink as 8 pairs of eyes would be judging me, silently castrating me.

So, fuck that shit - tonight I'm escaping to Lacie's to drink 1.5 litres of cheap wine and chill. 8pm can't come quickly enough.

Do I feel bad about leaving them indoors for the evening? A bit, but not enough to forego the thirst that can no longer be quenched. I have told Barış to go to his friend's house too as we all need a break, my olds included.

When I go to their house they still go out and meet up with their friends and do things without me, and I also see my friends too - so why do I feel so guilty about leaving them on their own? They have enough to keep them occupied; British TV, internet, a sparkling Christmas tree plus Gucci, so I'm sure they will be fine for one night alone right?

FFS Lei, start feeling less guilty and more pissed, that's the way to do it.

Don't misunderstand me 'dear diary', we are still having a grand old time of it visiting plenty of places, like on Sunday when we went to Datça Christmas Market. It was a complete and utter waste of time and we came away with a bag of bloody apricots alone, but we did have a lovely day outside of the Xmas market making it worth the hour's journey.

Monday was a rainy day so we didn't do too much, and Tuesday we had a home day but a busy one as Kate came round for a coffee in the morning, and in the afternoon Lorraine joined us for High Tea. It was a pleasant day, but why is it that some people just don't know when to go home?

Wednesday was Bariş's day off so we took the 'rents for a another good Turkish breakfast at 'Havuzlu Bahce' about 20 minutes outside of Marmaris and then drove on to Goçek - a quaint marina town. We had a lovely day and no stress in sight.

That was until today - Thursday.

This morning Mum and Dad showered Gucci – no problems there, well, not many anyway. This afternoon we headed to town. All was going well; we had soup at 'Yilmaz', picked up an adaptor for my Dad's electric razor, bought Bariş a pair of black chinos for an added pressy under the tree, had a coffee on the marina in the glorious sunshine and then got back in the car.

That's when it happened.

As I was driving correctly down a one way street, a female Turkish driver drove incorrectly up the street and point blank refused to back up even though it was my right of way.

I have absolutely horrific road rage and when it flares up there is not one thing I can do to stop it until the problem has removed itself - and the fucking bitch was not removing herself. Well the air was blue, absolutely fucking blue. Car horns behind were hooting and a tooting and this bitch was a yelling, and to top it off my parents were shouting at me to calm down making the situation 10 times worse.

Who actually calms down when getting shouted at to calm down? Not fucking me, that's who. Not the cars behind waiting for the bitch to reverse up the street, that's also not who. And certainly not my parents that were now so over the top reacting to my effing and jeffing that they got out of the car and informed me they were getting the dolmuş home.

Well that's bastard gratitude for you.

They walked away leaving me red faced and thoroughly raging.

The bitch eventually backed up but it took the driver behind to get out of his car, walk over to her and pretty much threaten her. Her face was a picture and she soon shifted her arse at that point.

Only one word for cunts like that...

The olds got home an hour after me. They said they wanted to give me additional time to calm down so went to 'Starbucks' for a festive coffee. Funny that as when I said I wanted to do just that they said they didn't fancy 'Starbucks' at all.

Is it me or what?

After hearing this I honestly couldn't take it any longer and so I called up Lacie, told her to prepare herself for my arrival and to push aside her no drinking on a week night rule that she has suddenly adopted. After all, I have done it for her.

As you can see we are speaking again, but it took a while, 4 days in fact before she replied to me. I may ask her tonight what was up, or I may sweep it under the carpet, but whatever I decide to do I'm sure I won't care as I will be good and wankered by that time God willing.

Tomorrow is Friday and it happens to be the Marmaris Christmas market. I'm hoping above all hope that I don't have a hangover as I'm neither use nor ornament in that state, but if we don't make it to the Xmas market, going by the shite Datça one, I'm sure we won't be missing much.

But what do I do with the olds otherwise?

A trip to Içmeler, 'winter city of the dead' perhaps? I doubt we could even find a coffee shop open at this time of year.

Ahh well, hangover or not, I will be forced into doing something. Let's just hope that the road rage stays at bay as another day like today will just about tip me over the edge.

Got to go now as I'm being summoned to look for a cooking dish that I probably don't have. Just another thing in the long list of bollocks that my Mum has informed me is wrong with my house...

ONCE UPON A WHISKY

Monday 19th December

Time: 16.44pm

Dear Pete Tong,

We didn't make it to the Christmas Market on Friday and yes it was due to my disgusting hangover. I was fucking green.

Damn you cheap red wine, damn you.

Mind you, Lacie and I had a bloody good night. Not good enough to warrant my disgusting hangover, but mighty good enough. I asked her about the funny turn and she gave me the answer, but I'm damned if I remember it now. Put it this way all was back to normal and the funny turn was left where it should have been, down the bog along with all my spew from that night.

Drunk lush. Me and Lacie.

Mum was not at all happy because as predicted, I was like a chocolate fucking tea pot - yup, we did diddly-squat on Friday because of me.

This was not a proud moment let me tell you. At 36 years of age I'm sure you are not supposed to willingly incapacitate yourself due to binge drinking. I mean why would anyone do this to themselves? I'm nothing but a greedy wine pig. The only thing I raised my snout at was to go out for dinner as the hangover needed feeding and we wanted to check out this particular restaurant as we had booked in for Christmas Day lunch.

Mum decided that with her bad knee she didn't want to cook as standing up for that length of time may finish her off (if reading my bloody diaries don't do so first), so the best offer that we saw so far was a newish restaurant on the beach front. All the trimmings plus Yorkshire Puds and vegetarian gravy (for me), for the very reasonable price of 42tl per person. It would cost more to do it at home!

Anyway, feed my face I did, but what a shockingly awful night we had that for once was not my fault!

I don't really know how it all started but I do know that we were in good spirits on the walk up to the restaurant, all of us laughing, joking and very much looking forward to dinner, Barış especially. After ordering our feasts it was obligatory photo taking time. How else would people know we were out and enjoying ourselves without uploading a few pics on Facebook?

That's when the night went Pete Tong.

Barış refused to smile or even take one more selfie with me and my olds. Embarrassing wasn't the word… I asked him to crack one little smile as the 2 photos taken previously had him looking like hated us all, but nope, he wouldn't.

From then the night turned to shit.

Mum was trying to speak to him but his one word answers were enough to put even the most positive person off bothering, so we didn't. He barely touched his food which annoyed me no end but there was no way I was asking him if there was a problem with his dinner… In fact I told him not to speak to me for the rest of the night. And he didn't.

PMS mixed with husband crimes is just vicious.

That evening we all went to bed deflated. I had hoped Barış would sleep on the sofa, alas he came to bed to piss me off further. I squashed myself over to the furthest edge of the bed and made sure not to touch any of his body parts all night, even when rolling over accidentally. I wedged Gucci in-between us for added annoyance as he hates it when Guch sleeps right in the middle as he rolls around and goes digging all night.

The next morning he was in a cunt of a mood. He didn't stay for breakfast and disappeared off to work after making the least bit of small talk possible.

Doesn't he know that I'm the only one that can behave like a stroppy brat in front of my parents?

And with that, I sent him a lengthy Facebook message stating that if he couldn't pull himself together and apologise to my parents for his ridiculous behaviour then he wasn't to come home after work. I also informed him that he would never have to be included in another photograph for the rest of his miserable life and that on Xmas day it will be like he didn't come as we will ask him to sit out of the way when the camera comes out, and when we have kids people will think that he must have died after impregnating me as there will be literally no trace left of him on this planet.

What was his response?

Apparently I took him to a restaurant that supports Kurdish terrorists and by doing this I have brought shame upon him, his friends and his family. I wasn't aware that we had taken his friends and family out to eat with us; maybe they were hiding under his blanket of shitty attitude?

Jesus.

I thought he was pissed off about selfie's damn it, I wasn't geared up for this shit. I know Barış has issues with terrorists killing innocents, don't we all, but this was just ludicrous. He has now refused to dine anywhere unless it can be proven that the owner is originally Turkish.

Not a problem fuck face, you will be left at home on your own from now on!

He did send my Mum a great big Facebook message apologising and explaining everything, however this left us with a problem - where the hell are we going to eat on Christmas day? I asked one of my friends at another beach front restaurant if they had Turkish owners (which they have) but Barış refused again as he thought I was lying. This happened 3 more times with 3 other restaurants all over Marmaris. We even went up to our old wedding venue 'Joya Del Mar' as it looked like it could be a great day and evening with live music and dancing, however I found out that the rival gang had booked. And that 'dear diary' would be a fate worse than death.

Mum couldn't take it any longer and informed us over the dinner table that night that if it would stop the stinking atmosphere then she would cook the dinner herself. I protested immediately but she took no notice. Oh the look on Husbando's face, like he had won the bastard lottery. I could have knocked him out.

I'm sitting there raging, he was sitting there like the cat that had got the cream and Dad was sitting there saying "well Gucci will be happy that Turkey day is happening in his own house".

FML, seriously?

So - we are having Christmas day at home.

Lorraine is bringing a trifle, I will help Mum in the kitchen as much as possible, Dad will keep Gucci out from under our feet, and Bariş can bloody well wash up - alone.

Mum has treated her and Dad to a Boxing night Hotel break at the 'Grand Azur' so she doesn't have to think about cooking again after Christmas day for a while. Quite right too.

It sounds as if I won't cook for them doesn't it? I have offered, believe me, but they were non to happy about the fact that they won't get any meat out of me - a nice pasta bake is as far as I can stretch what with being veggie and all. Alas no, my pasta bake has been outvoted in favour of an overnighter in a posh hotel. Not that I blame them.

Now it's Monday and I'm still raging. I didn't start speaking to Bariş 'till this morning when he asked me why my olds were going to a hotel overnight. The silly fucker thought it was to give us privacy for 'sexy time'; his face dropped when I told him the real reason and that my Mum would need a bloody long break after the hard work that is Christmas day...

Jesus Turks are stubborn! And it's not just my Turk either.

Fuck knows what we're going to do for New Year's...!

And to top it all off I'm bleeding like Mount Vesuvius. Yup, the period is here. Hmm, that may explain some of my hostility towards Husbando... Of course I knew there was no chance of being pregnant this month what with the wall being as shite as what it is, but does it have to have me doubled up in this much pain?

There really was no feeling of hope this time, no magical wonder - just a residing feeling of knowing. I suppose I should be grateful for this knowing, but I'm not. Me being me I am ever hopeful that an Immaculate Conception is about due a return and I could be chosen to be the new age Virgin Mary.

One can hope cant one.

Mind you, that would be a terribly heavy load to bear, raising a prophet. Heavier than the period pain I am going through right now I'm sure.

What a cunt. Period. Me. Pretty much everyone.

Thursday 22nd December

Current Weight: 63.5 Kilos. I'm shocked to say the least.

Time: 17.30pm

Dear Sprout stalker,

You will be happy to hear that things are back to normal in our household. No more bickering, no more bad atmosphere and no more withholding of sex. Well, I'm hoping my parents are abstaining whilst they are here as that would be pretty grim if they are bang at it in my spare room. Actually, I hope they don't do it at all anymore. It's just gross isn't it, the thought of one's olds doing it... I've heard them before you know, when I was 14 years old and living at home. The flash backs haunt me to this very day.

Anyway, it was touch and go there for a while but my Mum gave me a stern talking to and told me that if I didn't smooth it over with Barış then they were moving to a hotel for the rest of their holiday. The thought of having to cook for myself again so soon was simply too horrific to bear and spurred me right on to start speaking with Husbando.

So, we are back to our positive home once more. For how long is anyone's guess...

Plans have not been made for New Year's Eve as yet; we are avoiding the topic as no one wants to start any more arguments. I suppose we will wait to get Christmas out of the way first before we tackle the next obstacle.

In actual fact we should have been seeing in the New Year with Lacie as Lorraine is spending Christmas with us, however Lorraine has scored herself an invite to whatever we do for New Year too as she dropped in not so subtly that she would be alone, and what with Mum being nothing but a sucker, she invited her to join us. I'm not happy about this as plans are plans and this now makes for resentment on my part. Lacie won't join us now you see - she finds it hard to even talk about Lorraine let alone be in the same room as her, and this is kind of Lorraine's fault. It stems back my wedding day. Everyone knew that I wanted no friend agro, Lacie, Lorraine, the man on the moon - everyone. So when Lorraine came up to my wedding suite to change into her outfit, it was at the same time that Lacie and Kimmy were in full swing of getting me into my big black dress. Lacie knew what needed to be done so manned up and said a quick hi to Lorraine to ease the tension. Alas, tension is all that came out of it. Lorraine looked at Lacie, and then looked away, dismissing her. It was super rude, super inappropriate and super uncomfortable for all that witnessed it. I could have killed her, really I could. What was she thinking on my big day?

So you see, it's not really Lacie's fault that she refuses to be anywhere near Lorraine after that. And who can blame her?

Thankfully Lacie isn't ever alone and didn't hate me too much for the NYE cock up. I wouldn't have blamed her if she did as I sure would, but my girl understood.

At least I'm seeing her on Monday night while my olds escape to the 'Grand Azur'.

What's that, why am I not making the most of it and having a parent free night with Husbando?

Well, although I have nearly forgiven him I would still rather go see my bestie on Boxing night considering how I have fucked up the rest of it. And at least I can get good and pissed there. If I stayed home with Husbando I would be drinking alone and who the bloody hell wants to do that? No, sod that, its bestie night on Boxing night.

Other than the ridiculous above, I have had a busy few days which have proved that I can keep my cool when I try. My first test was when Kate came round on Tuesday to do my hair. I am now even darker with only snippets of blonde highlights showing through. Urm?

Apparently my hair still can't take bleach, so for now, I'm stuck like this.

She also dyed my new clip in fringe. Oh, didn't I tell about that? It must have slipped my mind.

I loved it when I had a real fringe, all thick and shaggy. I had what they call 'Half Moon Bangs'. It was too much maintenance for a lazy hair kinda gal like me, so I grew it out. I missed it terribly and wanted it back ever since, so when I saw this clip in beauty online I just knew I had to have it.

Not sure Barış thinks too much of it though as when he walked in the bedroom that very night, I heard a shriek, so I went running in to find the stupid mo fo standing on the bed shouting at my clip in fringe. Through the dimly lit bedroom light the tit though a rat had got onto the dressing table.

A rat FFS!

Rat or not, I literally can't wait to try it out.

Wednesday was a shopping day. We were on the hunt for two of the most difficult things to find here: A turkey and sprouts. Dad says that Christmas ain't Christmas without either, so off we went trailing round every supermarket in town.

We eventually found sprouts in 'Migros' in the centre, but the turkeys were all huge great big things of 7 and 8 kilos. Be Jesus there are only 4 and a half meat eaters on Christmas day (Gucci being the half), so who needs all that amount of meat!!! So, we left the turkey shopping 'till today when 'Kipa' told us they were getting smaller ones in.

FYI cooking at home is turning out to be a real pain in the arse...

Anyway, after enjoying a gorgeous brunch in the sunshine on the beachfront at 'Yunus' this morning, we eventually found a turkey of 5 kilos. We have all the veg, so all that's left to do is for me is to go to Rhodes tomorrow with Lorraine.

Rhodes? Sorry, another thing I forgot to mention.

I fancy a day out Christmas shopping in a real Christmasy environment, because as much as they try, Marmaris just doesn't quite pull it off. And why should it? They don't celebrate Christmas here after all.

Whilst there we are hoping to find Lidl and do a bit more food shopping. If not then it's clothes shops galore. Either way I'll be happy.

Plans for tonight: Easting toasties, playing with new fringe, watching the ultimate British Christmas movie 'Love Actually' and then bed early as up for Rhodes at 06.30.

Ewwww, I hate early....

My next update will be after Xmas. For the love of god, let's hope that goes well as I really can't cope with any more fall outs.

Saturday 24th December

Time: 15.07pm

Dear Venter chick,

I know I said I wasn't going to write 'till after Christmas but I need to vent somewhere, and being that this is my diary, it makes sense to do so here.

Yesterday Lorraine and I did indeed go to Rhodes. Although we didn't find Lidl, we certainly had a good old time clothes shopping and stuffing our faces with food that you just can't get over here.

I love Rhodes, what with its quaint little streets in the old town and its brilliant clothes shops in the new, it has loads more to offer shopping wise than Marmaris.

I've decided to visit more often, but when the weather is better. Yup, the universe decided to punish me for something because the spoiler of the day was the horrific rain. It literally poured from the moment we got off the catamaran to the moment we got back on again. But, weather isn't enough to stop 2 die hard shopaholics. We hit the new town, rain and all, and for once Lorraine didn't push any of my buttons.

I got home around 5.30pm that afternoon to Mum making dinner. They had a lovely day out and about; they went into the town centre for a wander, stopped for coffee, bought a measuring jug for the Christmas day gravy, visited 'Kahve Dunyasi', then had a walk along the marina whilst admiring the boats, got chatting to a guy standing outside a restaurant, and booked it for New Year's Eve.

WT Actual F?

I wouldn't mind but it's not even a restaurant that I like!

I saw red.

I tried to explain calmly that it might have been an idea to consult me before booking New Year's Eve, but Mum seemed to think not. I tried to clarify that this situation is plain ridiculous and it would be like if Barış and I had been into town in Spain for a day and booked New Year's Eve when we don't know the town well and don't know if the restaurant is good. Mum being Mum didn't get the comparison, or pretended not to at least.

Is it me?

I was left with a bitter taste in my mouth that no amount of cheese board could get rid of...

It also doesn't help that Mum has different TV taste to me and Dad. Mum likes soppy old love stories and we like thriller, action and alien films. She saw her arse when I suggested watching the film 'Snowden' last night. Me and Dad really fancied it, but it wasn't to be. In all honesty I don't think she was in the mood to watch anything, but we stuck on the film about the Tsunami 'The Impossible' and went with that instead. This was until she took a skype call from one of her mates and was on the phone for an hour, then we had to pause it again for 30 minutes so they could watch the news.

It takes the sparkle out of a good film when it's watched in 3 stages.

We didn't even get to finish it as when it got to 11pm they wanted to go to bed!

FML.

Today is Christmas Eve.

Mum has done all the veg prep ready for tomorrow, I have cleaned the whole house, laid the dining room table festively and washed my hair, Dad has taken Gucci out for a walk twice and Bariş is at work.

Mum has informed us that the kitchen is closed for tonight and we need to eat out. Quite right too, so we are off to 'Kervan' to fill our faces Turkish stylee.

Arse - my clothes have started to get tight and I feel like a heffer.

Nice one holiday food, you absolute turd you.

Thursday 29th December

Current Weight: No idea but my face has started to resemble a plate once more...

Time: 18.22pm

Dear Annoyed festive gal,

As this is possibly the last entry of 2016, I don't want to end the year on a shitty note, but somehow I can't seem to help it as I find myself sitting here annoyed again. I'm starting to see a pattern forming that I'm not particularly fond of.

Why am I annoyed? Take a wild guess...

Cracks are starting to show with this living with the parent's lark. There are too many people invading my personal space and I'm not used to this amount of attention, people or chat on a daily basis.

But before I get onto that I better start at the beginning, Christmas Day...

All was grand in the morning:

We got up, ate breakfast, opened our presents and waited for Lorraine to arrive. Once she was here we opened the Bucks Fizz and started the general merriment on the lead up to the main event - dinner.

I was on my way back from the toilet when I overheard Mum and Lorraine bitching about my drinking habits. Lorraine was in full swing of informing Mum that she does not go out drinking with me as she is not a drinker and doesn't condone it.

What's your game Lorraine?

They seemed to be having a right old 'Lei is shit' session and as you can imagine I was not a happy camper. I mean why the hell would my friend and my Mother choose to start this shit up on Christmas fucking day?

Why - why talk shit behind my back in my own fucking house? I know Mum wouldn't have instigated this as she's not like that - this was all Lorraine... It's not as if I was hammering back the booze FFS. Nope, I was sipping my Bucks Fizz and minding my own business. Well, I was 'till then anyway.

I started to see red again. I told the pair of them politely to keep their opinions to themselves as they have never been invited out to drink with me anyway, so why they felt the need to be arse holes about it was beyond me. Lorraine bit back telling me that she was not bitching, that she was simply informing my Mum that she does not tolerate my drinking habits.

OK love, if you weren't bitching what would you call it when you're throwing turds at the person who's house you're in for Christmas? Fucking poetry? Ahh fuck off.

Luckily for them, as it was Christmas I decided to pull my face round a lot quicker than usual, after all, 'tis the season of good will...

We enjoyed some nibbles, had a refill on the fizz and generally all went well. Other than my Yorkshire pudding coming out like a flat lump of lard, dinner was bloody marvellous. I, like everyone else, stuffed my face till I could fit in not one morsel more. We washed dinner down with a lovely couple of bottles of red, then coffee, then dessert which was Lorraine's Trifle.

About 8.30pm Bariş and I decided to go and find the big black dog that has adopted us and take him some leftover turkey. He enjoyed it immensely. Poor bugger wears a collar so he belongs to someone, but his human must be a useless fuck as the poor boy is painfully thin and his ribs are sticking out... Shame on that shitty human - seriously.

Lorraine took this as her cue to leave.

We had no major fall outs, but I won't forget her earlier snarky remarks easily. I'm like a camel that way - I store everything in my pot belly hump...

None of us were hungry that evening, but we were Christmas greedy and decided to opt for cheese board instead of Christmas pudding for supper. Did we need it? No did we fuck, but we had it anyway.

I ended the day slightly tipsy, stuffed like a barrel and ready for bed by 11pm.

Not a bad Christmas as they go. I wonder where I will be spending the next one?

Boxing Day was clean-up day. I was giving my dining room chairs a wipe down when I noticed that the chair in which Lorraine had parked her arse had severe clothes dye staining. I could make out the fringe detail that was on her new top so there was no denying who had sat there. I scrubbed as hard as I could with various solutions, as did Mum, but nothing was shifting this bloody dye. I felt the need to tell Lorraine but I didn't want to come across as a complete twat. So, as delicately as I could, I sent this message: 'Please be careful when you sit on your furniture as your new top seems to be leaking dye'. That was enough for her to ask what had happened and so I informed her. She didn't seem too concerned that one of my chairs was ruined, in fact she was mighty blazé about it.

What the actual fuck is wrong with people!?

After that I dropped my olds at the 'Grand Azur' for their mini break. When I came home I continued my clean-up before heading to Lacie's to indulge in pasta and duty-free whisky that I sly'ed out of the house because Dad would have been non to impressed that I was drinking his supply.

We got good and plastered while we caught up over the goings on of

Christmas and how she is definitely not getting back with wannabe - well, not this week anyway.

On Tuesday I collected the olds about 11am. After that we didn't do too much mainly because I had a stinker of a hangover.

Greedy whisky pig strikes again!

All I could manage was a little car ride down to the marina for a coffee in 'People 180' which I LOVE by the way as it sits right on the water and boasts the best views of Marmaris marina. Yup, my favourite place that end of town. And we received a free plate of chips too. Bonus!

Today is Wednesday and I'm all of a tiz once more. As its Baris's day off we decided to drive 30 minutes to Akyaka for brunch on the 'Azmak River'. I have always liked Akyaka, it's such a cute little town with really amazing little houses, the best beach of the area and a great 20 minute river trip for about 10tl per person. Today was a bit too nippy to do the river trip, but it will still be there in the summer.

We ordered a Turkish breakfast at 'Kordon' restaurant where we always seem to find ourselves when in Akyaka as it's such a delightful place overlooking the river with bleedin' marvellous food. No sooner had we ordered did it start pissing down and didn't stop. That put paid to our plans of walking on the beach front for the afternoon, so we headed back to Marmaris and went to 'Blue Port' shopping centre instead.

I finally found a balcony bistro table and chair set that I had been looking for for ages, and, which has just been delivered. Thanks Mum.

So, this leads us up to why the hell am I even annoyed?

It's an ongoing occurrence these days isn't it..?

As Bariş was removing our old deck chairs that inhabit the space in which the new balcony furniture was to be placed, I noticed that he was making a right old mess with his wet muddy boots, so my OCD infested self asked him to clean up after himself.

Nothing wrong with that right?

Well my olds seemed to think so and World War 3 erupted right there while I was trying to get the key in the frigging door to let us all in. They were shouting at me to stop raising my voice in public which in turn made me actually raise my voice in public - if you can even call the communal hall way of the apartment building public.

It's not unusual to hear arguments in the hall way, Turks really don't mind where they raise their voices, and I am very much the same these days, however when I am shouted at to stop raising my voice, this angers me and I tend to raise my voice.

I won't say the air was blue, but Mum did say the words 'fuck off' with force. I have now heard her utter the F word 4 times since she's been here. Not bad considering it's been nearly a month right? Wrong, as I have never in my life heard her say the F word until now.

And I mean not ever in my 36 years...

So, right now, I'm sat in the dining room avoiding all contact with Barış, Mum and Dad. I can hear them whispering in the lounge, more than likely ganging up on me.

Maybe I have overreacted again and I am the big cunt after all?

Oh I don't sodding know, but what I do know is as much as I try to convince myself to go back in the lounge and put a smile on my face, my pride simply won't allow me.

I feel the weight of the world on my shoulders today, or it could quite possibly be PMS.

Damn you life, damn you!

I'm sure a good night's sleep will cure all shitty attitudes by morning. And if it doesn't, then it's possibly set to get worse as we are going round to Lorraine's tomorrow afternoon for a finger buffet.

Please God let them hold their tongues about alcohol because if I start to feel ganged up on again I simply won't be held responsible for my actions.

At 36 years of age I really don't need to take that shit.

P.S: This month I've not been to my Doctor check-ups. I decided to give myself a month off bothering. Some may say that's when the magic will happen, I'm not so convinced.

So at the moment I have no idea if the patch is working or how big my wall has got, so I'm just winging it. Next month I will restart the baby making plans as in all fairness although I'm ovulating on New Year's Eve I doubt I will able to sly in a shag because I will hopefully be too pissed to do so.

Sod it, I'm obviously not going to fall this month, so I'm just going to hope for better luck in 2017.

New Year new wall growth perhaps?

January 2017

Sunday 1st January

Current Weight: 65 Kilos. Diet starts on Tuesday.

Time: 20.17pm

Dear Resolution maker,

Happy New Year!

I don't believe in writing big essay's rejoicing about seeing the back of 2016, because I'm not you see, rejoicing that is. I had a pretty good year when all said and done and I hope 2017 is going to serve up more of the same. Who wouldn't want more shenanigans, Sunday Funday's, good friends and mini breaks?

Of course I can tweak a few things as that's what the turning of a year is all about right; learning from the previous year's mistakes - hence the need to make New Year's Resolutions, which I will get to in a bit.

So, you will be happy to hear none of this 'New Year, New Me' bollocks ejaculating from my trap. Nope, I was a positive ray of fucking sunshine last year, and I aspire to be the same this year.

Positively pickled a lot of the time, but that's positive none the less.

Anyway, after re-reading my last diary entry where I absolutely realise I was miserable fuck, I have decided to make sure that I snap less at my olds and behave like the good only child that they deserve. Yup, it's time for my spoilt 'brattitude' to be put back in its box - after all, they don't have much holiday time left – T minus 2 days and counting.

I started my new reign of niceness on Thursday. I did not see red while waiting in the bank for over 45 minutes to be seen by a cashier that clearly didn't want to be there, and I did not see red when arriving at Lorraine's when asked if I wanted an alcoholic beverage and my Mother answered on my behalf. Inside I was cursing the foulest words imaginable, but outside I looked like a sweet mannered new woman - one that knows when to shut the fuck up.

Other than the alcohol ban imposed by Mum, the finger buffet went well. Thankfully there were no sly comments, at least none that I heard anyway.

On Friday we went to 'Kahve Dunyasi', or as Mum calls it, 'The Chocolate Shop'. That is their absolute favourite place in Marmaris to visit. We had lunch and, well, chocolate while sitting in the sun - another of my Mothers all-time favourite things to do. Being South African, Mum misses the heat terribly, and now that they no longer live in Spain, and with the sun in the UK being sparse, when she sees a spot of sun up her trousers are rolled in order to catch some rays. It was 10 degrees on Friday, but the trousers went up regardless. People walked by giving us funny looks while wearing their winter coats, scarves and gloves - but did Mum bat an eye? No, she continued to lap-up the sun.

Over lunch I was knocked for six when they asked if I felt that they had overstayed their welcome. Jesus, have my shitty only child antics really made them feel that way? How much of an arsehole am I FFS?!

So with that firmly in mind, no more cuntish behaviour will be displayed by this guilt ridden bitch till they are gone. After that it's a free for all.

Following that shocking revelation I needed a pick me up, so we headed into town to see if we could find anything new to wear for New Year's Eve, but as always, anything that I like looks like I'm stuffed in sausage casing.

XXL sizes over here are just lies - plain and simple lies.

Mum had the same problem, so home we went rather pissed off and with body complex issues.

If you didn't know any better you would think there are no normal sized Turks out here, that they are all petite little waifs of things. Not true as I have crossed paths with many a portly Turkish female before now, so what's with the shitty sizes Turkey..?

I decided to stick to the original clothing plan for N.Y.E, after all, I had no other choice. So I've settled on hair up with my new fake fringe, faux leather black pants, black vest top with a sheer t-shirt over it that reads 'Bad Bitch' (bought in Rhodes), new choker (also bought in Rhodes) and my long shiny thin jacket thing that looks more like a dressing gown. Yes, that will do nicely and no sausage casing in sight.

On N.Y.E itself I spent the day cleaning the house, fannying around with Guch, washing my hair and generally getting ready for the nights activities. Now it may just be me, but these days I would rather stay home on New Year's Eve as it always turns out shite - far too many expectations with usually too much booze and fake niceness, culminating in a bog, even substandard evening that occasionally ends in an argument caused by my over enthusiastic drinking and lack of giving a fuck. Yup, I would rather be home with Guch, however my olds love to go out on N.Y.E, and that's all they had been talking about since Christmas - so, allowances had to be made and smiles had to be slapped on.

We did indeed go to the restaurant that I wasn't so keen on at the marina. Lorraine joined and when she arrived I nearly died. Not because she looked amazing but because she was wearing her pair of faux leather black pants after I had told her on Thursday that I was wearing mine!

Seriously, what the fuck is wrong with people?

Seeing as though I was still on my reign of niceness I decided to say nothing about this situation. One day the time will be right to say my piece but it certainly was not then in front of my parents.

Lucky fucking Lorraine...

So, our night continued and we did the obligatory fake niceness as you can't talk about what you really want to talk about (which is usually each other), or it's not suitable for one of the parties ears. Yup, talk shite we did.

I totally believe that we went out too early as by 9.30pm we had all finished eating and yawns were travelling around our table like a Mexican wave. I must admit, this ole sad sack (me) suggested going home right there and then. It was a cold night, there was literally no atmosphere in the restaurant, plus I was pissed off with Lorraine. Alas, it wasn't to be; we stuck it out till just after midnight and the fireworks had gone off.

Much to my olds delight, a civilized yet bored me did not drink one's own body weight in booze. Much to my own delight I didn't make my mouth work as I was stone cold sober. Yup, I am happy to announce that no drunken nastiness escaped my lips. There may have been non-drunken nastiness desperate to be spoken, but like the smart 36 year old that I am, I kept my gob firmly shut - especially when Mum paid the bill for the lot of us, Lorraine included.

She's doing well out of my family isn't she?

I was home and in bed chatting to Lacie on Facebook by 1am.

What a New Year's Eve, so unlike me all round.

Today is Sunday, also known as the 1st page of a 365 page book - New Year's Day.

As I was up bright and early with no hangover in sight, I used this time to take down the Christmas tree and decorations. I was sick of looking at them as I stupidly put them up too early. Now the atmosphere seems flat, deflated somehow. I also felt a twinge of impending doom earlier and I can't even blame it on the booze (or the boogie). Maybe it's because my olds are leaving soon and I have just realised I have given them a shitty attitude filled holiday?

But, one can't wallow on that for too long as I don't want to add depression to their holiday shit list too.

So I thought what best way to spend a non-hung-over Sunday other than by giving my Dad something to do in his favourite shop in Marmaris - 'Tekzen'. It's a DIY shop a bit like 'Home Base' or 'B'n'Q' and my Dad can literally spend hours in there. I needed new light shades for our bedroom and dining room, and this is right up his street. So we headed to 'Tekzen', bought the shades, then he went on to fit them expertly giving him the first dose of satisfaction he's had since arriving nearly a month ago.

To end the day we went to 'Kervan' for their final Turkish bite - all the while Barış was working a 1-10pm shift on New Year's Day, poor bastard...

And now, I'm sat here in the lounge contemplating possible New Year's resolutions that I won't break while 'Dirty Dancing' is on in the background, because its either that or 'Harry fuck face Potter'. Gucci's blowing up the room with his farts and the olds are on their respective tablets Facebooking.

An early night me thinks as tomorrow I have a day filled with watching Mum pack cases before we head down to the marina for the last evening meal, and this time, with Lacie. Another tee total night ahead I'm sure, but it's all good as I don't want to upset the olds any further than I have already during their month long holiday...

New Year's Resolutions:

-Learn to be less hot headed, especially when it comes to my parents. I hate myself afterwards but can't seem to stop myself from being a prize prick at the time. Yup, the time to change is now.

-Get pregnant – This one's kinda obvious although it's down to my stinking ole wall really isn't it? My goal is still to be pregnant by February, so I have 1 month left. I still hold hope that this may happen being the law of attraction devotee that I am.

-To never ever put a Snap Chat filter on any of my photos - Why da fuck a grown woman would want to look like a fucking rabbit or whatever else is beyond me.

-Travel More – I've already planted the seed with my olds about joining their 2018 holiday to the homeland of South Africa, but other than the S.A. trip, I wonder who I can blag to fund a holiday to the States?

-Socialise More – And I don't just mean getting wankered (much).

-Stop being a fat cunt. No explanation needed.

That'll do for now.

ONCE UPON A WHISKY

Thursday 5th January

Current Weight: 63.5 Kilos. I'm not joking!

Time: 17.48pm

Dear Girl with a shit stained dressing gown,

I tried to give my olds a great last few days, I really did - but, life got in the way...

On Monday night we met up with Lacie and had dinner at 'Bono Marina'. It was my parents first time in their marina venue and they loved it. I'm not surprised as they decked it out really well and it just feels like a nice joint, you know, the sort that oozes class. The New Year's decorations were still up and it made it feel really cosy, especially where we were seated as we also had a nice warm halogen fire next to us. It wasn't busy, but then nowhere is on a Monday night in the middle of Winter.

I knew it was going to be a dry night booze wise so I made sure to pig out on the food side of things. It was, after all, our last meal out other than a Turkish breakfast planned for the following day, before the olds get picked up for the airport.

Dad and I are pizza fiends so we ordered the same 'Pizza Di Capra', while my Mum and Lacie had some Chicken Noodle creation. All was lovely; the food and the chat. Lacie really is great with people and never gets stuck for conversation; I suppose that's why she's in the job that she's in, customer service. My parents have always liked her, especially when they see how animated we are together, and in general we had a lovely evening.

We couldn't really catch up properly as our convo is certainly not appropriate for my olds, but we arranged a night of solid catch up gossip for Thursday. Glory days, Lei Lawson will return to the land of the alcohol fuelled wannabe socialites once more!

We were home early, around 9.10pm to be precise as the olds wanted an early night - I didn't mind in the slightest because it's not as if we were missing out on anything.

Oddly, I woke at 2.30am feeling queasy. I tried to shrug it off and go back to sleep but the feeling awoke me again at 4am. I decided to get up for some water to see if that would help. It didn't. By 4.45am I was hunched over the toilet throwing my guts up. Yuk, the pizza and its toppings were rimming the toilet water in all their glory. After a few retches I felt better and went back to bed. Not for long seemingly as by 5.45am I was back hunched over the bog again.

At that point it became 10 times worse as the other end started to gurgle.

Oh be Jesus, I wiped my gob and shoved my arse on the bog within seconds of it erupting - and by Christ, erupt it did! I found myself throwing up into the shower cubical and experiencing the worst case of the shits I had ever had simultaneously!

Barış and my Dad heard this ridiculousness and got up to see if I was alright. I really wasn't but after about 20 minutes it stopped for a break. I tried to get back into bed, but it wasn't to be as that's when the stomach cramps started. And from there on in I was crying with agony.

At 9.15am my upstairs neighbour Lucy knocked on to see if anything was wrong as she could hear the cries right at the top of the building! They tried to convince me to go to hospital but I didn't feel strong enough to even get dressed. Further convincing took place with everyone insisting to just go as I was, but I had no bra on, spew all over my PJ's and I swear there was watery faeces on my dressing gown. To put it mildly, I was a right old fucking state - but this right old fucking state was getting worse, and them there mo fo's took the option away from me and decided to shove my downtrodden arse into Lucy's car and just go.

Then Dad started to feel sick.

So there I was crawling on all four's to the car as even with the help of people I couldn't quite manage to walk, and then there was Dad who was now looking decidedly drained of all colour. We both needed the hospital and fast.

I didn't quite make it to the car. The cramps, sickness and diarrhoea got the better of me and right there in the middle of the street with cars driving past wondering what the hell was going on, in the midst of spewing, I may have shit myself. Not metaphorically, literally. Mind you, can you really call brown arse water shit?

At that point Barış decided to call the ambulance. I think it was a wise move as I'm sure Lucy would have been none too pleased had I have got arse water all up in her car - I mean I certainly wouldn't if the shoe was on the other foot.

The ambulance staff were all female and what a rotten lot they were. Firstly they yammered on about there being 4 cars available in our street to run me to the hospital so why was an ambulance called, and secondly when they stuck the needle thing in my arm (that the drip attaches onto), they fucked it up royally and it had to be redone in the hospital. They wouldn't even let Dad ride in the ambulance even though he looked like he was about to pass out, so him and Mum followed in Lucy's car, with Barış behind on his scooter. What a convoy!

Once at the hospital and fitted with the drip, you would think I would immediately start to feel better wouldn't you? I didn't. I suddenly got very hot and asked Dad to remove my Ugg boots. God love him he tried and was half way through taking one of them off when I said "oh fuck I'm gonna be sick, hurry up Dad", to which he replied with "too late girly, me too" - and with that he used my Ugg as a sick bucket and spewed his ring right there.

Needless to say the Ugg boot did not hold all the spew (which just kept coming) and it also flooded my hospital bed soaking my other Ugg boot, legs, and well my entire lower half.

FUCK MY LIFE.

Seriously.

What a sight us 'Yabanci's' were.

Once my Dad had stopped chucking up a look of terror crept across his face. By this time it was 10.30am and the taxi was picking them up at 1pm - he was shitting himself (not literally, not yet at least). I could see that both he and Mum were really worried for firstly if he was going to be OK to travel, and secondly were they going to make the pickup.

The staff at the hospital were great and leapt into action giving Dad an injection immediately to stop the sickness, plus prescribed him some tablets which Bariş went out to collect there and then. Thankfully they caught Dads sickness in good time - not good enough to stop me getting soaked in spew, but good enough.

Me on the other hand, I was still throwing up.

The nice people at the hospital also asked me for a poo sample. Ha, they didn't have long to wait. Thankfully me and my drip made it to the toilet for the next bout of brown arse water leakage and filled up their little sample pot within half a second.

Once the drip had finished, I did indeed seem to feel better. I sent my parents' home to finish packing plus hit the road as no one wanted the added stress of them missing their flight, while Bariş and I stayed in hospital for the rest of the day, finally getting discharged at 5.15pm.

Going home was fun. Well you can imagine can't you; I couldn't put my boots on as one was filled with sick and the other was covered in it - so barefooted I hopped on the back of the scooter and flung those disgusting Uggs in the bin. We had to go via the chemist to collect my pills so Bariş stopped outside one and told me to wait there while he ran in and grabbed them. Whilst I was waiting I caught a glimpse of my reflection in the side mirror of his scooter and nearly died. As well as sick and shit covered clothes, I also had sick in my hair. Nice one Lei, you absolute stunner you.

To make matters worse, I could see a pimple had taken over my chin and it needed squeezing desperately. As I couldn't look any worse if I tried, right there in broad daylight, looking like I did, on a busy street outside of the chemist, I squeezed my pimple. Fuck it.

I reminded myself of one of those memes that you see popping up on Facebook: 'Look at that girl in her shit stained dressing gown, puke in her hair, barefoot, on the back of a scooter squeezing a spot, giving no fucks'.

About right.

To top it all off, when I got home I couldn't even get in the shower to clean my stinking self up as the water had been cut off in our apartment building due to road works. There is only so much that wet wipes can do, so I kid you not when I tell you that I had to pretty much stay in that disgusting state for the next 3 hours as they failed to turn the water back on 'til then.

Dirty stinking bastards. Road works people and me.

At least Gucci was glad to see his Mum. He must have wondered what the hell was going on what with all the commotion, then my olds leaving and us not even back yet. Usually he becomes depressed for 3 days after the olds leave and refuses to eat. Not this time though. I'm not sure why that is; maybe he was glad to see me alive, or maybe he is starting to understand the ritual of the magical Christmas creatures that appear in December for a month every year, fill his belly full of meats and then disappear again 'till the following year - but either way he started tucking into his normal food which he had ignored for the past four weeks. Good ole Guch.

Thankfully I got to speak to Mum, she called from Antalya airport and also when they finally got home and it seems Dad travelled very well and did not throw up again. Thank God that's all I've got to say, I mean at his age it could have killed him!

When I did eventually get in the shower, I scrubbed my skin raw. Although it hurt, I enjoyed it more than anyone could ever possibly enjoy a shower.

On the bright side, I lost 1.5 kilos. That's near enough my whole weight gain since the parents arrived on the 6th December!

Was it worth it losing it in such a way?

Sitting here now, feeling mighty clean and no longer like death, I'm starting to think that it quite possibly was. God I'm just a tit aren't I. Not a question, simply a statement.

The only thing now that stands in my way of a jolly good Thursday is Barış as he has banned me from leaving the house to go to Lacie's to get pished.

Damn you Husbando and your caring ways, damn you!

ONCE UPON A WHISKY

Wednesday 11th January

Current Weight: 66 Kilos. Just fuck off.

Time: 13.34pm

Dear Jack Daniels drinker,

It has been nearly a week since my last entry and I have barely left the house. It's been a sad ole week truth be told, one filled with copious amount of rain (I bet you thought I was going to say vodka), and a Guch that refuses to get his paws wet so pisses up the sodding walls.

Thankfully, I have had a bit of company other than pissy paw soaked Guch.

On Friday Kate came round for coffee, a catch up and to add the last touches to my clip in fringe. It looks bitchin' by the way, and you would never know it was a clip in. Well, that was until Kate totally ruined the illusion and posted pictures of it not attached to my head on Facebook FFS.

On Saturday I actually left the house much to Barış's dismay, but come on, it was the first time since Tuesday! Cabin fever had set in and if I didn't go out then I couldn't be held responsible for my actions. What made it worse was he knew I was going out to party. I tried to tell him that it was just dinner with Lacie, but he has seen many a time how dinner ends up. No pulling the wool over his eyes, the all-knowing fucker.

I arrived at Lacie's at 7pm, clip in fringe an all.

If you're having a fat day then a fringe works wonders as it makes your face look chiselled and thinner. I sent a photo of this spectacle to Jenny and Mum before leaving the house and both totally loved the fringe and asked if

I had lost weight. Nope, in fact I have put it all back on and more since the sickness. Notice my weight today?

Anyway, nothing was going to stop me from enjoying myself and so I slugged back my duty-free whisky which always gets me in the mood. I thought I was going to be tipsy mighty quickly due to the length of time I had not had a drink, so I was shocked when by 10pm I still wasn't. Mind you, there was no time for tops ups as we just gossiped our way through a load of catch up and laughter.

It turns out that Lacie's still seeing the Kuşadasi fling - in fact she has just got back from a few more days away with him. That girl does mighty well for not having a pot to piss in.

We went out about 10.45pm. It was raining and the closest bar to us was 'Lighthouse'. As January is always a tough month, before ordering drinks we wanted to check prices, and as we wanted to continue the evening on whisky, we asked how much their cheapest was. 13tl for Jack Daniels and diet Coke. Fucking bonus! So Jack it up we did. But funnily enough, I was struggling to swallow my Jack, for some reason it simply wasn't going down. I had to ask them to keep topping it up with diet Coke as it was sticking in my throat. Lacie, on the other hand, was not suffering from the same affliction and was drinking 2 to my 1.

As we were the only two Yabanci's in the bar, we were attracting a bit of attention. You know what it's like, winter in Marms, British girls, lots of staring - you get the general idea. Lacie attracts this winter and summer, but for once I was collecting winks too! Colour me shocked. This never happens when I'm out with SVS. Must have been the fringe effect!

Anyhow, there were 2 blokes sat next to us at the bar, and as alcohol would have it, we were all drawn into conversation. They bought Lacie a Jack and Coke and me a Corona as I could no longer force Jack down - shocker I know.

The bar was buzzing and there were loads of people milling around totally lapping up the bitchin' atmosphere. Whilst in the midst of a sing-along to David Bowie's 'Let's Dance', I noticed Lacie's eyes glazing over, signifying only one thing - the girl was pished. From that point on she was up dancing, moshing and even got out the air guitar.

God I love that girl when she's drunk.

The fella's sat next to us were also up and at it; the only one that wasn't was me - ole non pissed boring twat over here.

It was 2am and I simply could not get drunk. Don't you just hate it when that happens?

I felt like I had wasted hard earned cash on sweet FA, so we asked for our bill. When it came, being the more sober one of the two of us, I grabbed and studied it. I did a double take and thought for a moment that they had put the bloke's drinks on our tab, but when questioning this they informed me they had not. How the hell was our bill 180tl FFS? I only had 2 Jacks and Lacie only had 4. I double checked how much the Jack was and nearly fucking died. We had only gone and misheard! We thought he said 13tl when in reality he said 30tl! I thought at the time that that was a bloody good price for Jack. Jesus!

I told Lacie how much her bill was and that's when it all went Pete Tong. The guys that had bought us drinks, well one of them anyway, had an argument with the bar man on our behalf - not that we wanted him to of course as little did he know we could sort our own bill issues out. We know the owner of the bar so decided to tackle the problem diplomatically.

Let me point out here that I don't mind paying for drinks, but I would never have agreed to order one that costs 30tl, not ever!

So, the owner of the bar joined us, we were very apologetic, informed him that the random guy arguing with the bar man was not with us, explained the situation, and our bill was sorted out. The owner is a bit of a fitty and I don't mind telling you that both Lacie and I may have snogged him some time long ago (not at the same time and not when we even knew each other as that's just grim and breaks girl code). He said not to worry about the mix up, pay the 13tl that we thought we were supposed to pay and let that be the end of it.

Fucking A! That past snog certainly paid off. Would have been better if it was free, but beggars can't be choosers...

As we were paying up, the guys were checking over their bill and decided to jump on our bandwagon.

Hmm, cheap skate mo fo's. Time to leave.

While we were walking out, we could see that a bit of an argument was going down between the bar owner and the likely lads - not my circus, not my monkeys - so continue walking away we did bumping smack bang into two of the rival gang; Larissa and Melanie. Neither of them have been over posting on social media of late and we actually thought that they must have fallen out, but no, here they were as thick as thieves looking us up and down taking in our outfits.

I was dressed in my usual Lei chic in Jeans, Doc Martins, a red T shirt, denim shirt and my black winter coat. Not really suitable for anywhere other than 'Lighthouse', but we weren't going anywhere other than 'Lighthouse'.

Thank God they didn't see me last week coming out of hospital!

Lacie looked great, then again she always does. She has a very casual style and was dressed in jeans, a turtle neck and a long cardi that resembled Josephs amazing technicoloured dream coat. I thought she looked bloody ace. The looks that we got from Larissa and Melanie told us otherwise.

They were clad in garish dresses with what was hopefully faux fur jackets, actually looking like twins. I will never understand why two grown women feel the need to dress so similarly. I know they both have their own personal style as my Instagram is filled with it, so why have they recently amalgamated into each other?

When we asked if they had been anywhere nice, possibly a wedding where they were bridesmaids, they took great joy in announcing that they were VIP's at an exclusive Netsel Marina party.

Oh please fuck off.

"Was that you Lei that I saw last week, outside of the chemist?" said Larissa, "It looked like you were wearing some sort of stained dressing gown and had been dragged through a hedge backwards. I think you were picking a spot in the mirror of a scooter".

YOU HAVE GOT TO BE FUCKING KIDDING ME.

I was speechless.

Why me? Why did it have to be *her* that spotted me?

I could think of nothing witty to come back with, nor could I explain myself. Thank Christ Lacie chimed in "Yes, yes it was Lei. She had been in hospital and she shit herself".

WT actual F Lacie!!

She continued "I have no idea why she was squeezing a spot in the mirror but if she wants to squeeze a spot looking like a hobo out in public, then who are you to judge".

FUCK MY LIFE.

And with that she turned around and power walked away muttering obscenities under her breath. I was left there like a complete cunt, speechless - but then again, so were Larissa and Melanie. Not quite sure what to do, I made my excuses and ran after Lacie. Do you know what; she had a go at me. Why? Because I hadn't pre-warned her. She reckoned that if pre-warned, she would have come out with a much better statement and wouldn't have been left to look like a fool.

Urm no Lacie, the fool look was all on me...

Although she wasn't proud of my hobo like status, she went on to say that no one other than her could rip the piss and make me feel bad. Which she then did. Big time.

#SquadGoals?

And so, the week has continued in the same boring way as the last. Rain, pissy paw prints and cabin fever. The only thing I have to look forward to is Friday night when Kate and I are going out. We have never been out alone before, so I hope it's not weird. I will however make sure to be pissed before I leave the house this time.

And just where is Lacie right now?

You will never believe it but last night she sent a photo of herself standing outside a shop in the 'Red Light District' of Amsterdam. The Kuşadsi fling has only gone and whisked her away again!

In the photo there was a couple fucking in the window, with Lacie posing next to the copulating couple with one hand over her mouth in a shocked pose, and the other hand groping her crotch.

She's a dirty bitch, but I love her.

Oh, and I think I'm coming on my stinkin' ole period 2 days early. Yup, day 25 in my cycle and I have a dull ache in the lower part of my abdomen and I have just wiped what seems to be the starting of brown period wee.

Although I knew I was not going to be pregnant this month, it's still mildly depressing.

Monday 16th January

Current Weight: 63.5 Kilos. What the fuck is going on with my body mass?

Time: 17.17pm

Dear Number noticer,

I'm here again, sat in my sitting room with the heater on because there is a nip in the air, watching the rain beat down outside, with a bored air of agitation about myself. It has literally not stopped raining since last week. This must be the 10th day in a row!

Rain in the Marms is not like rain in the UK, oh no, there is quite a difference. It can rain solidly for 10 days here but be constant thunder storms that drive poor Gucci to dive under the covers and howl for dear life. He just hates it. I don't mind a good thunder storm if it is only 1 - not like what we've had recently, day after thundery day. It puts a stop to everything you see. In the UK you somehow continue about your business, shopping, work, general life, etc. - but here all comes to a halt. One can't do a load of laundry as it just doesn't dry, and only the rich have a spin dryer. One tends not to want to go out as the streets get flooded easily due to shitty drainage, and I don't own a pair of wellies 'cos eww, why would I? It's just fucked all round really.

So, another mostly quiet period it has been for me.

I tell you what I have noticed whilst being stuck indoors - repetitive numbers. 11:11, 12:12, 18:18, etc. Just look at the time that I started writing today's entry! More than once a day have these numbers cropped up and I am finding it weirder and weirder. I consulted my old pal Google and discovered that I am spiritually awakening. I don't really know what that means but apparently that's what's happening. As you know 'dear diary', my religion lies with the universe, so it doesn't surprise me that something spiritual is a foot, but it would help if I knew what these messages actually mean…

Anyway, it stopped raining long enough for Kate and I to go out on Friday night to discover spirits of another sort.

We kicked off the night with pre-drinks round at mine and it wasn't odd at all. I feel at ease around her and that's a good sign. Mind you, her stories of the past are way out of my league. And I thought my younger self was a bad little bastard…

When I answered the door I instantly knew I had to get changed. We looked near enough identical; both wearing black blazer's and black leather pants. I mean FFS! After we laughed about it, I changed into my skinny blue jeans with a black and grey T Shirt style top. I kept the blazer as it looked different enough to wear without anyone passing comment (I hope).

Actually I felt good for a change. I had one of those very rare magical getting ready experiences where the makeup and hair just went to plan. Even my feline flicks didn't fuck up! I'm going to go as far to say that my makeup was on fleek (I hate that word, but it was), my hair looked good all piled on top of my head in a messy bun with the clip in fringe finishing the rock chick look. Yup, this here wannabe socialite felt good.

Even the selfie that I put on Facebook got over 100 likes! That only ever happens when Lacie is in the picture! There were some great comments too but thinking back now I'm not sure whether to take them as a complement or not? You see a lot of the comments were referring to how great my hair looked, and well, it wasn't really my hair now was it? Hmph, although it's great receiving a ton of likes and fabulous comments, when they are about a part of you that doesn't actually belong to you, do they even really count?

So, with both of us looking not bad at all, we went out about 10pm, heading straight for 'Lighthouse'. It was busy and there was nowhere to sit, so we leaned against the bar scoffing all the free pretzels and popcorn in sight. Kate had never been in before so it was a new experience to her. She said she liked it, although it wouldn't be the rival gang's cup of champagne - not posh enough for them mo fo's...

Once again we were near enough the only 'Yabanci's' in the bar, but this time we spotted a couple of people that were sticking out like sore thumbs. It's funny how a foreigner can spot another foreigner a mile off isn't it? In the summer they are a dime a dozen (that was very American of me) but in the winter there ain't many of us about, hence all the staring. We gravitated towards the other foreigners and ended up gate crashing their table. They were a nice enough bunch but one guy (that happened to look like Captain Birdseye) wouldn't leave poor Kate alone. It was rather irritating as we couldn't chat properly, not that the hound dog seemed to care. When Kate told him of her marital status, the ole fucker didn't bat an eye lid and was still trying to sniff her pits. He was pleasant enough with it I suppose so we shrugged it off.

From 'Lighthouse', we took the short walk to 'Davey Jones'. It's a good bar to end up in as it's always busy come winter or summer and they generally have a band playing. Unfortunately we had a cling on in the shape of Captain Birdseye, but that was OK as he offered to buy us a drink.

I always find when offered a free drink it makes up for a host of shitty situations.

So, we moshed the night away to mostly Turkish rock music. I personally think that the interval is the best bit about the band as that's when they play the cool tunes. It wouldn't be so bad if the band played a few more international rock tunes now would it?

I suppose you could say that the evening was good as far as nights out go, except when it came to us leaving...

When we announced that we were heading home, Captain Birdseye disappeared to the toilet. As we were getting our things together the waiter brought our bill, to which we said the Captain was settling. He went on to inform us that the old fucker had just left the bar, and with that, we were left with his bill. And can you believe it, the old bastard had been drinking Jack fucking Daniels!

Honest to God, what's fucking wrong with people?!

Saturday brought with it the standard hangover and I ate the entire contents of the house while having a sofa and 'Nashville' day.

On Sunday I actually managed to leave the house. I very nearly changed my mind as I knew I was going to be caught in the rain, but I couldn't be arsed cooking for myself and really wanted to have a catch up plus retail session with Lorraine. She really is the best to go clothes shopping with as she never gets tired of the hunt and tells you truthfully when you look like your busting out at the seams - which is quite a lot of the time here...

I hadn't seen her for 2 weeks, since New Year's Eve to be exact, and that's quite a while when it comes to the two of us. Not long enough seemingly!

Although we had lots to catch up on, she wouldn't shut up about the passing of George Michael. As much as I loved George, Lorraine's torrent of waffle was doing my head in. She bored me to tears for 3 hours - enough already, it's not like you knew him...

During the hurricane of George talk, we managed to feed our faces, shop, stop for coffee at 'Subway', and then when the thunder started we made our way back to the car. I got home at 8pm to a howling Guch.

A semi successful afternoon bar the barrage of bollocks from Lorraine.

So, today is Monday and guess what it's been doing all day? Fucking raining. So, I'm stuck indoors once again. If it's like this tomorrow I will just jump in the car and head to Lacie's. As much as I love a good sofa day, 9 out of 10 just ain't how I roll!

Oh, and I'm on cycle day 30 in the period saga. I know in my last entry I mentioned I was coming on, well that hasn't happened thus far. You won't get any excitement out of me; I know how this shit goes...

Thursday 19th January

Current Weight: 63.8 Kilos.

Time: 17.55pm

Dear Positively hopeful,

Just a very quick entry today as I'm going out of my mind. Today marks day 33 and still no period. I don't want to tempt fate here, but could this possibly be the month?

I have refrained from telling anyone as I get over enthusiastic, I have not Googled myself stupid as I usually would, and I have not bought any pregnancy tests. Why? 'Cos I know what happens when I do - I come on. So this time round I've done nothing. Like I said, I don't want to tempt fate...

Let's look at the facts here shall we:

Fact 1: I had brown period wee and period like symptoms since day 25 of the cycle. I thought I was coming on early and didn't.

Fact 2: This is the longest I have ever been without coming on before. The last time I assumed I was preggers, the crimson wave arrived on day 32.

Fact 3: I started using the patch at the start of this cycle. That coupled with the pills may have beefed up my wall, or it may have delayed the bastard period. Either way, I'm unsure...

Fact 4: And the biggy: We had sex the day before the big O.

So what do you think 'dear diary'? Could I possibly be knocked up?

I suppose only time will tell. I am telling myself that I am not and to keep expecting more brown period wee to show up at any moment, as let's face reality here - it probably will.

In fact I'm endangering it all by making a diary entry out of it, so I won't continue in fear of what may happen...

And the numbers! Still all I am seeing is repetitive bloody numbers! All of this has to mean something right?

OK, so to distract myself from pregnancy OCD, I will fill you in on what I've been up to for the last few days;

FUCK ALL.

Rain, rain, rain...! I have actually surprised myself with just how sick I am of the rain. Enough now - Yeter! Bring back the sun at a pleasant 22 degrees.

Monday I did nothing other than have a bit of a spat (if you can call it that) with Lorraine via Facebook. Basically I asked if she fancied going for brunch and a walk on Sunday, but that I had to wait for Friday to confirm. I received the following reply:

'I think I've told you before Lei, I'm no one's second choice. You carry on with your arrangements and when you're ready to put me first we can arrange brunch...'

WTF? As if she thinks' that way after she spent the whole of Christmas and New Year with me and my family! Maybe she was annoyed that I zoned out when she started with the George tripe, but come on, no fucker wants to be put to sleep with 3 hours worth of that....!

Since then I have been trying to find something to do on Sunday as 5 minutes later I found out that the plans I might have are not materialising. No one's biting. Lacie is having the weekend with the wannabe of all people, my old pal Sandie is busy and I don't fancy asking Kate as that may be conceived as a bit full on seeing as though we have only just started hanging out...

Damn you Lorraine.

I won't bother with her for a bit, it's absolutely the right time for a Lorraine cooling off period. But I wonder how long it will take for her to message me...? She is a stubborn cow, so I won't say watch this space as you would be watching for a mighty long time. Me, I'm not so stubborn, but I won't cave this time, not when she's the one with rocks in her head...

But it does leave me with a loose end for Sunday...

Tuesday I cleaned the house. I was planning to go see Lacie but she had gone to Izmir for a couple of days. Yup, another mini break. Where did I go wrong eh? Mind you, all that sex she's having is not my idea of fun. I simply couldn't be bothered with the fanny chafe.

Wednesday I watched shit on TV and obsessed about the possibility of being pregnant.

And Thursday, today, Husbando and I have been for a 'Subway' on the marina, then into town to do bank stuff, then over to the Lira shop as there was a 5tl sale on, and finally home - all whilst dodging the rain.

Tomorrow thank fuck I have plans. In the day I will give the house a clean and wash my minging hair, and for the evening Lacie and I are having a booze and food night here at mine. At least Saturday will be taken up with hangover so I won't mind the rain.

And then we come to Sunday - the only day that is due to be rain free and I have fuck all to do and no one to do it with.

What an absolute cunt. You can guess who.

Monday 23rd January

Time: 16.24pm

Dear Not so positively hopeful,

It is now day 37 of my cycle and still no period. I have finally stopped obsessing. Well I had to really after 1 negative pregnancy test (yesterday morning), a talking to from Kate (also yesterday morning), and a shit load of Googling (yesterday evening).

Yup, I have well and truly realised that I'm not pregnant and it's the patch fucking with my wannabe pregnant body.

Kate told me yesterday over brunch that although the period is missing, that I had disappearing brown period wee, and I have goings on happening in my tum - when you factor this in with taking hormone medication, this then puts paid to the whole lot as that's what's controlling my period.

So - I am not pregnant.

But am I dwelling on this shit? Hell's no. I decided to pull up my 'Bridget Jones' pants and shut the fuck up. I need to get my arse down to the Gynae for a check-up, however I will wait a few more days as I only took the patch off yesterday in the hopes that this will bring my period on ASAP. Should the period not arrive by Thursday or Friday I will make an appointment, as after all, one cannot become pregnant while waiting for ones bloody period to arrive. All the sex in the world is not going to help if I'm not ovulating...

So, other than the above, I've had an alright few days.

Friday was especially good. Lacie came over, picked me up and took me to the new apartment she is moving into next month. Finally she has a little home to call her own. Mind you, she should have had it long since but the ex-husband was not very forthcoming in the divorce settlement. We had a grand ole time thinking about what could be done with the place, what colour scheme she wanted and the type of look she was going for. And when we finished, it was back to my house for laughs, booze and Dominoes. Yup, Friday was a good day - plus it didn't rain!

Saturday I had the hangover that I knew I would, so I didn't mind at all having a sofa day. In fact the drunken plans made from the night before I decided to cancel as I just couldn't bring myself to go through the 2 hour hair and makeup ritual that this wannabe socialite is a slave to. No, it was better to keep my hung-over arse indoors and in the pyjamas that have become like a second skin these days. I'm that disgusting I even took Guch out for a walk in them. I swapped my dressing gown for my coat and waited until dusk to look slightly more incognito, but let's face it; here in Marmaris people wear their PJs to the shops, so I really didn't look out of place. Although, I could have given the armpits a quick roll of deodorant for the sake of poor Guch as even he was looking at me like I was a bin.

And Sunday, I finally got me some plans! Screw you Lorraine!

I decided to text Kate after all and she seemed quite happy to go for brunch. In fact we made a day of it as it was such a glorious warm sunny Sunday. We started out on the beach front where every man and his goat had the same idea as us. We decided upon 'Pukka' as there were less kids running riot.

How is it that 'local' families don't feel embarrassed when their kids are running around like raving loonies? They don't even scold them for making a nuisance of themselves - they just sit back, sip their çay and let someone else deal with it. What if one tripped up a waiter with a pot of scalding hot Tea? I suppose it would be the waiters fault! Had I of behaved in such a way as a kid I would have had the wooden spoon round my head, I kid you not.

Can you imagine putting up with that shit on a Sunday morning? Thank God I didn't have a hangover!

Now I know what you're thinking - this girl wants a baby but is hating on kids. Your half right - but more so the parents that I'm hating on. Why don't they keep their tribe in check? It infuriates me! Now, I'm not sticking up for my own here, but foreign kids are much better behaved, seriously...

Anyway, we made the most of the never ending tea supply whilst sitting in the sun, then went over to 'Blue Port' shopping centre to look at some garden stuff, before heading back down the promenade for a shandy right on the beach.

Rip Off Alert: Small shandy, wasn't even given the bottle, 12tl. Fuckers looked at us and thought 'Yabanci' so hiked up the price. This is an ongoing issue in Marmaris, probably the whole of Turkey - one price for Turkish, another price for foreigners. I'm sick of it. We didn't kick off but that bar has lost 2 customers.

We ended the day with a coffee at Kate's house where no rip offs occurred.

Still no word from Lorraine by the way.

I absolutely refuse to message her first, she can fuck off. I will become as stubborn as her in this game she's playing. Some people have very short memories don't they?

Well, lesson learnt, I won't be falling for that shit again. Don't get me wrong, I don't expect her to be indebted to me, but acknowledging the fact that I included her in special family time would be nice. Nope, colour me not impressed with her carry on. Now *she* has the audacity to talk about being second best? Fuck off Lorraine, seriously...

Oh dear, the rot has started to set in.

What was it I said quite some time ago, that we would not fall out so badly again? Well that statement is out the window as I have totally seen my arse.

Anyway, forget her. I have a nice busy week ahead of me and I don't want to enter it with a negative vibe. The sun looks set to stay and I feel like being a glass half full kinda gal.

So, I shall bid you adieu, and in my next entry I am hoping to report that the painters are in.

Saturday 28th January

Current Weight: 64 Kilos.

Time: 12.11pm

Dear Saturday afternoon beer drinker,

Well colour me impressed with my alright week. I have not had to slit my own wrists with boredom and the rain has been very sparse with only 2 days of it. So, I'm back to being positively delightful once more - well, as much as a plate faced, aging, wannabe socialite can be.

A bit of vitamin D really does go a long way.

That's what sun is right, vitamin D? Or is it C? Now I'm wondering if there is a Vitamin G? I've never heard of one but that's not to say that it doesn't exist?

So Tuesday I went over to my old pal Sandie's house for a catch up. Oh did we catch up. We didn't stop talking for 4 bloody hours, and even then we could have talked for more.

When visiting friends, Sandie is just like me - always choosing comfort over style. I love those sort of pals where I know I can rock up in my jogging bottoms, un-showered, no face on, spots red from being picked and not be judged for it. Sandi herself answered the door in her PJs and dressing gown at 1.30pm. Yup, long live friends that you can be a dirty old tramp with!

One of the things that we discussed in depth was Lorraine. I told Sandie about the shitty message and how I felt about the whole Xmas and New Year saga, and Sandie gave me her expert opinion. She said that if Lorraine has chosen to forget the holiday period and just go by one text (that really wasn't bad on my part), then she doesn't really deserve to be a friend. She's right you know. Thinking back, what sort of friend tries to bring my own

Mother into vicious conversation slagging me, her supposed friend off, on Christmas Day?

I have come to the conclusion that Lorraine and I tolerate each other because we both have a love for clothes and it passes the time, but I don't actually think we like each other anymore. I believe we are simply habit, and just like quitting smoking, bad habits need to be stopped.

But we did have a lovely afternoon, Sandie and I.

On Wednesday it was Barış's day off so we did the usual and went to 'Yunus' for a great big Turkish breakfast at 2pm, rain and all. It was so cosy in there that we stayed for a while watching the grey old sea batter the beach.

On Thursday it was a home day. I really enjoyed it and I'm not even being sarcastic. 2 days of being out makes you appreciate a day at home. I managed to clean the house, cook a bitching Quorn Spag Bol for dinner, take Guch out on a marathon walk plus watch my programs. Productive home days - love them!

Friday I was out and about again. I was dreading it as I was moving banks which is never an easy task here. It went a lot smoother than I thought and I walked out of my new bank with a big smile on my face as their customer service put my previous bank to shame.

When I emailed my old bank at the beginning of the week to give them notice on my account closure, the reply I got back was "OK, good". Whether that was lost in translation or not I couldn't rightly say, but the last time I had been in, I asked to speak to my account manager who refused to come downstairs and went on to have a full blown argument with me over the phone from her perch a floor above. Shocking, simply shocking. I made the decision there and then that once I received my interest for the month I was off next door to HSBC, and, that's exactly what I did.

I will not be shouted at by a Bank clerk, no fucking way! Customer service leaves a lot to be desired in this country...

So this brings us up to today, Saturday. I'm going out for beers this afternoon with Kate and Audrey. Its bloody cold out but I want to at least try to make an effort as one thing I have learnt recently is that you never know who you're going to bump into at any given time - and I really don't want to add any more fuel to the rival gangs fire FFS.

I'm sure we won't be out late as we are meeting at 4pm, but the lashes are going on regardless. I would rather meet at 7pm as what will probably happen is me home by 8, pissed up, and that can mean only one thing - Booze Blues.

Obviously I would prefer to go straight to bed when getting home from the piss, because sitting up and slowly getting sober ain't my idea of fun. No, I need to try to get the ladies to stay out till at least 10. That way I won't feel as bad going to bed when I get in.

And finally, I'm on day 42 of the missing period chronicles. I have just booked an appointment with the Gynae for Tuesday to see what the hell is going on down there. I have really fucked myself over with the stupid patch thing haven't I? I think I must have worn it for longer than I should have. To be honest, thinking back, I can't actually remember if he told me how long I should use it. Google stated 10 days for beefing up the wall; I wore it for 33. Ooops?!

A very small part of me thinks that I'm harbouring a secret baby and that my HGC levels are not high enough to prove pregnancy. I battle with this small part of me daily as I'm a hopeful kind of soul and believe in miracles. I'm trying really hard not to listen to that hopeful side, not in this instance anyway, as all it will result in is a great big let down when I do eventually come on.

Another small part of me thinks that I might have started the menopause. Yup, I can't kid myself any longer; age comes to us all. It's a depressing thought, really it is, but you know what, if I knew 100% that there was no chance of me growing a sprog, then it that would leave me in a better position than I am now - the ever hopeful, waiting for a missed period every month.

I bloody hate waiting.

So, as it stands - I may be pregnant, I may be starting the menopause and I may come on with not a moment's notice.

Jesus Lei - That's something to think about on a Saturday afternoon.

Thank fuck I'm going drinking eh!

Monday 30th January

Time: 16.41pm

Dear Girl with a hangover,

So Saturday was eventful..!

As predicted, Kate and Audrey did go home early, but not as early as I originally thought. We had a lovely chilled out afternoon starting with beers and food in 'Pukka', then over to 'Cheers' for vodka. This is where the night *should* have ended. I *should* have gone home right there and then, along with the girls at the sensible hour of 10.30pm.

Shoulda, woulda, coulda...

As I was in no mood to put a lid on my drinking, I called Kaan and tried my best to bribe him to come out. That phone call resulted in him calling me a knob and hanging up. That's nice isn't it? Lacie also wasn't answering, although I knew she wasn't planning on going out, but it did cross my mind to pop along to her house for a nightcap before heading home.

Again, that's what I should have done - but you guessed it, I didn't.

So what did I do? I marched along to 'Albatross' and walked in *alone*. It was quiet in there to begin with but I spotted a couple of people I knew immediately, waltzed on over and asked if I could join them. Thank fuck they said yes otherwise that would have been embarrassing wouldn't it?

Anyway, these friends are people that I rarely see these days as they are part of Jess the Mingers extended crew, and of course Jess and I don't see each other anymore, therefore our circles have changed and so have the places we frequent. But, it was lovely to see them none the less.

I mistook one of the people in the group for Jess because from behind her the haircut was pretty similar, plus it was dark and I'd had a skin full. This female did not take kindly to being mistaken for Jess, in fact she went on to inform me of just how vile she thought Jess was, calling her every name under the sun.

Had I of hated Jess I would have revelled in this, but I didn't and I don't. This 'ere chump did not join in with the Jess bashing and simply stated "We are all entitled to our opinions and if we all liked the same people the world would be a very boring place, but if you don't mind please keep your opinions to yourself". Very diplomatic of pissed me, I do make myself proud at times.

Unfortunately this wasn't enough for her.

Nope, she poked and prodded as she was clearly expecting me to say something in agreement with her, and when I didn't, she didn't like it. But why should I? Just because we are no longer Mingers doesn't mean I have to listen to someone else slating her. I can say things about Jess to a trusted few, but no fucker else can - no bloody way. We were Mingers for far too long for that sort of shite. So no, just 'cos Team Minger disbanded doesn't mean I have to diss Jess now does it? And I told this unpleasant female exactly that, to which she told me to fuck off.

Nice one!

Now I don't recall much after this encounter. What's left is vodka flash backs and they go something like this;

An overwhelming feeling of nostalgia, a possible phone call to Jess, shots, dancing on the bar, more shots, a plump blond woman singing on Karaoke, a disgruntled bar man, more shots, grinding with a random female, hugging, a bad attitude, spitting my drink out with laughter, weirdly more grinding and most definitely some slut dropping, shivering in the taxi home, looking at a text message from 'Marie' (?), rolling around with Gucci at 05.15am, waking up at 12.30pm with a raging hangover.

Random.

Sunday should be wiped from existence.

I didn't get dressed, I didn't wash and I certainly didn't attempt to move off the sofa. I did however receive a dose and a half of impending doom which seems to have lingered on even into today. What a cruel cruel world.

One thing that I did do was check my phone log. I was right about the phone call to Jess, but thankfully it seems she didn't answer said call, and all I can say is thank fuck for that. I wonder what I would have said if she did?

Funnily enough, while sat vegetating on the sofa last night, she sent me a Whats App message. I nearly didn't open it for fear of what was inside, so I was shocked to say the least when she enquired if I was OK. I didn't go into it, just said I was pissed and that's where I thought that conversation would end. It didn't. She went on to tell me she had met a new guy and she is happy these days, asked if I was, and wished me well.

I came away from that little to and fro with a warm feeling inside.

A Team Minger reunion is not on the cards, but I'm glad we have both moved on in life and we are adult enough to be civil with each other. After all, we don't have to be friends to be decent.

I have that New Year's Eve song running around my head, you know, the one about old acquaintances yada yada yada. I have never known what that song actually meant, but I think I do now and my interpretation is this: forgotten friends that are no longer part of our life, but we should remember them from time to time because at one point they were not strangers.

That doesn't make sense, does it?

What I'm trying to say is that I will always remember my friendship with Jess as a good one. That girl helped me through the shit storm that was my life back in 'The Final Summer of Vodka' days. She has wrestled me to the ground to remove the phone from my pursed fists when I was in desperate attempts to phone my ex, and she always gave me an excuse to get up, get dressed and get on with life. For that I am grateful.

So no, I don't take kindly to nasty ole bitches slagging off a Minger...

And that's where I'm going to leave it for today. I need to pull my finger out as I should have cleaned the house by now but haven't even managed to wash my face just yet. Day 2 of hangover you see. This aging rock star simply can't take the pace.

What a cunt. The hangover, the Jess basher and me.

The Final Chapter – February 2017

Friday 3rd February

Time: 21.18pm

Dear Girl that pulls no punches,

Welcome February, or as I like to call it, 'The Final Chapter'.

I have two things to say about your arrival:

Thing 1: I'm not ready for you.

Thing 2: I'm not pregnant.

So why have you arrived so quickly?

I still have no period in sight, I'm 3 weeks late and I'm definitely not harbouring a secret baby. So what the actual fuck man? Is it possible that I may not reach my baby goal by the end of this month after all?

Jesus, that's a depressing thought for his ever hopeful to have on a Friday evening.

But is all hope lost? Not if this wannabe pregnant socialite has anything to do with it. I do, after all, still have this month..!

So Tuesday at 2pm was the dreaded Gynae appointment. We have established that there is no undiscovered baby camping out unable to be seen, however my ever aging wall has grown to 6mm! The Gynae seemed mighty impressed with this and now seems to think that I stand at least somewhat of a chance of getting up the duff. I told him about my missing period and he said not to worry, and if it hasn't appeared in 2.5 - 3 weeks to go back and he will give me an injection to bring it on. I asked what that meant for ovulation with having a delayed period and his reply surprised me - apparently I may only have a period every other month while being on the hormone treatment. This off course cuts down my chances of getting pregnant by 50% as I may only have 6 periods a year opposed to 12 - and who the fuck knows when my actual ovulation is going to occur...?!

I don't know what to make of this, but the Gynae seemed happy enough, so I suppose I should be too, right?

Other than the above, I've had a good week in a number of ways;

My hangover lifted enough for me to get back on the booze on Tuesday night, but this time indoors so as not to inflict my ridiculous antics upon others. Lacie came round, I cooked my speciality pasta 'Gino D' Acampo's Spicy Tomato Rigatoni', we hit the booze hard and caught the hell up.

You will never believe it; she has only got back with the wannabe!

The last time we spoke about him she told me he made her flesh crawl. I remember having a similar feeling with my British ex fiancée, in fact I didn't sleep with the poor bastard for 2 months because every time he touched me I felt physically sick. In the end I had to be pissed to do it, and even then it wasn't a pleasant experience. I suppose that's when you know it's over...

It's like she's battling with herself when she says "But Lei, I really should be with someone that will do anything for me". Of course you should darlin' but not one that makes you nauseous when he puts his penis near your flangita!

Of course I get where she's coming from, really I do - she wants a good man that will treat her right, but at the same time, keep her on her toes. That's hard to find in this town as usually they go one of 2 ways; controlling or sickly sweet - either way is simply not suitable, and eww gross. No, girls like us need a bloke that will crack the whip and put us in our place when we try to walk all over them. Barış is as placid as they come until something bothers him, and then its 'Shut the fuck up Lei and do what you're told'. Hot..!

Anyway, I'm not sure if wannabe is the guy for the job and I told her so. I actually like wannabe, I think he's an alright sort, but to keep Lacie in check the dude is going to have to grow a great big pair of bollocks and be a lot less cringe.

I have not always been so glum on ole wannabe, no not at all. In fact I used to tell her to give it everything she's got, to submerge herself in the 'fake it till you make it' attitude, and maybe one day she could love him. But this time I didn't do that - no need you see. I know that girl well enough by now to be sure that by this time next week (or at the latest next month), she will have kicked him to the curb and have found a rich mo fo to replace him. That's just Lacie and her ever changing mind. The rich mo fo won't come to much, they never do, but I know one day a guy will come along that will literally floor her. He may not be rich, he may not be super attractive, but he will have the spark that she so craves. I just hope she doesn't have to wait too long...

We had a grand old night regardless and if your bestie can't tell you what she really thinks then what sort of a bestie would I be? After all, Lacie sets me straight when I relay my ludicrous shenanigans to her.

On Wednesday surprisingly I had no hangover.

Note to self: When drinking whisky moderately, I won't fuck myself up.

It was Barış's day off and my trainer pal Julia had invited us down to her house farm in Hisaronu (but not the Fethiye one). The last time I went to see her was just after I got back from Blighty as my weight was spiralling out of control, remember? Fair play, she set me on the straight and narrow. Mind you, I haven't done any kind of work out since November and I was supposed to start again on Monday 9th Jan, but that hasn't happened yet - no motivation you see. I would rather skip working out and sit on my arse vegetating on the sofa for an extra 45 minutes 3 to 4 times a week - that way, I can get through a whole new series on Netflix with the time I have saved not working out. Seriously, how the hell can I talk myself back into training when there is an option quite like that on the table?

But my weight was not the reason we went to see Julia and Zafer, this was all social.

Husbando treated me to a great big Turkish breakfast at 'Asparan' on the way down there. Had I have known that Julia was going to ply us with cakes on arrival I would never have had breakfast. In fact we bordered on rude as we could only squeeze in one ginger slice.

Bariş loved it there, I mean why wouldn't he? Their place resembles a small hippy commune, and this 'dear diary', was right up his street. What with having their pet goat 'Melek', plus 8 dogs and 10 cats running around like one big happy family - oh yes, Bariş could see himself taking root there - quite possibly in their greenhouse made entirely of water bottles.

It's peaceful, tranquil and a bloody good break from the norm, and I'm happy to report that Bariş and Zafer hit it off mighty well. They have met before off course; once at our wedding and occasionally when Bariş used to pick me up from training sessions when they still lived in Marmaris, but only ever for the briefest periods.

I knew Zafer would be Bariş's cup of tea, but it's a job trying to convince him of such. Luckily I won't need to again.

We left there with happy souls and a box full of apple crumble. Good times.

Thursday Kate came round for coffee and I took Guch to the vet as he had a dicky tummy. Trying to clean up diarrhoea when out walking with him is not just gross, but also damn near impossible. A couple of kids were laughing at me the other day while trying to pick up the sloppy vile shitty mess (with a bag of course). Jesus, I made a bloody the balls up that job! So off we went to sort out his tum, and now that it has warmed up a bit, he had a haircut too.

Guch is a funny little sod when he's has a shave. He behaves in a weird way, like he's bashful or something. To cover his dignity I put him in his favourite hoody. That boy loves clothes just as much as his Mum and these days he simply hates being naked. He adores November as its cool enough to wear his threads again. The clever little fucker opens his outfit draw and brings them too me when he is ready to 'get dressed' after the long hot summer, and I'm not even kidding.

Right now, in his hoody, he looks like the epitome of 'Thug Life' and I couldn't be prouder. All he needs is a big gold chain that reads 'Da Guch' and a spliff, and he would be Insta famous like his idol 'Doug the Pug'.

Talking about Guch, Barış and I were in the phone shop the other day repairing his Nokia when the phone guy asked to see my phone. It's nowt at all special, but as I was playing on it I assumed he wanted to see what I was doing (the nosey bastard). I clicked out of Facebook, turned the screen to face him and showed him my home screen. He cooed over the photo of Guch displayed and asked 'who's that' to which I replied 'my baby' - standard answer when anyone asks. This must have hit a nerve as he went on to tell me that a dog is not a baby and I should get busy making real babies instead of wasting my time with pretend ones and that when I have a real baby, the dog will be just a dog.

WT...?

Who the actual fuck does this abortion of a human think he is going off at me about my boy?

As you can imagine this did bode well and I blew up in his face, for 2 very different reasons:

Reason 1: No matter when I have a baby, Guch will still be my baby. At the end of the day, Guch is my first born and no jumped up little cunt of a phone shop guy is going to tell me otherwise.

Reason 2: As well as insulting Gucci, he also insulted me. He had no idea if I wanted children or not, let alone that we are struggling to conceive, so why feel the need to come out with such pish?

The fucker was left red faced when I went on to inform him that we are indeed trying to get pregnant, but for whatever reason it's not happening as quickly as we would like, and therefore he is a complete wanker for making such comments and how very dare he talk about my boy like that - then, I promptly burst into tears.

Barış proceeded to snatch his phone out of cunts hand, swore profusely at him in Turkish, shouted at him for upsetting me and told him that we would report him to the authorities.

OK, so the last bit was a bit extreme, but gotta love Husbando for taking a stand.

Seriously, what the fuck is wrong with people?

And finally, although not a good part of my week, it exists none the less. I shall to bring to your awareness what I have been dealing with in the form of a 65 year old attention seeker and her melodrama:

Lorraine has now resorted to childish bullshit in the hopes of gaining my attention. Obviously I still haven't replied to her last message sent in January, and from all this juvenile behaviour, it makes me see her for what she really is - a bit of a knob. In fact her adolescent ways are doing nothing but pushing me further away.

So what has she done exactly?

Well, she has clogged up my newsfeed with stupid quotes such as: 'If you hesitate between me and another person, don't choose me'.

I am forcing myself not to comment, but if I did, it would go something like this: 'I wish I had known that over Christmas and New Year'.

Part of me can't quite believe she is positing such pish, but another other part of me knows that for her this is completely normal behaviour. I also know she's restricting me from seeing some of her posts because she has told me that is exactly what she does with fallen friends before now. Why the fuck cant she restrict me from seeing the daily 10 dedicated to dearly departed George?

She won't succeed in getting a rise out of me. At 36 years old I know how to control my social media outbursts - it's just a shame some don't.

And that's about as much negative energy as I can bear for one day, plus the sofa has started to beckon. Guess what, it's fucking raining again, but today that simply doesn't worry me. All I care about is being available for Guch snuggles and chocolate.

Ohhh- maybe my period is on its way after all...

Wednesday 8th February

Current Weight: 63.7 Kilos.

Time: 14.02pm

Dear Bored winter girl,

So I woke up with a raging itchy nipple. It's not the first time I've had an itchy nip, but as this time it actually woke me up at 10.07am, I decided to Google it to see what's what.

Well I'm fucking dying aren't I!? Apparently I have a rare form of Breast cancer. Or it also could be Joggers Nipple, although that one would be hard to achieve considering I can barely power walk, let alone jog.

Or - I could have pregnancy Eczema.

Just fuck off body with your pregnancy trickery, I have had enough of you!

Do you see my issue here 'dear diary'? Everything I have is connected to sodding pregnancy.

One won't dwell on the fact that I am still period-less; one will power on through life like a boss and thank the universe for my Thug Life puppy love Gucci. He is my absolute one true love. Thank God Bariş understands. Most men wouldn't take kindly coming second place to a fur baby, but then again, most men aren't my Bariş.

Let's talk about him for a sec shall we;

We have had some rather large arguments in the last year. Some to do with cultural differences, some because of real life problems, and off course some to do with a wife's occasional hatred of her husband (and vice versa). It's never going to be all flowers and smiles 'cos life just ain't like that, but I am happy to announce that we are in one rather special happy place right now.

He didn't give up. I didn't give up. But by Christ, there have been times when I've come close.

Lorraine encouraged me to throw in the towel once you know. Probably because she was sick of my moaning - thankfully I didn't take her two bit advice. What sort of a friend actively encourages you to give up on your marriage FFS?

In the words of Cee lo Green, forget her because life is good again in the land of team Guch. I'm not stupid enough to think that it's always going be good, but I'll know better than to let the thought of giving up enter my head next time around. I will be armed with the knowledge that it can be pulled back again and that's good enough for me.

Talking about Lorraine, I decided to write her a letter to get off what was on my chest. I started it 3 days ago and probably got 3/4 of the way through, but now I can't be arsed to finish it. I guess all I really needed was to vent. I must add that the point of the letter was not to receive a reply - no, the point was so she could see my side.

I have also tried seeing it from her point of view, but that only angers me so I stop. Christmas and New Year keep getting in my way. Why aren't they getting in hers?

I have no idea if I will finish said letter, let alone send it as now the motivation behind doing so is sorely lacking.

That says a lot doesn't it?

Anyway, due to one thing or another, I have been bored since my last entry. It has been one of those weeks where I haven't seen anyone and I haven't done anything. I didn't go out on Saturday night and I didn't leave the house on Sunday. Basically the whole weekend was spent indoors. I was tearing my hair out by the end of it. I didn't feel like texting Kate and I knew Lacie was busy with moving, so I won't lie when I tell you that at one point I considered burying the hatchet with Lorraine just to escape the clutches of boredom, have a spot of Sunday lunch and a retail session. Then I came to my senses and thought 'go out and do it by your damn self'.

I was getting dressed to do just that and then it started raining. Now I could have gone regardless - I have a car and an umbrella after all, but the rain gave me the excuse I needed to stay indoors. Don't get me wrong, it's not as if I wouldn't go and do these things alone, but it's much more fun doing it as a twosome.

Damn me and my need to keep my circle small!

In these situations it would benefit to have at least one more friend living in Marmaris that I could call up on a whim to go out with. I have plenty of buddies on the other end of FB messenger should I fancy a chat, but that doesn't help when I want to go out and do something now does it?

Mission of the month: Make a new Marmaris friend. One that is not a know it all, doesn't want to wear me as a second skin, is not a psycho, and does not bring unnecessary drama into my life. I will also add that this new friend needs to have something about her. A girl with a personality like a wet dishcloth does nothing for me. No, my new friend needs to have a spark and she should be a sassy mouthed mo fo that does not take any shit from anyone.

Where oh where am I going to find me one of them as I think I may have discovered the last one in Lacie?

Can you write a personal ad for a new friend without looking like some sort of lezzer?

There is always Craig's List, but that's usually where the freaks and weirdo's congregate, and be Jesus, I don't want me any of them...

Wait a minute, who was Marie who sent a message after my random night out the other week? Was she the random girl I was slut dropping with, or am I barking up the wrong tree entirely? And if it was her, would I want to make a new friend out of her?

The jury is out as in all honesty, I can't remember what she looks like let alone if she is a wanker or not. Mind you, I'm sure I was a wanker that night, but that has nothing to do with this right now does it?

Anyway, Husbando and I have done a couple of things together over the last couple of days. I think he felt sorry for me as I was exhibiting signs of stir crazy cabin fever. After he finished work early on Monday afternoon, he took me to 'Blue Port' shopping centre for a Fro Yo and a look around the shops that resulted in us buying a load of seeds that neither of us know what to do with. The thought behind this was to create the balcony garden I desire, but as we are both clueless on what to do, I'm sure the seeds will sit in the shit drawer, in their unopened packets, for the rest of eternity.

Husbando's day off has now changed to Tuesday, so yesterday being Tuesday, we headed down to 'Yunus' to have breakfast on the beachfront and while a way a few hours watching the everlasting rain. We ate, we sat in a comfortable silence while each of us caught up on social media, and went on to make up stories about the people sitting around us drinking tea. It was an alright sort of afternoon.

And that's it - that is all I have done since my last entry.

It's a travesty really, and one that I plan to change as of tonight as I'm going to Lacie's new pad to be wowed with all her new home stuff and to drink my body weight in duty-free whisky.

Then on Friday Sandi is coming over for lunch, and Saturday I'm having a few afternoon drinks with Kate and Audrey on the marina. This week I have promised myself that I will get up to no shenanigans when they leave - in fact I'm going to tell them to watch me get in a taxi. That won't stop me from finding shenanigans as I can easily give the taxi driver the name of another bar to drop me at.

FFS I'm giving myself ideas here.

And with that in mind, it's time to go. I need a shower, some food and a new social agenda.

Monday 13th February

Time: 16.47pm

Dear Deep thinker,

What a difference a few days makes. Last week I was ready to slit my wrists with boredom and this week I'm praying for a quiet day! It's all or bloody nothing again!

Sounds like I'm complaining doesn't it? Well yes, I suppose I am - but instead of whinging about it, I will instead tell you what's been going down;

Wednesday night was spent at Lacie's new gaff drinking and catching up. There were boxes and bin bags full of shite everywhere, but that didn't stop my beady little eyes noticing the new furniture she has bagged herself. She has done alright out of that ex-husband of hers - finally. There is still more to do with the new pad but it's looking good. And, surprisingly, she is still with the wannabe.

I must have been pretty pissed because I don't remember leaving Lacie's or getting home. I asked Bariş the following day what time I got in and he said 02.30am, but when I doubled checked with Lacie, she said I left hers at just after 12am. Although when drunk it may take a little longer to get home, two and half hours is taking the piss - especially as Lacie now lives only 5 minutes down the road.

I'm not sure which one of them is wrong, or if they both happen to be right, but if they are both right then that means I have a secret place that I visit when I'm drunk. That would explain a lot as there has been many an occasion where 2 different times have been stated and I simply thought Bariş was over exaggerating to make me feel bad.

Interesting prospect or scary thought?

I can't quite decide, but I am intrigued as to where drunk me thinks it's acceptable to take me... It may be to time to invest in a video camera that I can strap on my bag...

Thursday I did a bit of food shopping. How is it every time I go to 'Kipa' I spend way over the odds? I was in there for all of 15 minutes and spent a total of 150tl. It's not as if I have much to show for it either. I am re-affirming my vow to shop elsewhere as it happens every fucking time.

In other non-related news, I also cleaned the house.

Friday was a bit of a mad one. Sandi came for lunch and also helped me take Guch back to the vet as his runny tummy wasn't getting any better. Poor bugger has only gone and got gastroenteritis and has to have a course of antibiotic injections daily until he improves - so guess what I did over the weekend? Talk about nursing my baby boy back to health and my poor wallet back to life. Jesus, vets must be frikkin' millionaires the amount they charge over here. They know they have us over a barrel when it comes to our babies. Fuckers.

Anyway, it was a grand afternoon with Sandi. I decided to be a better hostess than usual and instead of offering up my customary packet soup concoction, I put together a little afternoon tea that consisted of sandwiches, homemade scones (homemade by someone else, obviously), and Barış's own recipe of this weird but delightful pudding cake thing. Not a bad old effort from this 'ere Minger.

Saturday morning saw me take my boy for his second injection, and Saturday afternoon saw me in 'Lighthouse' drinking beer with Kate and Audrey, to name but a few. I got home at 8.30pm drunk and not particularly happy about it - but at least there were no shenanigans to report. Well not many anyway.

The look on Barış's face when I walked in at that time was priceless. He asked who I had fallen out with, was there a fire or was I just coming home because I had forgot something and was heading back out again? Sadly not 'dear diary', sadly not.

I have come to realise that afternoon drinking does nothing for me as I'm only just getting started when these mo fo's want to go home. We had a nice afternoon, yes indeedie, but arriving home at that time pissed up is just foolish on my part. It's too early to go to bed and too miserable to be in the company of a Husbando that is stone cold sober. I mean, how awful...

But, we turned it around and managed to have a date night none the less. We ordered Dominoes and watched 'The Girl on the Train'. I nodded off in a drunken slumber after 10 minutes, and woke up with the credits rolling.

You see, that's what afternoon drinking does for you - kills fucking date night.

Sunday was a sofa day. I re-watched 'Girl on the Train' and also 'Trainspotting'. Is it just me or is 'Trainspotting' not as great as I remembered?

The only thing that got me off my arse was taking Guch to get his third injection, and let me tell you, that was a ball ache. But other than that, I enjoyed my sofa day immensely.

Now I find myself right back here at Monday.

Considering I'm a girl that doesn't do very much, I just don't know where the time goes. I hate to get all philosophical here, but in the blink of an eye I will be 80 years old wondering where my life disappeared too. Yesterday I was a young naive 18 year old living it up in Marmaris, then I blinked and found myself here, at 36, looking in the mirror at an unfamiliar reflection - one that resembles the younger me, but different somehow. This new image has the beginnings of crow's feet, and what could possibly be considered wisdom behind those eyes. This more mature person staring back wonders just what the future me will think of the present me? After all, the present me doesn't really rate the younger me.

I am not one of those proud people that can't admit when they have been a tit - and believe me, at 18 years old living in Marmaris thinking I owned the joint; I really was nowt but a tit. A young tit with no weight issues or wrinkles - but a tit none the less.

And it doesn't stop there; I also have other not so pleasant thoughts. Today I'm filled with them. I think of death, and not just my own. Gucci, Barış and my parents are all lumped in. How will I cope without my olds FFS? What on earth will I do if Gucci passes before me? Will me and Barış die together leaving Gucci alone in the big wide world?

Fuck me.

I often wonder how I will die; will it be from a vicious attack, possibly a stabbing of some sort, or maybe from a nasty disease? Obviously I'm hoping for asleep in my bed at 1001 years old. That's right - 1001. I'm not an idiot by the way (debatable) because my Dad read somewhere a couple of years ago that the first person to live to be 1000 has already been born. That person could well be me. I have just as much a chance as anyone right? I'm sure it will be a case of trialling a pill of some description and I'm quite happy to sign up for it as long as they have one for Guch and the rest of the clan too.

Can you imagine how much knowledge a person would have with that amount of time on the planet?

Now then, here's a thought: I wonder if the human race will still be blowing each other up, or if our fixation for watching cat videos will still reign supreme...?

Fuck me, all of the above is simply too much speculation for a Monday afternoon. I think I may need to pour myself a little whisky to take the edge off.

It's definitely time to change the subject, and what better way to do that than by telling you of my plans for the week. Oh yes, big plans have come my way!

Firstly Lacie and I have decided we need another weekend out of the bubble that is Marms before things get hectic for the summer. Couldn't come soon enough if the above is anything to go by. So, we are planning a long weekend in Bodrum in April. It's more expensive to stay at home than go on a 3 day holiday at only £40.00 per person for a 5* all inclusive!

Secondly its Valentine's Day tomorrow so Barış and I are heading over to Kate and her Husbando's house for pizza and beer. I won't lie, it was a task getting Barış to agree, but as soon as I mentioned Kate's dogs, the deal was sealed.

Thirdly I'm going to Lacie's on Friday for a few drinks and quite possibly a bitch about Lorraine. Yup, she's at it again with her Facebook quotes.

And fourthly, its Kat's birthday night on Saturday. We are booked in at 'People Marina' so I get to dress myself right up for a change. There will be no shabby blue jeans in sight. Oh hell yes, I'm going all out in the outfit stakes. In fact I'm planning on nipping into town tomorrow to see if I can find something new.

And with that I am going to take my shit infested puppy out for a walk and hope to God he doesn't go through another 6 bags worth of puppy poo.

Ciao for now.

ONCE UPON A WHISKY

Saturday 18th February

Current Weight: 63.5 Kilos surprisingly.

Time: 14.26pm

Dear Tramp girl,

What an odd few days. Social calendar wise all has been great, however the Husbando bonding session on Valentines night at Kate's house went down like a lead balloon. Yup, it totally crashed and burned. Sometimes I wonder why I bother, then I remember I like to booze it up while being a social mo fo, and it all comes back to me.

I had better explain...

So Tuesday night we rocked up at Kate's with 1.5 litres of cheap red wine & diet coke to mix up a sangria style cocktail. You can never go wrong with sangria. We heard the music blaring from right down the road, well before we arrived at the front door. It sounded as if a party was going on indoors, but nope, just the 2 of them awaiting our arrival.

It was like walking in to a 90's rock festival. Now that's my sort of music, abso-fucking-lutely, however when one can't hear the reply when asking where the drinking utensils are located, this could have caused a mini break down. Too loud to find a glass? Whatever next..!

Had I have thought the music would be lowered to a chatting level once comfy in the sitting room, I would have been mistaken. Kate tried, she really did, but her husband Mehmet was in the zone, loving life and loving his tunes. Every time he got up and left the room she would grab the remote and turn it down, but on his return he would attack the house like a bull in a China shop in search, so much so that Kate had to cave every time in fear of the sitting room being trashed.

Noticeable Point: I always imagined Kate to be the boss of the household. Now I'm not so sure.

I wondered if the whole evening was also forced upon Mehmet?

If they could only hear each other to chat, Barış and Mehmet would have realised they have more in common than they know - what with both being forced into socialising and all.

All conversation fell upon music deafened ears - no fucker could hear themselves think, let alone speak, so after some time, we gave up trying and embraced the tunes. We ordered pizza, we drank the sangria concoction, and Mehmet and I sang along very loudly to some of my favourite hits of the 90s including Erasure and INXS. I was quite happy with this scenario. Barış on the other hand was not. When it came to 11.30pm he could take it no longer. He shouts at me when my tunes are too loud in the house so I'm not surprised that his head was totally fucked and he wanted to leave.

Mehmet couldn't understand why we were heading home so early as he was having a ball, but when you are not used to this volume of sound, it makes for a sore headed Husbando.

Barış informed me the next day not to play 90s tunes for the next year and not to ask him to double date for the same length of time. Fuck sake.

Ahh well, I tried...

This has now put me in a bigger predicament. I was over at Lacie's last night when she suggested that the four of us do something. Just to be clear here, she meant me, her, Barış and the wannabe. We came up with a death defying plan to hire a party villa in Akyaka for an overnighter, take a shit load of food, a shit load of booze and just party. This appeals to me no end, but when I presented this fabuloso idea to Barış he flat out refused. I knew it was going to be difficult to approach, but I didn't think it was going to be impossible.

So to compromise, I suggested a 2 hour trial run on home turf and if he didn't like wannabe then, I would take his decision as final and never bother him about it again.

Nope - flat out refused that too.

I am yet to inform Lacie, but I'm on my way round there for pre-drinks later, before we head down to 'People Marina' for Kat's birthday. I'm not looking forward to telling her as she was so excited about it last night. Maybe when it's not so fresh Bariş may cave slightly, however that could easily take a couple of years, and considering we were planning on going in a couple of weeks, that's time we simply don't have.

In other news I found sweet F.A in town to wear for tonight's birthday bash and it's the rival gang's fault. Yup, I managed to bump right into them in my favourite shop 'Ambar'.

Can I just ask - what the fuck is wrong with me? Why is it every time I see them I look like a fucking tramp? And how do they always look so God damn glam even after completing a 5K run?

Unfortunately for me, I decided to leave the house with not a scrap of makeup, 4 day old unwashed hair scraped on top of my head, wearing jogging bottoms that I fished out of the washing basket and a sweatshirt that was 2 sizes too big as I had sod all else to wear being laundry day. Yup, hobo alert.

I tried to avoid them, I even hid my shame behind a clothes stand, but that Larissa is a bug-eyed bitch and clocked me straight away. Oh how she revelled in walking over to me giving me the once over - twice!

"Have you left the gym without showering and changing again Lei?"

Gym - as if, but that'll do, I can live with that "Larissa, I am a woman on a mission today and didn't have the time".

"Well I hope you're not planning to trying on clothes in that state, that's a shame for other shoppers in the fitting room plus the ones that have to try on your cast offs once you have finished".

I didn't think it through very well did I?

That northern troll had me trapped like a deer in the headlights and she bastard well knew it.

I stuttered and stammered my way out of there sharpish, found Barış in the Lira shop eyeing up the tools and informed him that we needed to leave town before any other fucker spotted me in that 'state'.

Really - this shit can only ever happen to me. I should learn a lesson from this and always wear makeup when leaving the house, alas, I'm a lazy cow and sometimes can't be arsed primping and preening if I'm only taking on a 30 minute shopping dash around town.

So, back to tonight's outfit. I have fuck all new to wear due to my tramp shame, so I'm opting for black plants, black camisole, black cardi and a black lace choker. There is nothing like a bit of black to make you feel slim, vampish and less bum like.

I have a slight hangover from last night's drink-a-thon but no cause for concern re tonight. I am, after all, nothing if not a diehard party animal.

So, that's where I shall leave it for today. No doubt I will have shenanigans of some description to report after the birthday bash, so watch this space...

Or - I may be home by 11pm.

It could go either way these days...

Thursday 23rd February

Time: 14.52pm

Dear Mother of a prophet,

Today is cycle day 68 in the disappearing period debacle and I have started to symptom spot again. Can't help it - wish I could, but I can't. What makes it worse is that I don't have the feeling of coming on anymore - that stopped about 10 days ago more or less. I get it very fleetingly now so it makes me forget I'm even in this situation.

What it's been replaced with is a sore throat that has now turned into a minor cold. Oh, and headaches. All apparently typical pregnancy symptoms...

I won't jump for joy as I'm simply not that lucky.

Nope, I know what all this cruel trickery is, and pregnancy it is not. The headaches I'm guessing are down to the copious amounts of dodgy vodka consumed on Saturday night. I swear I would recover quicker from a facelift than I do a hangover these days. And the cold? Well, Lacie had a cold when I saw her this weekend, so it stems back to her and her vicious snots.

But, what if it's not?

What if..?

I mean, there is neither sight nor sound of the MIA period, that's got to mean something right? I know I shouldn't be torturing myself, but really, what if..?

Good thing I am heading down to the Gynae on Tuesday isn't it. That will put paid to all of the above. I desperately need the period kick starting considering it doesn't want to appear on its own, and I imagine I will receive a prick in my arse for that. That's the way they do it here, injection in the bum for bloody everything. But, at least I'll come on and that means the baby making can resume.

I have a fear though. What if I'm preggers and the Gynae doesn't realise, gives me the period booster and that takes away the possible pregnancy? Gynae's ain't that stupid, surely?

Oh shut the fuck up Lei and come to terms with the fact that the patch fucked you up will you?

I agree with myself - it's about time I stopped this nonsense, so on the no period / pregnancy drama that's just where I'm going to leave it.

Anyway, Saturday night was good.

It was us vs. them. Us being Lacie and I, and them being Kats group of friends that she does everything with. You could say that we were the odd ones out, the only 2 that were not part of 'The Golden Group' - but do'ya know what, it didn't faze us at all. Why? Cos we foresaw this situation and got our pre-drink on. Had we have arrived straight laced things might have been different, however we arrived half cut and in a rather cheery mood. Even after my mother of all hair and clothing meltdowns!

I don't do classy, but I thought I would make an effort for Kats birthday as we were going somewhere so nice and all. But as soon as Lacie passed comment that I looked the most sophisticated I had ever looked, I instantly regretted my choice of outfit. All I needed was my black faux leather pants instead of the chic trousers I was wearing and life would have been worth living again. Alas, it was too late to go home and change and Lacie's clothes don't even fit my big toe, so I was stuck like that for the duration.

And the hair? Oh fuck me. I used my new curling tongs that I got for Christmas and it somehow added to the elegant look! I thought by giving myself a bump at the crown with a shit load of back combing it would somehow replace the classy factor - sadly not.

Lacie couldn't get enough of my lady look - I on the other hand, hated it. So much so that I decided right there and then I needed a new doo in the hair department, STAT. One that could never be confused with classy...

Anyway, our night continued and the us vs. them divide wasn't too noticeable with the more drink that was consumed. That's the thing about birthdays, you are forced to go out and party with people that you wouldn't usually as they are not in your social circle. Sometimes it can make for an awkward night, and other times (like when you're already drunk) it can make for a fun night. Thankfully this was a fun night.

The food, music and vibe were pretty cool down at 'People Marina'. I must add this to my list of favourite restaurants. From there, the birthday girl opted for a bit of Karaoke in my favourite chav bar 'Albatross'. See, I definitely didn't need the classy pants!

When arriving at 'Albatross', some of the group swapped vodka for coffee. I mean what the actual fuck? When you have been drinking booze all night, how does one end up on coffee? I just don't get it. I however, made up for their lack of boozing and was drinking 2 to everybody's 1. As I got drunker, the feeling that I was Axel Rose got greater, and this resulted in some mighty fine air guitar and a bit of 'Paradise City' on the Karaoke.

It's funny the things you do when pissed isn't it? I would never dream of singing when sober, but when inebriated, I'm frikkin' Adele. Hello?

As the group started getting smaller, my need for partying unfortunately didn't. I did my usual trick and latched onto anyone that was staying out, which happened to be Cathy the Karaoke hostess. Thank fuck she's an alright sort as I could get myself into no end of trouble the way I carry on, with this time being no different. I managed to insult an 80 year old woman when she introduced me to her 12 year old boyfriend. Honest to God, this is how it went down;

"Lei, I'd like you to meet Mustafa my boyfriend".

"Ha-ha, good one! It's so farfetched it's ironic. I love it when people take the piss out of themselves considering what this town is like for old women shagging young boys. Brilliant, cheers for the laugh".

"Lei, Mustafa really is my boyfriend, we have been together 3 years".

"Oh". Hangs head in shame and orders vodka.

Yup, you simply can't take me and my mouth anywhere. But can I just add, what the fuck does she expect?

I sneaked through the door at 04.30am. Not bad considering.

Gucci woke up immediately and came a running to greet me. We had a 5 minute love in on the sofa before we both hopped into bed. I thought I was being super quiet but apparently not as Barış rolled around to face me, and calmly but firmly asked me to refrain from singing 'Mother of Pearl' by Roxy Music to Gucci while he was trying to sleep.

Fuck sake, we were enjoying that sing-along.

Sunday was a sofa day with movies and crisps and chocolate and lots and lots of bread. These days I find the only thing that aids me when in full swing of hangover is a ton of bread products. Crumpets and Marmite would have gone down a treat but this is Turkey and you can't sodding buy crumpets here. But I did make myself the biggest crisp sandwich known to man.

Monday I still had somewhat of a hangover because that's right, I get 2 dayers now, so I didn't leave the house. Instead I cleaned it and went on to binge watch 'Girlfriends guide to Divorce'. Good times.

Tuesday was Barış's day off so we did the usual and went for a dirty big breakfast at 'Şahin Tepe'. Then, because it was raining (yes again), we hit 'Blue Port' shopping centre and bought a bamboo blind for the balcony, went home and Barış installed it like the good Husbando he occasionally is.

Wednesday Kate came round and gave me the new look that I desperately needed. I now am white blond with a LOB. Jesus my hair feels short, but I like it. In some twisted way it makes me look younger. How I couldn't tell you, but anything that makes a 36 year old gal look fresh faced is definitely worth considering. And without having to resort to a facelift a la Larissa!

So, this brings us up to today - Thursday. I have not done a lot. I was thinking about going food shopping but instead I find myself just sitting here simply thinking about it. Fuck it, a job for tomorrow.

In other news it has been nearly one month with no word from Lorraine. She is of course still posting stupid quotes, plus the usual George Michal tributes as it seems she will never get sick of boring us all...

With the shit she posts you would be forgiven for mistaking her for a young silly teen - until you see her profile photo (that she changes daily). Mind you, the app she uses knocks 20 years off...

Moving on, I have no plans for boozing this weekend because I fancy giving my liver a break. This week Saturday night means date night, and Husbando and I are going to 'Kervan'. We haven't been for a while and it's nice for a change to eat out with him as opposed to my buds. I may even bribe him to take me for a walk on the beach front after, or possibly a movie? I wonder if 50 Shades of shite is still on?

And next week is a busy one so I'm not sure how much time I will have for you 'dear diary'.

Anyway, I suppose I better go and get on with doing sweet F.A, but before I do, let me leave you with this;

The end is nigh. Not of life off course (I hope), but the end of this diary. It is after all, nearly the end of February. So dear universe - I am making one final plea for you to knock me up. I vow to be a better person, I vow to stop some of my shenanigans and I vow to be the best Mother of a prophet that you can imagine - just do me this one solid.

Mother of a prophet, fuck I crack myself up!

And just like that, it was over...

Friday 3rd March

Time: 21.52pm

Dear Diary,

Well, here we are at the end of the road.

The fact that I am still writing means at least I have lived to tell my tale, but didn't that tale's end come around quickly? That's time for you I suppose, apparently it's all relative.

I can't quite believe that this is my final entry. I'm not sure how I feel about it. I could continue of course, but we all have to draw the line somewhere, right?

Once more, I have lived through a rollercoaster of emotion during the last 6 months, and once more there have been good times, great times, and fucking loathsome times.

How have I come out at the end of it? Pretty much sunny side up - I am, if nothing else, a mostly positive speck of stardust. Don't get me wrong, one can't always remain positive when looking despair square in the eye, but one can choose not to be a dick about it.

I think it's fair to say that I have learned a lot during this 6 month period of diarying, especially about myself, marriage and friends. Let's have a look see shall we;

Me: I have come to the conclusion that although married, I am still me, Lei frikkin' Lawson, and married Lei is an entity all on her own. Although still fiercely independent, it has taken me by surprise to find that I enjoy being someone's wife. I am still the outspoken, headstrong female that I always have been, but can I also add that this married biatch occasionally enjoys cooking for her man when he comes home from work - as long as I chew said meal silently of course.

Being married has also not changed the fact that I am still as obsessed as ever with weight. Alright, I have come on leaps and bounds as I no longer leave orange arse oil everywhere I sit due to ditching the diet tablets years back - but that doesn't stop the mind from wishing that the body was stick thin. I always did like the emaciated look. Off course I know that if I eat healthy I shouldn't need to diet, but I am an obsesser all said and done, and obsess I do over crisps and chocolate.

I have come to terms with knowing that living in Marmaris is never going to be easy, but I should do wise to remember that I do in fact, live in a foreign land. As Barış likes to remind me, this is not my home turf and should something go wrong then I'm pretty much fucked. When out partying, my mouth is not always my friend, hell, drink is not my friend, and it's about time I learnt that I am not indestructible.

I have never paid attention to the 'Foreign Wives Cliques' until I got hitched, and now, I sometimes catch myself looking around said cliques and I can't help but think that I just don't belong. Some like to revel in others misery, some like to judge from their high and mighty perch, and some are just active wearing, Frappuccino drinking cunts. Fuck me I don't belong in those kind of club's - oh no, I belong in my own - and you know what - that's absolutely OK. Some may find it comforting being part of an ex-pat gang of wives to survive life in Marms, but that's just not my box of frogs. The bitching, backstabbing and gossiping about each other alone serves me no purpose. Give me 2 or 3 solid friends and I'm happy as a pig in shit.

And, if I've learnt anything from reading back through my diary, it's that sometimes it's best to keep silent until one knows exactly what to say. I may have to remind drunk me of this, but kicking things off with sober me is a great place to start.

Marriage: I have learnt that no marriage is rock solid apart from my Mum and Dad's. Now there is a relationship goal if ever I saw one. Mind you, they have been together for 40 plus years so they should have learnt how to deal with each other by now.

So in an average marriage such as mine, I know it's never going to be plain sailing. I can cope with this. What I can't cope with is people whispering in my ear that I would be better off alone, because as much as I hate to admit it, little seeds start to take root when watered.

The truth is I would not be better off alone. I am better off right where I am. I have found my lobster and he is the absolute correct lobster for me. Hard times and arguments are a given, but I believe it's how we whether the storm that shows strength not just of character, but of marriage. I'm glad I didn't give up when times got tough because I would have been devastated to have missed the right now.

Yup, married life is pretty good atm, long may it continue.

Friends: Well them fuckers come and go. At the start of this diary I would never have believed that Lorraine and I would not be speaking again. I am still in disbelief that it has got this far, but I know Lorraine, and I am totally aware that she cuts off her nose to spite her face. Do I? Quite possibly yes - but when I'm right I'm right, and in this case I'm fucking right. Who knows, she may still receive that letter from me (if I ever finish it), but for now that is well and truly pushed to the back of my mind as I have bigger fish to fry.

Never one to be disheartened, I take the rough with the smooth and I have made me a new friend in Kate. For a gal like me I find it near enough impossible to make new buds, but this one is my cuppa whisky. I love the little meet ups that Audrey, Kate and I have, even though I'm never ready to go home when they are. In fact the next one is this weekend and I couldn't be more excited. And who knows, maybe one day Barış will enjoy couples dating too.

And back to the old; I will always have my trusted few that date back to when time began. As much as I get annoyed with Kimmy, that girl is my rock. She'll be back before long and I literally can't wait to see her. She is after all, my voice of reason.

Unfortunately Jenny is no longer part of our Marmaris shenanigans, and that's OK - she needed to sort her head space out, and by leaving Turkey I hope that's exactly what she's doing. We keep in touch off course, but it's different now. I suppose that's just the way it goes when someone leaves and is not set to return. On the other hand, 3 always was a crowd when it came to us.

And then there's Lacie. We wind each other up, we call each other the most horrific names known to man, and we love each other fiercely. She is just as cracked as me, if not more - and that 'dear diary' is a friendship quality that is mighty hard to find. There are limited few similar to me, but at least with Lacie I have found me one soul on fire. We don't do cliques, we don't do fake friends and we certainly don't do what we are told. What we do is laugh our fucking asses off, we party, we take off on random weekend long benders and we create memories. I like us. Actually that's an understatement - I bloody love us.

More friends will come and more friends will go, but the ones that are meant to be will remain sturdy, just like ole Ataturk statue in the centre of Marmaris.

And the Rival Gang, whatever happened to them?: Well, they got theirs. I was out on a beachfront walk with Gucci last week and for a change I decided to put my face on. In fact I was looking A-OK for a usual hobo. I was dressed in my non smelly, on trend jogging bottoms, funky Def Leppard T Shirt, hoody and baseball cap. I actually looked the part.

It was a lovely sunny day and I was strolling along listening to a spot of 'Queen' with not a care in the world, when out of the corner of my eye I spotted Larissa and co. I couldn't quite make out what they were doing until I got a bit closer - if my eyes were not deceiving me, it looked as if they were raking through a large communal outdoor steel skip. In fact Larissa was inside it and I must say it looked very much like she was going through bags of rubbish! Within 60 seconds she noticed me stood there gawping and shouted over "It's not what it looks like Lei, you can put your bulging eyes back in their sockets. At lunch with the girls my wedding ring flew off my finger and landed in the bin, and what with the cost of it, I clearly can't leave it for the bin men. The diamond is the size of one of Gucci's eyes, so you would do the very same if your man could only afford such a ring".

Fucking cunt of a bitch.

As per usual, I came up with fuck all witty to retort and went with "It's all good Larissa, when I have a tiff with my fella I occasionally look at my ring and wish to do the same".

You see, I'm simply shit when put on the spot.

But what that bunch of bastards didn't realise is what I did prior to them noticing me. I had taken my phone out of my bag, angled the camera to get the best selfie ever and snapped away.

That bad boy got over 150 likes on Facebook. And yes, I tagged each of the 5 rival gang fuckers in the photo 'cos I'm a cunt like that. It doesn't matter that they untagged themselves when they noticed what I'd done because by that point the sheer social destruction was already accomplished, and the photo shared over 10 times. Yup, this wannabe socialite couldn't be happier, and that 1 selfie took down those pretentious arse holes in one fell swoop!

So you see, karma was on my side all along!

And the last point that I would like to address before I sign off is about the goal that I set out right at the beginning of the diary;

Just because I want something badly enough, doesn't mean it will happen. I have learnt that dealing with a bloody red let down on a monthly basis is just part and parcel of life and not to be dragged down by it all. In sheer mortal existence, these things happen - except in this case off course, because guess what mutha fucka - this 'ere wannabe socialite is 6 weeks pregnant! I know, I can't quite believe it either!

All my love,

Lei & Gucci

XOXO

TO BE CONTINUED...

ONCE UPON A WHISKY

Memories...

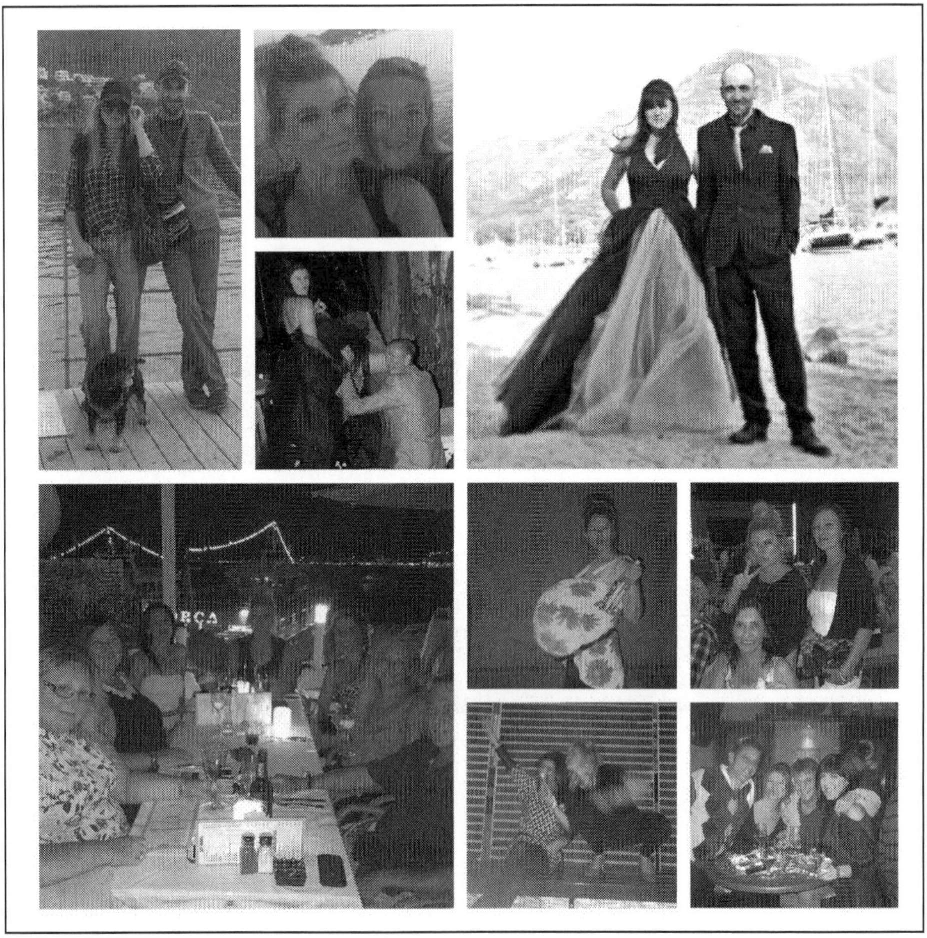

ABOUT THE AUTHOR

Louise Bell lives in Marmaris / Turkey and has done since the sweet age of 16. She is an ex rep, has a dog called Gucci and is married to a Turkish chap named Mehmet.

She is one of the more positive people that belong to this world and enjoys a glass of whisky and vodka from time to time, although these days sipping a Long Island Ice Tea is much more her favourite tipple.

Connect with Me:

Friend me on Facebook: https://www.facebook.com/Louise-Bell-274618615897440/

Subscribe to my newsletter: http://louisebellauthor.weebly.com/

PLEA FROM THE AUTHOR:

Hello fellow booze lover! So you have got to the end of my book - I hope that means you enjoyed it? Whether or not you did, I would just like to thank you for giving me your valuable time to try and entertain you. Thank you for giving my book a chance and for spending your hard earned cash on it. For that I am eternally grateful.

If you enjoyed this book and would like to help, then you could think about leaving a review on Amazon, Goodreads, or anywhere else that readers visit. The most important part of how well a book sells is how many positive reviews it has, so if you leave me one then you are directly helping me to continue on this road as an alcohol inspired writer.

Thank you in advance to anyone who does, you are helping out an aging rock star :)

Printed in Poland
by Amazon Fulfillment
Poland Sp. z o.o., Wrocław